My Dearest Duke

KRISTIN VAYDEN

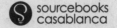

sourcebooks
casablanca

Published by Sourcebooks Casablanca, an imprint of Sourcebooks
P.O. Box 4410, Naperville, Illinois 60567-4410
(630) 961-3900
sourcebooks.com

Printed and bound in Canada.
MBP 10 9 8 7 6 5 4 3 2 1

Dedicated to my grandmother, Nadine Lainhart, who, through every season in life, found a reason to be joyful, even when it seemed impossible.

One

England, 1815

"YOUR GRACE, THE INCIDENT HAS BEEN resolved." His mother's nurse spoke succinctly, eyes averted. "Your mother is resting now. The doctor would like to talk to you."

The fire crackled as the silence stretched into several moments before Rowles Haywind, Duke of Westmore, acknowledged her words with a nod. "I'll meet with him shortly. You're dismissed."

The nurse gave a quick curtsy and took her leave.

When the door to his study closed, Rowles let out a pent-up breath. His mother had grown progressively worse since his older brother's untimely death. Robert, the late Duke of Westmore, had lost his life with several others in a fire at a party. The loss had cascaded through several powerful families in the London *ton*, shifting the mantle of titles to several younger sons—himself included.

His mother, Amelia Haywind, Duchess of Westmore, hadn't been well even before Robert's death, and once she learned her favorite son had passed, what was left of her mind fractured into shards like broken glass. It was frustrating to keep her under the watchful eye of her nurses and doctor, but Rowles saw no other way. Left to her own devices, she would run stark naked through Hyde Park.

She'd done it before.

And she'd tried it again today before being thwarted by the footman stationed outside her bedroom door. But unlike earlier times, on this occasion, she wasn't as easily persuaded to return to her rooms. The doctor had been called and had laced her tea with laudanum to calm her down.

Rowles stood from behind his desk and knocked on the mahogany surface with his knuckles. He released a wry snort of irritation as he looked to the door, then to the crackling fire. It had been hard enough losing his brother. His mother too? Wasn't that too much? A mirthless chuckle escaped his lips as he thought how condescending he'd been to his students at Cambridge when they posed similar questions.

As a professor of divinity at Christ's College in Cambridge University, he was expected to have the answers, or at least know how to pray for them. But even with all his knowledge, his study, and his researched answers, he was coming up empty on the questions that plagued his own soul.

A person could be crushed under the weight of

it all. Yet maybe that was the unfortunate secret: A person never really broke; they bent till they had nothing left. Was that what was happening to his mother? Her mind hadn't broken, had only become bent so far it no longer was able to think straight?

Worse yet, the thought he didn't want to dwell on, the one that haunted his moments of weakness was: Will the same happen to me?

"Your Grace?" Himes, their new butler, bowed low.

Rowles tugged on his shirtsleeves, straightened, and forced the unwelcome thoughts from his mind. "Yes?"

"The doctor asks for you—at your leisure, of course," the butler finished, then slowly rose from his bow.

Rowles nodded. "I'll come directly."

Himes stepped back from the doorway, allowed Rowles to exit first, then followed close behind.

The hall extended to the main entrance and then flowed to the grand staircase. The living quarters were on the second floor, in the western wing of the Elizabethan-era house. Built in an E shape, the house had undergone several renovations to keep it modern. However, the grand staircase and the location of the family apartments had remained unchanged.

Rowles took the stairs slowly, not looking forward to the conversation with the doctor. He was sure it would be a different rendition of the same advice: sedate her, keep her comfortable, post a guard at the door.

The white-haired doctor was frowning at the wooden floor as Rowles approached him. Upon realizing the duke's presence, the doctor straightened, then bowed.

"Your Grace."

"Doctor Smithe." Rowles waited for the doctor to begin.

The doctor's bushy eyebrows drew together, covering his bespectacled eyes. "I'm afraid it required more laudanum than I usually have to administer, so she will be sleeping for several hours." The doctor paused, seemed to consider his next words. "The agitation she exhibited was abnormal. Was there perhaps some sort of event that troubled her?"

Rowles shook his head. "Nothing of which I'm aware." Rowles studied the doctor. "It's worse, isn't it?"

The doctor met his look, and Rowles appreciated the lack of pity in his expression as he answered with a directness often absent in others. "Yes. And it will likely continue to progress, Your Grace."

Rowles bowed his head with the weight of the truth. "Is there nothing to be done, then?"

"At this point, no. Unless you wish to—"

Rowles's head snapped up, and he met the doctor's stare, which had shifted to a look of wary concern. "Hell will freeze over before I send my mother to Bedlam. If there's nothing else?"

Rowles didn't wait for the doctor's response, but spun on his heel, gave the doctor his back, and left.

He doubted the doctor would suggest such a preposterous idea again. As if he could relegate his mother to within the stone walls of that institution legendary for harboring insanity. His mother wasn't herself, but she wasn't a danger. And she would be prey in a place such as that. Never had he been so grateful for the privilege of his rank. Because of it, he wasn't forced to consign his mother to Bedlam, but could provide a better way to care for her needs.

A shudder racked his body as he thought about the implications that would course throughout the London *ton* should he make such a move. His mother's infirmities were whispered and laughed about, but he didn't begrudge the murmurings. They were all accurate, or at least mostly. It would be like a tiger without stripes if the London *ton* didn't gossip about a widowed duchess who had a bent mind.

But that didn't mean he found it easy to deal with the furtive peeks in his direction from people wondering if the infirmity was in his blood. Though apparently that wasn't enough of a threat to keep the mamas of the *ton* at bay when it came to throwing their daughters in his direction. How his late brother had dealt with such officious attention was beyond comprehension.

Rowles descended the stairs and returned to the quiet solitude of his study, welcoming the sight of shelves of books all well-worn with use and appreciation. Life had been so much simpler when his brother carried the mantle of the family title. Rowles missed teaching; missed it with an intensity that was too similar to resentment to be healthy. He would be a better professor now, he was certain. Life had taught him some harsh lessons, and humility had been one of the most powerful lessons.

If he'd learned anything, it was that he truly didn't have all the answers. And maybe that was the greatest lesson of all. Knowing how little one knew. But damn and blast, it was a difficult lesson to swallow. His eyes drifted to the hearth, the embers glowing in the evening light, and he felt a kinship with the charred wood. Could anything be made from ashes?

He struggled with the answer that rose from his long study of the Bible.

Beauty. Beauty came from ashes. Perhaps his and God's interpretations of beauty were vastly different. It wouldn't be the first time. And unfortunately, it likely wouldn't be the last either.

Two

JOAN MORGAN STUDIED THE TWO PIECES OF
linen paper on her brother's desk as she considered his
question. One missive was written in broad, feminine
penmanship with little care for efficient space usage on
the expensive linen paper. The writing on the other
was more linear, with clean lines and perfect flicks
across the *t*'s and evenly spaced dots above each *i*.

"Well?" Morgan, her elder brother and the Earl
of Penderdale, asked impatiently. His Christian
name was Collin, but she'd only ever called him
Morgan. It suited him better, she thought, and he
apparently agreed.

"Left. The one on the left," Joan answered, then
lifted her eyes to meet her brother's gaze.

"You're sure?" he demanded. He was so temperamental these days, like an irritated stallion constantly

snorting and pawing the earth as if restless deep in his soul.

"Yes." Joan nodded, then clasped her hands in front of her, willing a peaceful demeanor against her brother's irksome one.

Morgan held her gaze for several moments before looking down at the papers and collecting each one carefully. "I'll let them know."

Joan nodded, not that her brother was looking at her, but out of habit as he slid the papers into the leather folder from which they had come. After closing the folder, he took a deep breath through his nose and met her scrutiny.

Joan sighed. She knew that look. Dear Lord, she'd dealt with that expression her whole life, and was certain she knew the lecture that was about to follow.

Holding up a hand, she tipped her head and met his look with a frank stare of her own. "Before you break into the 'Joan, we're playing a dangerous game' lecture, please remember that I'm the one who's anonymous, and you're the one who takes the risk. So if anyone should be lecturing, it would be me giving the speech to you. And so help me, if you begin one sentence with anything regarding me being of the feminine sex, I will take this letter opener and—"

"There's no need to threaten me, Joan." Morgan's look shifted into one of amusement as he deftly slid the gilded letter opener away from her reach. "You're right—"

"Say it again," Joan demanded.

"I don't think I will." Morgan lifted the leather folder and smirked. "I'll be back this afternoon, long before we need to prepare for the ball."

Joan folded her arms across her chest. "You better not be late. You think my warning with the letter opener was hostile, but I will do far worse— I'll find you a wife."

Morgan stilled. "Don't remind me. But, since you did mention the *w*-word, I do believe it would be wise to remind you that since tonight is your come-out, less is more."

Joan narrowed her eyes and tipped her chin lower, as if bracing for a verbal fight. "What exactly do you mean by that?"

Morgan shrugged. "I think you know very well. As it is, I wanted to wait a year, maybe two before you started this whole debacle—"

"I'd be on the shelf before I even had a chance!" Joan retorted. "Nineteen is late enough. There are ladies married at nineteen!"

"Other ladies are not you, Joan." Morgan's voice sliced through her argument.

She froze, then slowly nodded. "Exactly. Which is why I will be a sensation. Don't you think? After all, I'm not simpering, limpid, and boring. I fancy myself to be fascinating, really. And I think others might as well. Having a secret always makes a person more interesting, don't you think?"

Morgan sighed. "I know. Believe me, more than anyone else in the world, I know. Which is why I'm taking this seriously, as should you. Just…do me a favor, please?" He turned his brown eyes imploringly to her, and some of her bravado faded into affection for her now only brother. They'd lost Percy; all they had was each other now. She might fight Morgan, but in the end, she knew he had her best interests at heart, so with a nod, she waited.

"Even if you *know* something, see the details that others missed and piece together some scandal, or read someone's expression that makes you think they're lying, you must keep it to yourself. When you find the right man, I'll help you talk with him about your remarkable work for king and country in the War Office, but till then, protect yourself, protect your heart. Likely you'll see through all the bad apples, but in case…"

Joan took a few steps toward him and placed her hand on his shoulder. "I understand, and I will be careful. Chances are even if I slipped up, it would be easily explained as a coincidence. I've worked with you long enough to know how to be on my guard."

"True, but multiple coincidences lead to suspicion, and I don't want you to be the focal point of any of the *ton*'s bile in their gossip."

"Thank you." Joan squeezed his shoulder. "I'm thankful for a big brother like you."

"Even if I'm an overbearing tyrant?" Morgan asked, releasing a tight chuckle.

"Even if you're an overreacting, overbearing, maniacal tyrant," she answered.

Morgan released a breath. "With Father and Mother gone, and then when Percy died in the fire... I don't want to lose you too. Even if only to heartache."

"You won't, but you will be taking your life in your hands if you don't leave now so you'll be back in time for the ball," she teased, attempting to lighten the mood, but the mention of fire had her on edge slightly. Ever since they'd lost their brother in the blaze, she'd been fearful of that element.

Morgan's eyes widened, and he clasped the folder to his chest, then took his leave. "Be back in two hours at the most."

"We'll see," Joan called out as he disappeared from the library.

Releasing a breath, she looked to the desk where the papers had rested. Her skill was hopefully going to save a life today. The missives were two letters sent from the same source; one was a decoy, the other the real message. Without information concerning which one was a ruse and which was accurate, the War Office didn't know which location was the correct one, since each missive held a different destination. It was a smart precaution in case the messenger was caught—which he had been—but it wasn't enough. Not when the War Office had someone like her in their ranks. Though any information and questions were passed through her brother, Joan had developed quite a name within the office.

It was Morgan who had coined her alias, Saint. It was brilliant, really, since she was named for Joan of Arc, thus giving a fitting nod to her namesake.

It had started when she was in leading strings, when her father had worked for the War Office as a handwriting analyst. As a student of graphology, he kept Camino Baldi's book *Trattato* on his desk as a reminder of the power of the written word in deciphering clues about the writer. Baldi's book, coupled with Charles Grohmann's treatise on inferring character from handwriting, had been elemental in her father's work of studying the handwriting of a potential criminal or threat given in writing.

The late earl had traveled to Germany to talk to Professor Grohmann and returned with piles of notes, which had fascinated her. Thankfully, her father had encouraged her reading, and as she watched him work, she'd learned how to apply what she'd read. One day, she was in her father's office looking at the same paper as him. When he denied finding anything suspicious about it, she'd placed her hand over his, halting him from shifting the parchment to the side. The memory was still strong in her mind as she recalled the scent of his tobacco that clung to his jacket and the crackling of the fire in the hearth. There was a small discrepancy, one that was almost imperceptible, in the second line of the missive.

"Father, look." She pointed a dainty finger and lightly traced the shape of the T. "See, it's different from this one. Look at the slope and angle." She paused as her father looked closer.

It was the first time she had spoken up, had dared to prove she understood and that she could apply such knowledge.

The earl had nodded his approval, made a note, and from then on, welcomed her assistance. They had worked together until he passed away suddenly and the War Office lost a valuable mind. Morgan, aware of her penchant for deciphering and studying handwriting, offered her an option for continuing the work she'd loved so well. He had begun working for the War Office the year before, under the careful watch of their father.

Through his connection, Morgan devised a plan—one that both protected her and set her free to do what she loved, an arrangement that made her feel like her father was still somehow close by. Her brother gave her a job.

The War Office was desperate for another analyst. And as it so happened, there was one available.

Morgan said the person wished to remain anonymous and went by an alias: Saint.

It took some convincing, and a little hint that perhaps the anonymous person was actually Morgan, before the War Office agreed, but agree they did and Joan went to work.

Her learned skill wasn't glamorous. She didn't see visions like her namesake, or have waking dreams of archangels, nor did she anticipate saving all of Great Britain in some heroic crusade. No, but it was satisfying to make a difference.

Even if she was never given credit for it.

The clock chimed two, and she jumped at the sound of it. If her mother were alive, she'd be bustling about, reminding Joan to be ready for her potential callers.

But her mother wasn't alive. Nor was her other brother. Or her beloved father. It was only Morgan and her now, the last of them. Her heart pinched at so much loss. The fresh loss of Percy, Morgan's twin, was the most potent as it was only a year and a half old. Closing her eyes, she took a moment to mourn their memories, and then breathed deeply through her nose. No, they wouldn't wish for her to pine away for them. They would encourage her to move on, to live a joyful and full life. So, with that truth in her heart, she started up the stairs to her second-floor rooms.

Her suite was in the same wing as that of her

brother. Her lady's maid was waiting with a brush, a determined gleam in her eyes. Joan took a seat in front of the vanity and closed her eyes, wishing she had remembered to grab a book from the library.

Too bad, she'd have to endure an hour of hair brushing, tugging, and pinning without anything to read. As the maid began, Joan's mind wandered.

Tonight was her debut and so much could happen, or nothing at all. Which was the beauty of it… One never knew. And for someone who *usually* knew, it was a delightful adventure.

The unknown.

Three

THE CARRIAGE MOVED AT A SNAIL'S PACE IN THE long line of attendees for the Penderdale rout. Rowles had already been waiting for fifteen minutes, and likely it would be another ten before he made it to the front of the drive. It was the event of the week: the debut of Miss Morgan, an heiress in her own right. But Rowles knew her as his best friend's little sister. It had been an age since he'd seen her, his teaching at Cambridge taking up most of his time and energy. And when he did visit London, a ballroom was the last place he wished to be in attendance.

Even now, he was attending as a favor to Morgan, and out of responsibility to his title. He welcomed the wait, however. With his mother's condition widely known, he was certain to draw a few whispers and side looks. No one would dare say anything to him about it, for he was a duke after all, but that didn't make the situation any more comfortable. It wasn't as if their whispers weren't based on fact.

The carriage inched forward, then rolled to a stop as he continued to wait. Torches lined the short circular driveway, and if he closed his eyes and concentrated, he could hear the barest whisper of music from the main hall. Surely the doors on the balcony were open, allowing air in and music out. It would be a crush, he was certain of it, and already a trickle of sweat slid down his back at the thought. Of the two of them, his brother had been the one who enjoyed social gatherings. Rowles missed him. But life moved forward at a faster pace than the carriage, and didn't halt for emotions or pain. It carried on.

And so must he.

At last his carriage stopped before the grand entrance. Footmen swung open the carriage door and waited for Rowles to disembark. As his feet hit the gravel, he straightened his spine and drew a fortifying breath. Women with feathery hats and men in shining Hessian boots filed through the door, the dull roar of conversation already welcoming Rowles into the mayhem of a more crowded ballroom. Nodding to several men he knew, he took the stone steps to the door and passed through, the scent of beeswax and humanity greeting him.

The sound of music carried over the buzz of conversation, and he followed the long hall, illuminated by hundreds of candles and reflected by mirrors that lined the wall. Even if he wished to avoid the ballroom, the methodical flow of foot traffic toward the grand room would have made it impossible to do anything but follow. As he entered the room, a footman passed by with a silver tray of claret. Rowles lifted a glass and sipped it slowly. It wasn't his drink of choice, but it was a far cry better than nothing at all.

The stares of hungry matchmaking mamas made his skin itch under his evening attire. The prospect of a duke for a son-in-law overcame the stigma of him having an infirm mother, apparently. Avoiding their predatory looks, he scanned the room for Morgan. Being tall, he had an advantage in searching. After a few moments, and several nods to familiar faces, he made his way to the opposite corner of the room where Lady Joan was holding court and Morgan was dutifully standing by. As the Earl of Penderdale, his place was beside his family, presenting his sister.

Rowles understood the weight of responsibility, and a rush of kinship with his friend washed over him. Sipping the tepid liquid from his glass, he snaked around the milling people and skirted the ballroom floor where a Scottish reel was being danced. He ignored the stealthy attention from several others and kept his focus ahead.

"Ah, Your Grace." Morgan bowed, but his brown eyes sparkled with relief.

"Penderdale." Rowles nodded, then went to stand beside his friend and whispered, "Damn and blast, I hate it when you call me 'Your Grace.'"

"I'm only protecting my hide since my sister will

have a fit if I make any faux pas at her come-out," Morgan replied, sighing with resignation.

Chuckling, Rowles returned with "Ah, I should have known."

"Yes, yes, you should have." Morgan groaned, then tensed.

"What is it?" Rowles followed his friend's attention and frowned.

"Were we ever that wet behind the ears?"

"Pardon?"

"Green, untried, and full of our own stupidity. Look at him. Bloody fop is mooning over my sister, and if his eyes stray south once more—"

"Ah, it's times like these I'm thankful I don't have a younger sibling."

"It's a trial," Morgan replied through clenched teeth.

"Want me to cut in?"

"You can't, not without making a scene, and then you'll have to deal with the aftermath of people wondering if you are favoring her."

"Oh. Yes, well then."

"Chivalrous of you to back off so quickly," Morgan said with dry sarcasm.

Rowles chuckled. "Tell me you wouldn't do the same if the roles were reversed."

"I can't," Morgan returned after a moment's pause. "Are you going to ask her for a dance?"

"Does she have one available?"

"I've been very selective in granting my permission to those allowed to dance with her," Morgan answered.

"And the milksop—"

"Was an error in judgment."

"I see. At least it's a reel, so there's no prolonged touching." Rowles shrugged. "Or real conversation for that matter."

Morgan stilled in his agitated manner, then turned to Rowles. There was a gleam in his eye that made Rowles's cravat seem tighter. "Waltz with her. That dance is still open. I've made sure of that, but I didn't consider the…touching…as you put it."

Rowles gave a deprecating chuckle. "So you want me to do the touching?"

"You're not interested, so you're harmless."

"And here I thought we were discussing how we didn't want to start talk, or—"

"This is higher priority, and I'll explain that I wanted her first waltz with someone safe if I hear the rumor mill start to buzz. One bloody dance won't signify a courtship." Morgan turned back to watch the dancing.

Rowles fought against a scowl. Safe? He wasn't sure if he was being insulted or disregarded with such a label. He'd been called many things, but safe? That didn't sit well with him, but at the same time, he understood his friend's quandary. In that context, *safe* was an accurate word, much as he hated to admit it.

He wasn't interested, nor was he even looking for a wife. If his mother were in her right mind, he was sure she'd be after him to find a duchess, but as it were, there was no pressure.

And he was in no hurry.

The Scottish reel ended, and Joan curtsied, then turned toward her brother from her place on the dance floor. Rowles studied her. Eyes the sparkling green of moss and a bemused expression on her lovely face were all that lingered of the girl Rowles remembered from years ago. She'd made the transition from girl to woman with uncommon grace. She met his look with a curious expression but then turned her attention to her brother as she approached, escorted by her dance partner. When the gentleman bowed and left, Joan raised her hand ever so slightly to hide her wide grin.

"What's so amusing?" Morgan asked, his scrutiny raking over the crowd.

Joan's giggle was light and playful as she shook her head. "It's quite overwhelming. And odd, if I'm honest. It's quite difficult to converse during a reel, but I must say my partner made a valiant effort."

"I'll bet he did," Morgan ground out.

Joan smacked her brother with a fan she'd lifted from a nearby table.

"What did I do to deserve such treatment?" Morgan frowned.

"I'm not sure, but it sounded insulting so I assumed."

Rowles bit back a chuckle at the banter between the two siblings, then straightened his coat as the first strains of the waltz began.

"May I have the pleasure?" He turned to Joan, offering his arm.

Her look darted from him to her brother, then back. "Why am I suspicious?"

"Because it's in your nature," Morgan replied. "Are you telling me you're going to turn down a duke wishing for a waltz? Come now, His Grace is giving you an honor."

Joan quirked a brow to her brother, then turned her attention to Rowles. "I'm honored." As she took his arm, he led them toward the center of the ballroom.

His hand circled her waist, an odd sensation of awareness dancing through him at the touch.

"Thank you," Joan stated as she placed her hand on his shoulder and met his eyes unflinchingly. She was taller than he remembered—of course it had been several years. It was a rare day he didn't see clearly over a woman's head. Her touch was light and delicate, like her voice as she continued. "I know my brother asked you to do this." She gave a little shake of her head. "One would think it was *his* debut, the way he's been acting."

Rowles chuckled, amused at her insight. "He's wound tight, is he not?"

Her eyes widened with agreement. "Yes! Good mercy. Shall I tell you a secret?"

"If it's concerning your brother, by all means."

Her eyes darted to her brother, then back to him. "I called him a tyrant today."

Rowles laughed, then restrained his reaction. Her words had caught him off guard for a moment. "Truly? And what did he say to refute such a claim?"

"He agreed."

"Ah, and that is the true shock! You have achieved what others have failed at trying."

"Proving him wrong?" she asked, bestowing him with an easy grin.

For a moment, he became distracted by the pink swell of her lower lip, curving up into a perfect Cupid's bow. "Er, yes. Often I'm rebuffed when I present him with facts."

"Aren't you a professor? I'd think proving someone incorrect would be part of your daily work."

"Do you think so little of those who taught you to make such a claim? No. Rather, I'm often proven incorrect. But the difference is, I appreciate the opportunity to learn. While your brother appreciates the opportunity to prove himself right."

"Ah, I see the difference," she replied, then tipped her head as she studied him. Her scrutiny was piercing, as if she were seeing right through him and reading his very soul. The sensation of being evaluated didn't sit well with him, and his cravat seemed tight as he swallowed. When people studied him in such a way, they usually were looking for some link to his mother, some thread of the infirm in his features, expression, or mien.

"You're a good friend, Your Grace. My brother is lucky to have you." She looked away, her cheeks graced by a becoming hint of pink that hadn't been present a few moments ago. But there was a spark in her eyes, as if she wanted to say something but chose to withdraw.

Testing his theory, Rowles pressed her. "There was something more you wished to say, wasn't there?" He added a teasing lilt to his tone, even though his heart beat strangely in his chest.

"You read people well, Your Grace."

"I've had to learn. It's part of the weight of the title."

"I believe that."

"But that doesn't answer my question."

"But it relates to it." She hitched a shoulder, adjusting her hand on his upper arm. "I'm afraid it's personal, and it's not my place."

"And now I'm more curious," he answered.

"I suppose I did not put myself in a winning position, arousing your curiosity by attempting to dodge the question."

"For one so astute, you did miss that repercussion," he teased.

"Ah, this is true. Don't tell my brother. He will pester me mercilessly," she answered, a giggle interrupting.

"Ah, that is another thing I wouldn't have

expected from you, seeing as you have an older brother."

"Oh? And what is that?"

"You gave me ammunition," Rowles answered, a smirk spreading across his lips. The movement was so natural he nearly missed it, but joy seeped into his soul, calming his restless spirit ever so slightly.

"Ah, and what makes you think I did that unwittingly? If I'm as astute as you say, wouldn't it follow that I didn't miscalculate my words but chose them intentionally? What have you to say to that theory, Professor?"

His blood heated at her flirtation. Hearing her call him *professor* was oddly erotic, and he tamped down his instinctive response. She was Morgan's younger sister, and her brother was trusting him to be a "safe" choice for her first waltz.

He felt anything but safe at the moment. Rather, he was certain that if Morgan knew the inner temptation Rowles was currently fighting, he'd have a facer to show for it come morning.

"Hmm?" Joan asked again.

"You've still not answered my question." Rowles turned the conversation, needing some sort of distraction.

Her flirtatious expression faded into a more serious one. Ice chilled his veins as she met his eyes unflinchingly. "Are you sure you wish to know?"

An odd foreboding tickled his senses, but not

one to back down, he nodded. The music ended, yet he held her for a moment longer, waiting.

Joan released a breath, then leaned in ever so slightly and whispered, "You're not."

Frowning, Rowles tipped his head in confusion. "I'm not...what?"

She paused, as if weighing her words with great care. "You're not...your mother."

Shock laced through him, and he released her from the frame of their waltz. It took a moment, but he pulled his wits about him and offered her his arm as they walked back toward her brother in silence.

"I was afraid I would say too much," Joan murmured. "I apologize."

Rowles slowed his steps slightly as he replied. "No apology necessary. Rather, thank you. You've said the very thing everyone—save your brother—has avoided speaking about in my presence. And...I believe you. Thank you."

As they reached Morgan, Rowles bowed and offered Joan's arm to her sibling. Thanking her for the dance, he went to stand beside Morgan as another young buck came to collect her for the next round of the cotillion.

As she walked onto the dance floor, Rowles watched. And when her attention darted over her shoulder and met his look, he took a deep breath, unsure what odd sensations were fighting for dominance within him.

Only when he heard Morgan's sharp intake of breath did he break his stare from Joan to find Morgan's eyes intent upon him.

Seeing too much.

Rather than face his friend's questions, Rowles took control of the conversation. "She's perceptive."

Morgan froze, then gave a jerky nod. "She is that."

"It's…refreshing. You'll have your hands full with suitors."

"Are you a prophet as well as a professor now?" Morgan asked tightly, but the stark suspicion faded from his expression.

"In this, yes," Rowles admitted. Then he patted his friend's back. "Best of luck with that."

Morgan's expression bordered on hostile, but then he turned to face his friend fully. "Tell me, then. Will you be one of them?"

Rowles took a step back in surprise. "Pardon?"

"Should I expect you to come calling at the social hour with sonnets and flowers?"

Rowles noted the sarcastic tone to his friend's voice and sobered. "Judging by your tone, you already know the answer to that."

Morgan narrowed his eyes, but didn't press his friend further.

For that, Rowles was thankful, because the truth would have been a lie, one way or another.

Because he wasn't sure of the answer.

Because half of him was intrigued.

The other half was terrified.

He couldn't remember the last time someone saw through him so clearly. And that begged the question: If she looked closely, what would she see?

And did he want to know?

Sometimes demons were better left buried, rather than faced and set free.

Four

IT HAD BEEN TOO FAR.

She'd known it, but he kept pressing her for the answer and now all she had was regret. They had been having such a lovely waltz, her first one, and with a duke no less. But she'd ruined it by looking too deeply and seeing too much. Hadn't she learned? People hid things for a reason; they didn't want others to know. And just because she could observe and make assessments based on various traits she'd studied in her research didn't mean she should tell others what she saw when evaluating them.

Did it?

Joan tossed in her bed, unable to find a comfortable position in the midst of her mental turmoil. It had been the perfect evening, save that one trespass. The lights and music were dazzling, and her dress was ethereal and angelic—several gentlemen had said as much. And each and every dance had been partnered. The event was a success in every way, except for her ability to keep her thoughts to herself.

Maybe her brother was right; maybe she wasn't quite ready.

Yet, even as she berated herself, part of her wasn't

sorry at all. If there was one thing she'd learned in her study, it was that people often went to great lengths to hide the truth.

Even...*especially* from themselves.

But the Duke of Westmore was different.

Oh, there was confusion and uncertainty—that was clear in his expression, in the way his eyes scanned the room for those judging him, in the way he held his back perfectly straight as if daring any accusations to try to hit a target—but he wasn't intentionally trying to hide his soul.

It was as if he'd been at peace with it.

But there was one tightening of his expression that bespoke of a concern, a hint of pain that ran deep.

Fear.

From there it was simple to deduce the root of it. After all, everyone in London knew about his mother's ailments. And if she were in his place, the one question that would plague her would be... what if?

What if it happened to me?

Is that my future?

What will happen if...?

It was deduction.

And those fears were unnecessary.

His heart was as solid as the vivid blue of his eyes, his expression and mannerisms clear. It was in the way he held her gaze and the peace that she saw residing deep within. Those who harbored the weight of deception didn't display such a demeanor. Didn't he deserve to know the truth so he could release the burden he carried?

She had used that as justification to tell him… when he pressured her. But again, doing so had been going too far.

And it revealed too much of herself, of what secrets *she* kept.

Morgan had cornered her after the ball as they made their way to find their beds for the night.

"Anything I should know about?" he'd asked.

Unable to lie, she cast her look to the floorboards.

Morgan had sighed, then tried a gentler tone. "Is there anything I should know about?"

"No."

It wasn't a lie because sharing personal information about others didn't pertain to her brother…so she could refuse with a clear conscience.

Sleep had eluded her ever since and was still persistently avoiding her, so she decided to rise from bed and find a book. She lifted a leather-bound copy of *Ivanhoe* and sat in her wing-backed chair beside the crackling fire, careful to enjoy its warmth but not get too close. Warily, she pulled her knees in tight as she flipped through the pages to find the last one she'd read.

The lines became blurry after the second page, and before she started the next chapter, Joan was startled awake by the sound of the book hitting the floor after slipping through her drowsy fingers. She picked up the book and then climbed into her bed, thankful sleep was finding her at last.

The soft morning song of birds slowly called her awake as morning dawned, but a moment later their song was interrupted by her maid's voice.

"Miss? Your brother is asking for you."

Joan's eyelids were heavy as she fought against the sleep that sweetly called her back into oblivion.

"Very well," she mumbled, then forced herself to rise and blink.

In short order, she was dressed and her hair twisted into a simple knot as she took the hall stairs to the breakfast room.

Morgan would have to wait till she had her tea.

And toast.

And perhaps a few rashers of bacon.

"Ah, there you are. I thought you'd been swallowed up by your bed," Morgan said by way of greeting. He lowered the *London Times* only enough to see her, then returned to whatever article he'd been reading.

"What's so dreadfully important that you needed to send my maid to pester me awake?" Joan replied without preamble.

"Aren't you jolly this morning."

"I'll be jolly when I have tea and breakfast."

"Then by all means." Morgan released one hand from the paper and waved toward the sideboard.

Joan breathed deeply of the sweet scent of bacon

and jam, then selected several items for her plate before finding a seat beside her brother.

She poured herself a cup of tea, breathing in the steam with a greedy impatience as she sipped the hot liquid. Then she sighed and turned to her brother. "I'm ready."

"Took you long enough. I thought you'd want to see this." Morgan carefully folded the paper in half and laid it beside her plate, pointing to a bold headline on the third page.

FRENCH SMUGGLERS CAUGHT OFF THE COAST OF CORNWALL

Joan read the article. "It was a smuggling operation?"

"Yes, and thanks to your efforts, they were easily located and arrested. You saved the War Office much time and many provisions by eliminating the need to set up surveillance at two areas. Well done, Saint." He winked.

Joan smirked at her brother. "Well, that is a great start to the day, is it not?"

"I thought so, but you needed some convincing."

"I've changed my attitude," Joan replied saucily as she took another sip of tea.

"Oh, and this might be of some interest as well." Morgan lifted a society page from beside his empty plate. "The society papers work harder than the actual news, I believe. This was a quick turnaround as far as gossip is concerned."

Joan plucked the single sheet from his hand and read it. It was the *Tattler* page that often circulated after notable events or parties. That it came the day after her come-out was an indication that the party had been a very important one. Joan blushed at the implication.

It was a lovely evening, with lovely people with lovely gowns and evening attire. But the highlight was the way the pure English flower danced with a duke whose name bears a dark, ominous cloud. Can beauty overcome the stigma of blood? One has to wonder... and we'll be curiously watching from afar.

"That's odd." Joan frowned as she reread the phrasing that most intrigued her. "I'm not sure I'd insult the Duke of Westmore in such a way. It's utterly inaccurate as well."

When Morgan was silent, she turned her attention to him.

Joan smiled. "*He's* not infirm, but his mother likely is." She flicked her wrist. "I've never met her, but he's not. I can tell you that for certain." She went back to her tea and took a sip. "I recently read Juan Luis Vives's—"

The silence made her stop and look from her plate to the newspaper and then finally to her brother. His expression indicated that Morgan was mulling over her commentary. He folded the paper and braced his hands on the table as he leaned forward. "Explain."

"Explain what?" Joan asked, an uneasy sensation unwinding in her belly. Morgan's talents included relentlessly ferreting out the truth.

"What you said so casually concerning your dance with Rowles."

"Waltz, actually. If we're to be as detailed as you're attempting to be."

"Cheeky thing," Morgan drawled. "Very well, you *waltzed* with him, and even the society gossip pages took notice."

"May I remind you that I waltzed with him because he was obliging you?"

"Not important." Morgan waved off her words impatiently.

Joan sniffed at his rebuttal and took a sip of tea, eyed the laid out food, and started to fill a plate. She needed a moment of distraction to collect her thoughts.

"What did you do? Because for you to be so sure of something—"

"Do you think he's…like his mother?" Joan asked impatiently. She set her teacup down and leaned toward Morgan.

"Heavens, no." Her brother had the good grace to look offended by such a question.

"Why?" she asked, her dry tone earning a scowl from him.

"Because I've known him for over a decade. You, on the other hand, know him only through my acquaintance, so forgive me if I question my very…perceptive sister"—he looked around, taking into account the servants present—"about her convictions."

Joan twisted her lips.

Morgan's stare pierced her. "Are you finished?" He gestured to her still-full plate.

"No. I've been arguing with you and haven't had much opportunity to do anything else," Joan replied, then took an exaggeratedly slow bite of bacon and chewed methodically. It was amusing to watch Morgan's ears turn red with irritation.

"Bring it with you and follow me." He gave a pointed look to the footman beside the sideboard and stood, indicating for her to rise as well.

She sent him a scowl. "You're awfully pushy today."

"I'm sure I could come up with some accurate adjectives for your behavior as well, seeing as my 'pushy' attitude is a reaction to you." He resettled her chair under the table for her, then led her down the hall.

Joan lifted the last rasher of bacon to her mouth and chewed as she followed Morgan to his study. He closed the door behind them and took a seat. Drat, she was in for a lecture and it wasn't even half eleven in the morning.

"I forgot my tea." Joan rose again.

"You don't need it," Morgan replied and sat

across from her in the smallish seating area near the fire. "Joan, we've discussed this. In social settings, you mustn't let on that you—"

"I'm mindful. I didn't do anything wrong. Why must you be so sensitive—"

"Because I know how people work, think, and react." Lines formed along his forehead. "And I don't want you to be on the receiving end of their speculation or ire," he finished.

When he put it in such a protective way, Joan struggled to find her righteous anger against him. *Drat the man.*

She sighed softly. "It was your friend, someone whom I know you trust. I didn't say or do anything that would give way to speculation, and even if I did, don't you have faith in your friend not to use it against you...or me?"

Morgan studied her, then looked down to his hands, folding them and then unfolding them. "So you said nothing to him?"

Joan glanced to the side.

"Damn it. What did you say?" Morgan asked, his sharp words echoing in the room, even with the quiet way he had spoken them.

"I tried not to."

"Oh, it's bad, isn't it?" He rubbed the back of his neck, then stood from his seat and began pacing.

"No. Stop fussing. You're worse than a mother hen."

He gave her quite a sarcastic expression as a response, but halted his pacing.

"I was curious," she said, defending herself.

"Which killed the cat, you know." Morgan began pacing once more.

"Meow," she replied smartly and continued, "I hedged a bit."

"Which only whetted his curiosity." He snorted.

"Probably."

"And you said?"

"Well, I could see this sort of aura." She hedged.

"I regret giving you books on Greek etymology," Morgan replied and set his head in his hands as he sighed. "You're not answering the question, and I know damn well you saw no aura. You're far too fond of your facts and science."

"There's a severe deficiency in women's education. You know this. You were giving me the freedom to study that which interested me and expanded my mind."

"Which I'm utterly reaping the benefits of currently."

"It was never for your benefit, Morgan."

He made an impatient movement with his left hand. "Carry on."

"It was in the way he carried himself, confident, yet expectant and...almost bracing himself for some attack." She lifted one delicate brow in query. "The battlefield is within one's mind. That was exactly what I saw in him. Sometimes you need something…someone…to point you in the right direction. So…I did."

"By saying?"

"Simply saying what I saw!"

When Morgan didn't reply, she hazarded a look up to him.

"And what was his response?" he asked quietly.

She shrugged. "I don't think he believed me, but he will. It's a burden he shouldn't have to bear when it's clearly a lie."

"He didn't question how you came to such an observation?" Morgan asked skeptically.

"I tried to go about it in a way that didn't reveal how perceptive I am, an observation that anyone could make. I'm smarter than you give me credit for, Morgan."

"It's not your intelligence I've ever found wanting. It's your lack of sophistication that I fear will lead you astray."

"I call that your inability to give humanity the benefit of the doubt."

"And I call it covering my…self." He smirked and then shook his head. "Very well, it seems that the crisis I imagined is not forthcoming."

"Shocking, that, since you're so often the optimist of the two of us."

A smile slid over his face. "As I said, cheeky."

Joan's lips quirked to the side as she nibbled the last part of her rasher of bacon. "Will that be all?"

"For now. I'm sure I'll find another reason to rake you across the coals, but you're free for the moment," he teased, then tipped his head to the side. "I should think you'll be expecting some company later today."

"I should hope so. If not, my come-out was a complete failure," she replied. "But I do expect I'll have a few callers."

"With their sonnets."

She gave a thoughtful sigh. "I think I should like to have a sonnet written for me. To be one's muse… It's a heady thought."

"Yes, well…"

Joan smirked at how her brother didn't come back with an articulate response. "Have you ever written a sonnet for a lady, Morgan?"

He gave her a withering glare. "I have better things to do with my time."

"Ah, yes, saving the world and all."

"It's a team effort, I like to imagine."

She giggled. "Indeed. Speaking of which, have you any other need of my assistance?"

"Not at the moment." He paused. "But I'm sure it's only a matter of time."

"Very well. If we're finished here, I need to dress for my prospective visitors this afternoon." She reached for her plate but paused, one finger raised. "You asked me to remind you the next time I plan to attend a meeting…"

Morgan's expression darkened. "Don't tell me you're still involved with those bluestockings who are papering London with their voting demands."

"Are you so against a woman having a voice?" Joan stood and placed a hand on her hips while the other held her plate.

"No, which you very well know. I don't believe that society's way of going about change is the most effective."

"Well, try not, succeed not." Joan nodded. "It's our motto."

"And a good one it is. However, I wish you would support it from afar. It's unfashionable and frowned upon for a lady of the *ton* to participate in bluestocking endeavors."

"As you've said. On multiple occasions. I suppose I'm a bit unique… Oh wait." She gave a wry expression. "We already knew that, didn't we? I cannot change my spots, Morgan. Besides, knowing what you know about me and my insight, doesn't that indicate the importance of such an effort? That I see its soul-deep merit for others should encourage you to support women's rights."

"I do, but I am concerned about you. And of the two priorities, you are my first." Morgan nodded, then stood as well. "Be cautious, and don't take the family carriage."

"I've already hired a hack and Mrs. Gunthrie's sister is my chaperone."

Morgan nodded. "Well, then you are all situated. Be safe."

"I will." Joan hitched a shoulder with a cheeky smirk. "And I'll be back in plenty of time to hear all the sonnets the gentlemen have worked to write since the ball last eve."

"At that, I'll take my leave." Morgan chuckled. "Goodbye."

Joan watched her brother leave the study and sighed. The plate was heavy in her hand even though it held little. Perhaps it was her mind that was heavy. She wasn't dishonest about the women's rights convocation, but she knew that Morgan was correct; it was a difficult path ahead. But difficult did not mean impossible. How often were the right things the very ones that required a fight to be achieved? Usually, so Joan chose to fight for those causes.

The hall clock chimed, and she straightened her spine and nodded to herself. Never let it be said she backed down from a worthy challenge. Rather, let her be the one to rise to meet it!

After all, what good was it to be named after someone significant if you didn't do your best to honor the legacy that person left? Joan strode to the breakfast hall and considered the idea. She might not be working to free France like Joan of Arc, but working to expand women's freedom? That was certainly a worthy cause.

And one worth all her effort.

Five

It was fascinating how four words could have so much power.

Rowles watched the steam curl upward from his teacup, disappearing into the air as he thought over the previous night. It had been a crushing success, the come-out for Lady Joan, but all of the evening faded into the background at the memory of her simple words.

"You're not like her."

Dear Lord, he'd felt infirm, had feared it for so much of his life he couldn't remember anything prior, but to have someone speak that fear out loud and renounce it so confidently... Well, it nearly made him believe it as the truth.

He wanted to, desperately.

But the greatest enemy to truth was the simple question, "What if?" And thousands of those questions peppered his mind with doubts. Yet he continued to remember Joan's words, and the tone with which they were spoken.

Quiet, unassuming confidence.

It reminded him of his theology professor at Cambridge, Professor Dory. Joan's words had carried the same soft-spoken assurance. Professor Dory's lectures were Rowles's favorites, and he'd adored the way Professor Dory spoke with conviction that came from a solid truth, a firm foundation for knowledge that left only room for faith to believe it. Rowles shook his head at the memory. He would never have expected that years later he would take over those lectures in that very hall after Professor Dory passed away and teach those same principles to his students.

And though Rowles had tried, desperately tried, he couldn't replicate that same soft reassurance of his predecessor. But Joan—rather, Lady Joan— spoke with it effortlessly.

It was alluring, captivating, and frightening as hell. Because what peace surrounded her mind and heart to put such unshaking resolve in her words? Perhaps she didn't notice it. Maybe he wouldn't have noticed either, had he not already been exposed to that same sense of conviction by his predecessor. But it called to him.

Made him want to believe whatever authority gave her the raw intensity in her words.

He gave a self-deprecating chuckle. He was the professor, the educated one. He had studied at Cambridge, had spent countless hours in the library poring over books and memorizing whole chapters of the Bible to grasp the truths he sought. Only to later teach them, and still lack the principles the slip of a woman presented last night. It was humbling.

Rowles took a sip of tea, his mind wandering to the events of the day ahead. His mother had been at rest for the past few days, not leaving her rooms, even to break her fast. It wasn't unusual, but in the past, she would at least have ventured to the library where she'd stand in front of the wide window that faced the front of the estate. For hours, she'd watch the carriages pass, but even that didn't currently interest her.

Guilt laced through him. If he were a better son, he'd take a deck of cards upstairs to at least attempt to play with her, or even bring along a book and read to her. But he'd hired people to do that in his stead. It seemed like a good choice but he wondered if his true intentions were to avoid her. Resolved, he took a final sip of tea and set the cup back in its saucer. He could very easily take tea with his mother, rather than sit in solitude in his study. Leaving the quiet of his sanctuary, he took the stairs to the second floor and then turned right to take the hall that would lead to his mother's rooms.

Mrs. Owens, his mother's second nurse, was sitting outside the room knitting. She stood and curtsied as Rowles approached. "Aye, Your Grace. Your mother is well this morn."

"Good, good." He paused, tucking his hands behind his back. "Would you have tea sent up for us?"

Mrs. Owens blinked, then nodded. "You wish to have tea with yer mother? Of course, Your Grace. I'll see to it directly." She curtsied once more.

Rowles turned the brass knob on the door and took a deep breath. The room was dark, thick with warm and stagnant air that carried the tang of medicine. His clothes felt constricting, as if suffocating him as he made his way inside. Candles flickered, and the fire in the hearth cast its cheery glow on the otherwise silent room.

"Yes?" His mother's voice was little more than a frog's croak, as if rusty from disuse.

He cleared his throat delicately. "Hello, Mother." Rowles spoke in a gentle tone as he approached her bedside.

"Son? Ah, come here, let me see my beautiful boy," she whispered, and the rustling of bedcovers followed as she shifted.

Rowles stood beside the bed, his attention on the shadow of the woman his mother had once been. Her skin hung loosely over her limbs, and he noted she'd lost more weight. It was difficult to convince her to eat, her malady making her suspicious of all food, convinced it was poisoned. He'd asked one of his mother's maids to taste the food in front of his mother before serving it, but that tactic must not be working as well as it had been last week.

He released a soft sigh of hopelessness, even as

he continued to force a peaceful expression for his mother's benefit.

"So beautiful, you were always such a beautiful boy." She tried to smile, her dry lips stretching across her teeth.

"I take after my mother," Rowles replied, grasping her hand and squeezing it gently.

"Where's Rowles?" his mother asked suddenly, and looked behind him as if searching.

"Pardon?" Rowles gave a start, then eased out a slow breath. Ah. She had forgotten. Again.

"Robert, don't tease your mother. It isn't kind. Where's that brother of yours? I'm worried about him."

Rowles sighed, then decided to play along. As much as it grieved him, it wouldn't be helpful to try to convince her that her son was gone forever. Who knew what episode such a revelation—again— could bring about!

"I'm sure he's simply reading. You know how he can be." Rowles shrugged, tucking his hands in his pockets like his brother used to do. A tight ache in his chest reminded him of how much he missed Robert.

"That boy." His mother clicked her tongue as she gave her head a slow shake. Her mobcap went askew at the movement, revealing silver curls that had escaped their confines.

Her pewter eyes narrowed as she looked to

Rowles, seeing him, yet not. "Can I tell you a secret?"

Rowles nodded. "Only if it's a good secret," he teased, using his brother's words as he remembered them.

His mother only frowned further. "I think he might be a bit balmy."

Rowles froze, then frowned at his mother's words, rather the irony of them. "Say what, now?"

"Daft, addlepated, not quite right." She sighed as if the long explanation was a great source of fatigue. "There's something about him... Even when he was a boy, I worried. He's not like you, Robert, so kind and handsome. His mind is too...over-worked." She closed her eyes and relaxed into her pillow. "Watch over him. And if he goes too far, you have my permission." She nodded, then opened her eyes and speared him with an observant look that left his bones chilled.

"Permission?" Rowles asked, not certain he wanted to know the answer.

"Don't look at me that way. It's nothing we haven't discussed before." She waved a bony hand dismissively.

"Discussed what, exactly?" Rowles asked, his cravat itching his neck.

His mother blinked once, then twice. "If he's as crazy as I think he might turn out to be, put him in Bedlam. Don't worry, he won't know the difference." She sighed. "But we can't have our family the laughingstock of the *ton*. At least you're the heir, Robert." She chuckled. "Can you imagine if Rowles had been the heir? God help us." She gave a dry laugh that changed into a cough.

"I'll get your nurse," Rowles whispered, his mind churning with the implications of her words, the irony of them and the pain as a result.

"She won't care. They hate me, all of them," she wheezed. "But mark my words, watch him, Robert. Watch him."

Rowles didn't respond, but backed away from his mother's bed and started toward the door to get the nurse.

"Wait."

Rowles stopped, then turned toward his mother. "Yes?"

"Come closer," she demanded, her words icy.

Every instinct in him said to leave the room and let the nurse attend to her, but instead he took several slow steps toward her bedside.

"No." Her eyes widened.

Rowles tipped his head in confusion, then took a step back as his mother lurched forward from her bed.

"No! Deceiver! Where's Robert? Where's my son?" The words were a shriek as she grasped his shoulders and pushed him backwards with surprising force. Caught off guard by her assault, he landed on a wooden side table as the nurse came in with the requested tea.

"Oh my!" the nurse exclaimed and rushed back out the door, calling for footmen.

Rowles stood from his sprawled position on the floor, casting a furtive glance at the now-shattered side table and the splintered wood that had embedded itself in his skin. Wincing in pain, he watched his mother cautiously as she continued to advance toward him.

It was a difficult position; he didn't want to harm her but also didn't wish to be assaulted further. Yet he knew that he'd gladly take more abuse rather than defend himself against her. She let out a loud screech and lunged for him. Rowles reached out and grasped her in a hug, pinning her arms to her sides as he held her tight. Three footmen rushed in, followed by two nurses.

"Your Grace!" one of the footmen shouted and then started forward at the moment his mother took the opportunity to Rowles in the shoulder.

He howled in pain, releasing her reflexively.

The footmen held her fast and then guided her to her bed as she spat epithets at them all.

Rowles panted with shock as he watched them pin his mother to her bed. A nurse poured a dose of laudanum into a cup, then added water. With shaking hands, she took the cup to his thrashing mother. He watched as the nurse all but forced the liquid down his mother's throat, amid her gagging and coughing, with a good measure of spitting thrown in, till at least some portion was swallowed. The footmen held fast for several minutes as they waited for the opiate to take effect.

Slowly, his mother ceased her fighting, and her protesting became weaker as she relaxed. None too soon, the only sound was the soft noise of her snoring as she fell asleep.

The footmen gently released their hold and stood cautiously, then turned to face him. "How can we assist you, Your Grace?" one asked. His livery vest was open, the gold buttons of his uniform scattered across the floor from the duchess's assault as he'd held her fast. Another footman's lip was swollen, a trickle of blood at the corner of his mouth.

The third refused to turn, standing vigil over the duchess, making sure she didn't awake and renew her assault.

"I... That is, I'll address my situation in a moment." Rowles nodded. "I am grateful for your assistance."

The two footmen bowed, and the third turned and bowed as well, acknowledging their duke's words.

"See to your own needs." Rowles motioned to the door. He then turned to the two nurses, who were watching him with wary eyes. "Please keep her sedated, and I'll confer with the doctor."

They curtsied, then shared a look with each other.

Rowles winced as he took a step toward the door. "I will be making different arrangements for her from now on," he murmured.

The nurses nodded, then relaxed their rigid posture as if the words gave them stark relief.

He paused and turned to the nurses. "Has she been this violent before?"

The older of the two stepped forward. "Your Grace, this was more severe than usual, but her behavior *has* taken a violent turn as of recent."

Rowles nodded. "I see." He glanced from the nurses to the laudanum to his mother's sleeping form. "Keep footmen beside the door and do not come in to care for her without assistance."

"Yes, Your Grace," agreed the older nurse.

Rowles took his leave then, his leg hurting like the devil. He made his way to his rooms. Thankfully, his valet was waiting, no doubt having heard about the fiasco from the rest of the house staff.

"Your Grace." Lowson bowed as Rowles closed the door to his bedroom. "Where is your injury? Should I summon the doctor?"

Rowles nodded. "Send a missive to the doctor, but not for my injury. That, I am certain we can manage on our own. But I need to discuss my mother's behavior and…" He paused, not wanting to say the words out loud but not having any other recourse.

Lowson waited.

"And see about assistance for my mother, more than we currently are able to provide."

Lowson's eyes lowered to the floor as he nodded. "I see, and I know you don't make such a decision lightly, Your Grace, if I may be so bold."

Rowles gave a shrug. "Be as bold as you wish. It won't change a damn thing."

"I'll have a footman send word to the doctor, and then we shall discern what sort of injury you have received."

Rowles nodded, and as Lowson quit the room to find a footman to take the missive to the doctor, he started to undress. His breeches had slits where the wooden table had split and splintered, ripping the fabric, and dark blood was drying the frayed cloth to his wound. As he removed the garment, the wounds reopened, seeping blood. Several long slivers peppered his thigh, and he withdrew some easily enough, but a few more remained, needing more than fingertips to remove them.

The flesh on his thigh was turning purple, and he growled as he noted how his boots were scuffed, possibly beyond repair. He took a deep breath and pinched the bridge of his nose, focusing on calming his churning mind. He didn't want to think about his mother's words, nor did he wish to remember what had just transpired, but it haunted him on the edge of his mind.

A sarcastic scoff escaped his lips, and a dry sneer teased his lips. Hadn't he been musing over the confidence in Lady Joan's words? Choosing to spend more time with his mother, be a better son? It was all for naught.

He'd known that Robert was the favorite, but for her to so clearly indicate that was heart-wrenching.

Lowson knocked once and then let himself back in the room, giving a quick nod to indicate the missive had been sent. "Shall we address this, then?" He gestured to Rowles's leg.

Rowles nodded once, not trusting his voice or much else at the moment. He was still reeling with shock from the whole fiasco. But one thing was for certain: something needed to be done. His mother was a danger, and he couldn't, in good conscience, continue to let the nurses address her violent behavior.

Lowson poured water into a bowl and began to dab the blood caked on Rowles's thigh. "No stitches, I'd say. But we'd best get this splintered wood out, Your Grace."

"Do what you must," Rowles rumbled.

In short work, Lowson had removed the splinters and bandaged him well, with only the faint sting reminding him of the earlier pain. A knock sounded at the door as Lowson finished tying Rowles's cravat as the final touch on his new and cleaner clothes.

"Enter," Rowles called, tugging on his shirtsleeves.

A maid entered and curtsied. "The doctor has arrived, Your Grace."

Rowles nodded. "I'll be down directly."

The maid curtsied and left as Rowles let out a tight breath. "This is not how I imagined my day going," he muttered.

"I'm sure, Your Grace," Lowson murmured.

As Rowles exited his bedroom and started for the stairs, he steeled himself for what he was about to do.

God have mercy on them all.

Six

Men are sometimes hanged for telling the truth.

—*Joan of Arc*

JOAN RESISTED THE URGE TO FIDGET OR twitch or nervously tap her foot as she held court in the green salon for all her callers. The previous night's party had been a smashing success, if only because no fewer than five suitors had called, and it was only half past four. The clink of china teacups sounded throughout the room as she scanned the occupants. Three earls, a viscount, and a baron, all vying for her attention.

Lord Archby addressed her. "Do you enjoy horseback riding, Lady Joan? If so, I must tell you about my lovely stables in Sussex." He punctuated the words with warmth. Of the five, he was the most charming.

Alas, horseflesh was the least of her interests. However, to be kind, she nodded. "Do tell me about them."

"My stallion is from a champion bloodline, quick

as lightning and every bit as temperamental." He gave a wry smirk.

"And you know this from experience? Has he ever thrown you?" she asked, flirting only a bit.

Lord Archby shrugged and cast a sideways glance to his competitors. "Not once have I been unseated, my lady," he replied with a confident tone, his hand shifting slightly as it rested on his knee, his eyes darting to the left.

Beside him, Viscount Burton snorted softly as he sipped his tea.

Liar. Joan suppressed the impulse to shake her head at the falsehood Lord Archby had told. If she wasn't convinced by his body language, the viscount's reaction would have told her the same. The light from the windows dimmed around him, as if swallowed up by the sin he'd committed. Irritated with the lie, she breathed calmly through her nose and turned her attention to the viscount. "And what inspires you, Viscount Burton?"

He greeted her question with a twitch of his lips. "I enjoy the fox hunt."

"A noble sport," she replied politely, wondering if anything of true interest would ever be introduced as a topic. At least, of interest to her. "And you raise foxhounds, I assume?"

"Yes. Which, I might add, are the most adorable pups you'd ever see."

Now that was intriguing. "And that I have no problem believing." She grinned.

"Do you enjoy animals, Lady Joan?"

"Indeed, especially those of the adorable variety."

The viscount nodded. "Then I shall notify you when I have a new litter to display for your adoration."

"I look forward to that," Joan replied, feeling more at ease.

The social hour carried on in a similar fashion, leaving her quite exhausted from all the attention and conversation when it was finished. At last, she took her leave from the parlor and went to seek solitude in the library.

As she turned the brass doorknob and pushed the door open, the evening light filtered across the rug-covered floor. The chaise lounge near the fire promised respite, and she made her way over to it with gratitude. Joan reclined on the soft brocade fabric, allowing her mind to wander to the afternoon's events.

She was able to eliminate her interest in several gentlemen and found several others diverting. It was an odd season in her life. She was reminded of the verse in Ecclesiastes: "To everything there is a season, and a time to every purpose under the heaven." It was a season, hopefully, for love. What a worthy adventure.

She sighed wistfully, only to be startled when the library door swung open wider, revealing a quite determined-looking Morgan.

"Ah, there you are. Finished with holding court and not a moment too soon. Come with me, will you?" He waited for her nod and then left the room.

Joan stood and followed him to his study.

Morgan closed the door with a muted click and then went to his desk, his forehead furrowed.

"There's a situation, and I am at a loss for what to do, Joan," he started, his stare lingering on the desktop as if searching it for clues.

"I will help in whatever capacity I can," she assured him, curiosity nibbling at her thoughts.

"It's not that I doubt your ability. Rather, I doubt whether it is prudent to ask for your assistance." He met her look.

"You fear for me?" Joan asked, reading the truth in his eyes.

"Yes."

She nodded once, then leaned forward, splaying her hands upon his desk. "I fear nothing but treachery."

Morgan's lips twitched, not with amusement but with the weight of decision. "With the War Office, all is loyalty or treachery. There is no middle ground."

"Then it is good that I fight on the right side of it."

Morgan sighed. "That you do. That you do."

"So? What is it?"

Morgan withdrew a rolled linen paper from his

front coat pocket. It was held fast with a single red ribbon. "We have received several…riddles. They all are related to different parts of the Bible, and we think they hold some sort of significance for those who wish to create dissent in England. Napoleon is on St. Helena and will not escape again, but that doesn't mean the French loyalists and the few French sympathizers in England are willing to give up completely on their cause."

"I see. Is that one of the riddles?" Joan held out her hand.

"Yes." Morgan handed the paper to his sister.

The ribbon slid off easily, and Joan unrolled the paper and held it flat against the desk as she read it.

"A time to be born, a time to die." She glanced up to her brother, then back to the words and kept reading. "A time to plant and a time to harvest. A time to be born and a time to kill." She frowned as she reread the words.

Hadn't she been thinking about that same passage? It was from the very book and chapter she'd been musing over before Morgan had come to find her. "What makes you think it's a message for dissent?"

Morgan waved his hand over the desk. "We intercepted it from a long-standing French sympathizer."

"I see." Joan studied the words again, then closed her eyes. "This isn't as easy as figuring out which is the ruse and which is accurate, like last time."

"No, no, it is not. Which is why I was hesitating to ask for your help."

"Because you know I'll need to see them, face-to-face." She remembered her recent encounter with Lord Archby. She wasn't as well-versed in behavior as she was in handwriting, but she was willing to try.

"Yes."

Joan nodded to her brother. "Then lead the way."

Morgan sighed. "It's not that simple."

"You say that, but isn't it? After all, what if I was born for this? What good is my education and skill if I refuse to take the risk of using it to protect my country? My family? I refuse to back down because my brother sees a potential risk. And yes, let us emphasize the word: *potential*. Not a sure risk. A possibility. Besides, you'll be with me, won't you?"

Morgan tapped his fingers on the desk and studied her. "Yes, I will." He hesitated for a moment and then gave a nod. "Very well. Let's get this over with."

"You have the messenger in custody?"

"Yes. You'll have to...change."

"Ah, you mean a disguise."

"Yes, exactly. In fact..." He frowned. "I can't believe I'm going to say this." He paused, then straightened. "Yes, that will be best. As unconventional as it is, that will be best."

"What...what will be best?" Joan asked, her tone skeptical.

"Sister dear, you're going to be my groom."

"Pardon?"

"I'll go and collect livery for you, and that way you'll be unrecognizable."

"I'm to dress as a groom? For your carriage?" She blinked. "And a male one, to boot?"

"No one will be the wiser, and you'll be safe."

"This is not how I imagined this afternoon playing out," Joan replied with a shocked tone.

"I thought you were willing to do whatever was necessary," her brother challenged.

Joan glared at him. "Very well. Do your worst, but don't cut my hair."

Morgan had the good grace to look offended at the thought. "We won't need to go that far. Go to your rooms, and I'll knock and leave the uniform by the door when no one is looking. Dress quickly and then knock three times on your door when you're finished. I'll collect you when the hallway is clear, and we'll escape through the back. I'll have my curricle ready."

Joan giggled. "Why do I feel naughty, like I'm doing something wrong rather than doing something right? I surely won't tell anyone," Joan replied as she started toward the door.

"Nor will I." Morgan gave her a wink. "Go. I'll be by shortly."

Joan nodded and took the stairs to the second floor. Once she got to her rooms, she waited.

As promised, Morgan knocked and left the navy-colored livery of their household servants outside her door. Scooping it up, she said a brief prayer of thanks that her dress didn't button up the back, making the solo costume change much easier. Once dressed in the breeches and buttoning the coat, she turned to the mirror and studied her reflection. The clothes were, thankfully, a little large, hiding her feminine form. Still, she took off the jacket and wrapped her chest with a long cloth, binding her breasts to make them even less noticeable under the coat. Approving of the change, she turned her attention to her hair. Morgan had left a top hat beside the clothing, and she fleetingly wondered if she could pin it in place. Surely it was similar to a ladies' hat, was it not? If she could tuck her hair into a high knot, then pin the hat, it should work.

Several minutes later, she studied her reflection and decided it would have to do. The hat was tipped forward so that it would be easier to hide her face if she lowered her chin. This was an addlebrained idea, but it would prevent anyone asking questions about why Lord Penderdale would take her to the holding place of criminals.

Good Lord. A shudder rippled through her. She couldn't imagine what the tattle papers would say about such an event. She tugged on white gloves and smoothed her pants much like she'd smooth her skirts. Then she rapped three times on her door and waited for Morgan to open it. Less than a minute passed before the door swung inward to reveal him waiting for her, and she followed him out the door, down the hall, and into the back alley of their home.

"You'll sit here." He pointed to the groom's seat.

"Obviously." Joan allowed a bit of dryness in her response as she took her brother's offered hand and sat on the small seat.

"Now, keep your head down, and I'll take a bit of a roundabout way to the holding place. We've not moved the culprit into the prison yet, which makes this easier. I wouldn't dare take you to that hellhole."

Joan nodded and adjusted her placement on the seat, keeping her eyes and face averted downward.

Morgan snapped the ribbons and directed the horse to the front. Soon they were traveling through Mayfair toward Whitehall. They passed Charing Cross of Central London, moving down to Horse Guards, the seat of the War Office. Joan kept her head lowered, only her eyes darting about, taking in the scenes of a bustling Westminster.

Morgan took a small side street and then turned right onto a larger lane. The curricle coasted over the cobblestones and then came to a stop in front of a very ordinary black door. Upon his arrival, a man stepped out from the building and studied

Morgan coolly. "I'll see to your horse," he said after a moment, his voice deep and gravelly.

"I'll take the lad inside, see if he remembers anything important," Morgan replied, then indicated with his head to the door. Joan stepped from her perch, fleetingly taking note of how odd it was to have no help alighting from the carriage.

She kept several paces behind Morgan as they approached the door. It was maddening, for she wanted to ask Morgan a million questions but she had to wait, silently filing them in her mind for later. How did the man know that the groom, who was usually the one to mind the horses, was the one who had information? Had Morgan sent a missive ahead? Or had this been the plan all along? She wouldn't doubt the latter. Irritating that he had worked out this adventure in his head long before approaching her to participate, as if he'd known she'd agree.

Which, of course, she would.

And had.

But that wasn't the point, was it?

She pushed her thoughts aside and took in her surroundings. The hall floor creaked with each step, and the scent of pipe tobacco hung in the air. The walls were a dingy white with plaster peeling where they met the ceiling. Morgan stopped beside a door and opened it, revealing a worn wooden table and four chairs.

"Sit." He motioned to a seat and then took one

beside her. "Now, let me explain what is going to take place," Morgan whispered softly, as if the walls were thin or had ears. "I will bring in another gentleman. He will be an assistant, should the person you are to see become belligerent. I'll remain by your side, and I ask you don't speak. Your voice will give you away. Merely listen, and when you have what you need, lay your hand on the table and drum your fingers, agreed? Oh! I nearly forgot. Keep your gloves on. Those dainty hands of yours will tell our secret quicker than a word."

Joan nodded, her heart beating fast.

"Charles," Morgan called, and soon there were footsteps echoing in the hall. The door swung open and two men came in, one in handcuffs. The handcuffed one was set in a chair across the table, a wide toothless smirk distorting his features with sarcastic mirth.

"Ah, James. We meet again." Morgan reclined in his chair, giving the appearance of one utterly at ease.

"Ya got more questions? I tol' ya, I won't sing." The man crossed his beefy arms and then turned his attention to Joan.

Joan could feel his gaze like a slimy touch along her skin. It was foul, permeating the air around her. Morgan spoke, interrupting her urge to scoot farther away from the offensive man.

To begin, Morgan asked some innocuous questions. Joan watched carefully, noting his demeanor and using it as a foundation to build upon.

"What day is it?" Morgan asked calmly.

Other than a furrowing of his brow, likely from the lack of importance in the question, the man answered swiftly.

Morgan asked a few more similar queries before launching into the important subjects.

"Who are you working with?"

Joan studied the man, noting the way his hands flexed on the table, not into complete fists but enough to show tension. On the next question, his eyes turned upward, not in recall but to avoid eye contact. His posture was alert, not relaxed, and the small details of his answers didn't coincide.

When she had seen enough, Joan set her hand on the table and lightly drummed her fingers.

Morgan asked several more questions, likely to deflect any suspicion of their signal, and then dismissed the man.

In short work, they were walking out to the waiting curricle. Joan stepped up, took her seat, and breathed deeply the air of freedom.

"So?" Morgan asked as they started back toward home. "I tried to ask the sort of questions that needed a yes-or-no answer to make it easier."

Joan considered what she'd learned. "That did help, but I'm afraid I don't have the specifics. I'm not a mind reader."

"Anything is helpful, Joan." He turned his attention back to her.

Joan released a pent-up breath. "It would be best to wait till we're in your study. I have a feeling you'll need to send out several missives."

"Drat."

"Yes. You were right, Morgan. They haven't given up because Napoleon is on St. Helena. All the things you wished were him speaking the truth had clues, little mannerisms that can mean they are lies. And that, my brother, does not bode well."

Morgan sighed. "I wish you were wrong."

"So do I. So do I," Joan said and, not for the first time, wondered if maybe her skills were as much of a burden as they were a blessing.

Seven

ROWLES SHRUGGED INTO HIS GREATCOAT AND quit his chambers, refusing to look down the hall to where his mother rested. First, the doctor had attended to his mother, adjusting the dose of laudanum and its frequency while monitoring the bruising on her arms where the footmen's hands had held her in place to prevent her from attacking anyone further. Then the doctor had a frank conversation with Rowles concerning her care.

It was one of the most difficult moments of his life, listening to and honestly taking to heart the extent of his mother's condition. For the first time, he was candid with himself about his mother's malady. The only positive aspect of the whole sordid mess was that the doctor did not recommend Bedlam. They were in the process of moving the Bethlehem hospital to a new location, and the doctor didn't approve of the methodology of Thomas Munro, the chief physician, in any capacity. Dr. Smithe suggested separate living quarters and staff to address the needs of Rowles's mother.

Rowles commissioned the doctor to find a

suitable staff to address her condition, and an apartment would be easily procured for the stricken duchess.

With all that out of the way, Rowles needed a drink, a strong one and in large supply. The carriage was waiting out front to take him to White's, and it couldn't convey him there quickly enough for his taste. As the carriage cantered to the side, probably due to a hole in the cobbles, Rowles shifted to retain his seat. His leg protested the movement with a sharp pain, reminding him of the earlier events of the day.

Yes, he needed a drink. Badly.

White's was crowded and perfectly distracting. Rowles nodded to several gentlemen and found a table. In short order, he was lined up with a glass of Scottish whiskey and another on the way.

The amber liquid reflected the firelight of the room like a glowing ember, and he inhaled the aroma of Scottish peat and smoke. The Scottish island of Islay had the most superb whiskey because of that peat moss that they used when distilling. Rowles closed his eyes and took a long sip, savoring the burn down his throat and praying it would help him forget, even for a few moments, the hell of the day.

By his third whiskey, his body was warm and relaxed, his memories far less sharp and demanding of his attention. When he finished his fifth, he frowned at the empty glass, wondering if it was actually his sixth glass. Rounds seven and eight were less memorable, but what he did notice was he was no longer alone at the table.

It took a moment, but his look focused on a familiar face. "Morga'?" He blinked, then wondered if perhaps he forgot the last consonant of his friend's name. Ah, to hell with it.

"Bad day?" Morgan asked, downing a glass of what looked like brandy.

"Yes," Rowles answered and raised his eyebrows when another round was placed before him.

"It must have been. It's been an age since I've seen you flat-arse drunk."

Rowles lifted his eyes to his friend, wondering why it took so long to finally focus on his facial expression. "I'm not drunk... I'm not drunk *enough*. Yet."

Morgan lifted his glass in a toast and took another long swallow. "Want to talk about it?"

Rowles scoffed. "What's there to talk about? My mother attacked me. And before that, she thought I was Robert and told me—rather, she was talking to Rob—" He frowned. That was bloody confusing.

Morgan saved him. "I think I follow. Continue."

Rowles shrugged. "She said that she'd always worried about me being"—he whispered—"like her. And then she said that if I went all cocked up, Robert was to put me in Bedlam." Rowles closed his eyes and leaned back in the chair. It was a bloody disaster, and no amount of alcohol would change that. More was the pity.

"I see," Morgan answered.

"So now I have to move my mother into a separate apartment with a trained staff to care for her so she doesn't hurt anyone." Rowles looked to him.

Morgan leaned forward. "What do you mean, hurt anyone?"

Rowles gave a dark chuckle. "Oh, I left out that detail. All this happened moments before she attacked me and three footmen. She's quite strong for her frailty." He rubbed the side of his leg at the memory.

"Heavens." Morgan breathed out a lengthy sigh. "Old chap, that's a bloody awful day."

Rowles lifted his glass to salute Morgan's words, only to find it empty. "Damn and blast."

Morgan observed him, as if evaluating a decision.

"What?" Rowles asked. "I'm not one of your prisoners to cross-examine. Don't look at me that way. It makes me feel more cocked up than I probably am." He sighed.

"You're not."

Rowles froze. "Say what?"

"You're not." Morgan shrugged. "And I'm an excellent judge of character." He ticked off the words on his fingers as he added, "I know infirm, I know misguided, and I know foolish. You, my friend, are none of the above. So stop your needless fretting. You'll turn into an old man."

"I already feel like an old man." Rowles sighed.

"Feeling like and reality are two separate things," Morgan corrected him gently. "So, decide which one will rule you."

Rowles nodded slowly. "Thank you, old chap."

Morgan raised his glass, then realized it was empty and waved for another round.

Rowles frowned and turned to Morgan. "So why are you here?"

Morgan hitched a shoulder and nodded his thanks as another round was placed before them and the empty glasses collected.

Morgan swirled the liquid in his glass. "Between my sister holding court to several young bucks this afternoon and then business at the office, I'm finished with today."

Rowles nodded sagely. "That deserves a drink."

"Indeed."

"So she had quite the turnout, did she?" Rowles asked, a strange sort of tension scratching along his belly at the thought. It wasn't surprising that she'd attracted attention with that clear observation skill of hers that saw through to one's soul. In truth, he was still haunted by her words and the way she'd spoken them.

"Yes, which is not surprising, at least to me. But I must say, I don't fancy this season of my life."

Morgan's expression went thoughtful, as if the words had reminded him of something else entirely.

"Season, eh?"

"Yes," Morgan replied and then sipped his drink. "I'm sure she'll find a good match. But the process might kill me."

"You mean might kill others." Rowles chuckled.

Morgan raised an eyebrow. "That too. But we'll keep that between us. I don't wish to scare off any prospective suitors because word gets out that her brother has a hot temper and is quick on the draw," he said with amusement.

"Your secret's safe with me." Rowles lifted his glass in salute.

"I know. And your secret is safe with me as well."

Rowles's forehead furrowed as the words brought him back to the earlier conversation. "Much obliged. You know…your sister said something quite similar to your own words."

Morgan paused swirling his glass, then started back up. "Oh?"

"Yes. She said I wasn't." Rowles tipped his head to the side. "She's usually so talkative, but it was difficult getting her to explain what she meant."

"Oh?" Morgan said again, taking a slow sip.

Rowles noted the way his friend's hand moved from the table and held the edge, as if gripping it tightly. Odd. Even in his inebriated state, he'd noticed. It must not have been a subtle movement.

"Yes. But eventually she explained herself, and I must say she's…intriguing."

"In what way?" Morgan's expression went blank, as if he were hiding his emotions.

"Are you well, ol' chap?" Rowles asked, leaning forward to take a closer look.

"Well enough. Continue." Morgan waved his hand impatiently.

Rowles frowned but continued as instructed. "I was saying, it was like she was looking through me. I've never had that happen before. It was disconcerting, yet I'm grateful she did."

Morgan didn't reply, only worked his jaw as he swirled his glass.

"She reads people well, doesn't she? A family trait, that, and I do believe you'll have your hands full of young bucks all fascinated with her," Rowles mused, then took a sip of his own drink.

"Is that so?" Morgan asked, an odd grin on his face. "Disconcerting, eh? Anything else?"

Rowles thought about the question, then reading his friend's expression, decided to leave it unanswered.

"No, tell me." Morgan's tone was sardonic. "Being able to read people well doesn't mean she's different or anything of the sort. It takes so little for a lady's reputation to be tarnished, and the last thing she needs is someone like—" He paused.

Rowles stilled. "Someone like?" he asked, pain lacing through him at the words left unsaid.

"I was wrong," Morgan apologized, though his tone was anything but apologetic.

"What were you going to say, Penderdale?" Rowles asked, his hands clenching into fists.

"I wouldn't want to offend, Your Grace." Morgan took the final sip of his drink and stood.

Rowles stood as well, easily towering over his friend. "'Your Grace'?" he scoffed. "Since when have you cared about my title?"

"When you're pissing me off," Morgan replied with a scowl.

"And what have I done to offend you?" Rowles asked with a biting tone. "Or do you still let that temper of yours run away with your mouth?"

Morgan glowered, stepped back as if about to leave, then swung. His fist landed a nice facer on Rowles's jawline. Stumbling back, Rowles rubbed the mark and swore under his breath. "Is that how it's going to be?" He lunged forward, landed a right hook on Morgan's cheek, and blocked a blow to his own. It had been an age since he'd boxed, but the moves came back instinctively, and while Morgan had the advantage with swords and pistols, Rowles had always won in fisticuffs, even if the whole sordid mess was blurry from his drinking.

After all, this wasn't the first fight they'd had, and it likely wouldn't be the last.

Rowles landed a punch to Morgan's gut and then another to his head, effectively blocking his friend's advances. Morgan spat blood, then reared back and at the last moment switched fists. He bypassed Rowles's block and landed a punch to the corner of his left eye.

Rowles blinked back the bright light that exploded at the impact. "Always want the last word and the last punch, even if you still lose," he said, sneering.

Morgan spat more blood. "Better a man assault you than your own mother," Morgan whispered, then paused. He took a few steps back.

Rowles blinked at the powerful onslaught of his friend's words pummeling him from the inside out.

"That…that was too far. Pardon me," Morgan apologized, his expression one of anguish. "I shouldn't have said such things."

Rowles nodded once.

"Truly," Morgan added, and then took several more backward steps before he turned to leave.

Rowles watched his friend's retreat, his face, leg, and abdomen aching, but it was nothing compared to his heart.

Whoever said words were meaningless had certainly never had them aimed like arrows.

Because words could destroy faster than any weapon ever could. And it felt like he was bleeding internally.

Eight

If I ever do escape, no one shall reproach me with having broken or violated my faith, not having given my word to any one, whosoever it may be.

—Joan of Arc

JOAN HAD FINISHED BREAKING HER FAST AND was walking down the hall when the butler answered the door. Curious, she lingered to see who was paying a visit at such an unsociable hour. It must be some emergency or pressing business, perhaps from the War Office? Her thoughts tumbled as she walked toward the door to see what was transpiring.

"The earl is not at home, Your Grace," the butler replied, looking quite uncomfortable at turning down a duke, if his posture were any indication.

Joan stepped forward. "Ah, Your Grace," she greeted, then hesitated upon noticing the purplish bruise circling his eye. "Merciful heavens," she said breathlessly, then collected herself. "Come in, won't you?" She turned to the butler. "Please have tea sent into the red parlor, along with Mrs. Hiddleman." The housekeeper would serve as chaperone.

"Right away, my lady," the butler replied and left to do her bidding.

"Will you follow me?" Joan asked, gesturing to the hall.

"Thank you," the Duke of Westmore replied softly.

Joan silently led him to the east-facing parlor. Early-morning sunshine filtered through the sheer curtains and filled the room with light, making the red settee and chairs seem to glow. "Will you sit? Tea will be in shortly," she said conversationally.

"Thank you," the duke repeated.

After Joan took a seat, she leaned forward. "So, who looks worse? You or my brother?"

The duke blinked, then the tips of his ears flushed with color as he sighed. "That is the nature of my early social call, Lady Joan."

"Ah." She offered pleasantly, "That is an interesting shade of purple."

He chuckled. "I thought I looked dashing and dangerous, like a pirate."

Joan giggled softly. "Certainly like a pirate. And my brother will look like one, too, I'm assuming?"

"Possibly. Though he tends to bruise less than me. Unfair if you ask me, since I usually won the fistfights."

Joan shook her head. "And what caused the altercation?" She leaned back into the settee.

The duke paused, his amused expression shifting

to uncertainty. "That's the thing. I don't know. What I think we were fighting about doesn't seem to be the real reason. Not that any of this makes sense." He shrugged. "Nonetheless, we shouldn't have come to blows."

"No, you probably shouldn't have. You'll both cause talk, and somehow I'm sure Morgan will find a reason for it to come back to me." She sighed.

"Pardon?"

Joan worried her lip, torn between wanting to tell the truth and not disclosing too much information. It was always a fine line, one for which she rarely found the middle ground.

"It's only that he can be very protective of family."

"Of you," the duke stated.

She nodded.

"That's not a terrible thing." He shrugged.

Joan gave a small sigh. "Anything excessive can be bad, Your Grace."

He leaned forward. "Do I sense a challenge?"

"Challenge?"

"Yes, you postulate that anything in excess is bad, am I correct?"

"Ah, I should have remembered you're a professor. Very well, do your worst." She mimicked him, leaning in as well.

Mrs. Hiddleman came in with tea. She set the service on the side table and took up a seat in the corner, the perfect silent chaperone.

"Tea first or debate?" Joan asked, her tone cheeky.

The duke narrowed his eyes, then shifted his gaze from the tea to her and then back. "Trick question, but one I will answer. Tea first."

"Excellent choice," Joan replied. "Shall I pour for you?"

"Thank you."

Joan served the tea and then sat back with her own teacup and waited. "Proceed, Professor."

His expression froze for only a fraction of a second before he seemed to collect himself, and then a pleasing smile lifted his lips. "Very well. I agree that *some* excesses can be detrimental. Some examples would include whiskey, laudanum, greed, the famous seven deadly sins, if you will."

"Agreed." Joan nodded. "But it sounds as if you are proving rather than challenging my point." She sipped her tea. "I'm waiting to be impressed, Your Grace."

He smirked. "That's 'Professor,' to you."

"Ah, apologies." She tilted her head and studied him through lowered lashes.

Good Lord, she'd flirted. With the Duke of Westmore. No. She *was* flirting with the Duke of Westmore. Her brother's best friend, the one who had, by all evidence, had quite the altercation with her brother. His next words interrupted her internal revelation.

"I said 'some.' Now, I can agree with a fraction of your premise, but the whole is incorrect. As a wholly applicable statement, it's false."

"Why?" she asked, fascinated.

"What about kindness?" he asked, then grinned as if he knew he'd won the battle before the fight had even started.

Joan twisted her lips, then took a slow sip of tea, stalling and allowing herself time to come up with an intelligent reply. "Ah! Yes. Kindness in excess isn't a good thing."

"Defend." He gestured to her and leaned back, sipping his tea. When he lowered the cup, a welcoming expression illuminated his face, adding a twinkling depth to his blue eyes. Even with his purple-ringed eye, he was handsome. Distractingly so.

Joan turned her attention down to her teacup to collect her thoughts. "If I am kind to my own detriment, then I might be kind to someone but not to myself, which, in fact, negates the kindness, does it not?"

The duke nodded, his expression thoughtful as if considering her words. "Indeed. However, would that be kindness? As it is defined? Or a lack of self-preservation?"

Joan frowned. "How would one define either? What decides the line between kindness and it moving into something less of a virtue?"

"Excellent question. What is a virtue? And can those be in excess?"

"Virtues are purity of action and thought, selfless in nature."

The duke spoke with warmth. "So eloquent. Indeed. But can they be, in their pure form, excessively used to the point where they are no longer good? Say, forgiveness. Can you forgive too much?"

"According to the Bible, no."

He nodded.

"But it also depends on how you define forgiveness."

"Well, I'd argue that one is forgiveness, and one is counterfeit."

"It is too bloody early in the morning to be discussing the finer points of theology." Morgan's voice broke through Joan's thoughts, startling her.

She gave a jump and leaned back, smoothing her skirts. "Maybe for you," she replied.

The duke stood abruptly and set his tea service to the side. Joan's scrutiny shot from her brother to the duke and back. It would have been comical if not for the tension pulling the room into a tight knot. Morgan had the opposite eye sporting that same shade of purple, only his lip was split as well, and he took a seat with some tender care, as if his abdomen were sensitive.

"Sit down." He waved a hand toward the duke. "I'm not in the mood to wax romantic over

apologies. We're both idiots, and I started it, so…"
Again, he waved off his friend.

The duke sat back down, but kept a watchful eye on Morgan. "I apologize."

"We were both quite drunk," Morgan added.

Joan gave an irritated snort. "Drunk? Really, Morgan?" She couldn't exactly chide the duke, but her brother? That was a different story.

"I'll take your tongue-lashing later, dear sister. And I'll take it without complaint as long as you let me suffer in misery for the moment."

"Headache?" Joan asked, remembering the aftereffects of her brother's drinking from an earlier escapade.

"Severe," was his only reply.

The duke relaxed, and Joan noted the way the room seemed to shift back to normal, the tension unwinding like yarn from a ball.

Joan giggled softly and then turned to the duke. "Speaking of virtues…" she said with a laugh.

"A well-placed verbal spar. I concede defeat on that point. But you must admit, my challenge goes unopposed."

Joan narrowed her eyes playfully. "Very well, I will concede that one cannot make a statement about excess being universally malignant."

"You made a very convincing argument," the duke said.

Joan's cheeks heated at his words, since the

statement was coming from someone who would certainly know about worthy debates. Surely he'd seen his share of brilliant students and ideas in his time at Cambridge; he was likely one of those brilliant minds. The compliment washed through her all the way to her toes, far more than if someone had called her beautiful.

The duke had praised her mind, her intelligence, the intangible things that didn't fade with time.

"Thank you," she murmured, meeting his look. There was such warmth there, captivating her. So many times she looked at people to uncover things, or to find the truth, but in this moment nothing was required of her. Everything he had said was true, and she was basking in the glow of it all. His body language said even more than his words.

"Does that mean this theological discussion has ended? Please say yes." Morgan's words broke the spell, and she turned away, wondering how long she'd been staring at their guest.

She hazarded a peek back to him, observing the way he glanced from Morgan to her, likely noting the same thing she had, Morgan's closed eyes. Never before had she been so thankful for a headache. If Morgan had seen her behavior, he would certainly have questions.

Questions she wasn't ready to answer yet.

Because she wasn't sure of it herself.

But one thing was for certain.

This conversation, this precious half hour of time, was more enchanting and tempting than all of the hours spent with her potential suitors. Which left her with one question, the one she was most afraid to answer.

Was she fascinated by the duke? Or was this what it felt like when one fell in love?

Nine

ROWLES WIPED ONE HAND DOWN HIS FACE AS HE thought back over the events of the morning. What had begun as the worst sort of way to start a day—apologizing and looking after a friend he'd assaulted—ended with the brightest conversation he'd had in an age.

Joan didn't only see through to one's soul, she bloody well interpreted what she saw as well. Her premise was brilliant and well defended. And he took the challenge as a way to tease her, test her, and see a little into that wit he'd enjoyed when they'd waltzed. And she'd not only risen to the challenge but done so brilliantly and with such articulate prowess. She was enchanting.

But good Lord. When she'd called him Professor... Hopefully, he'd collected himself quickly enough, though she was painfully observant, and she might have caught on to the expression on his face. For his mind had taken a seductive turn, and abruptly so, catching him wholly off guard. He'd liked her calling him Professor. He'd liked it far too much, and it had taken concentrated effort to school his features and keep his wits about him. She was a temptation he hadn't expected and wouldn't soon forget. Even now he was anticipating seeing her again, which only led to further problems. He'd mended his friendship with Morgan. It wasn't the time to ask permission to court his sister.

Good heavens. He could only imagine the fight that would possibly follow. And that didn't bode well for a potential suitor.

Rowles decided to wait, test, and see if perhaps Joan had felt the same sort of attraction. He had time, and if there was nothing on her end, no need to alert Morgan. It was a long stretch, he reminded himself. Joan had a plethora of suitors clamoring for her attentions, and he wasn't necessarily included in their ranks, at least officially.

It wasn't worth destroying a friendship for a possibility. But he could still ask for a dance, could he not? He'd already waltzed with her. Rowles thought back to Morgan's original description of him.

Safe.

He felt anything but safe at the moment, not after enjoying her lively conversation, and certainly not after hearing her call him Professor. *Safe* was not an accurate word. It had taken severe restraint on his part not to cross the room and kiss her right then and there, in front of the bloody housekeeper, God, and everyone.

And for the first time, Rowles felt dangerous. But

in the way the gothic romance novels portrayed the tragic hero. Black eye and all.

He could play the part.

It was a little too close to home anyway.

An ill mother, a title that weighed heavily on him, a love interest that was completely out of reach, and a hero with nothing to lose but his best friend.

Yes. That could certainly be a gothic story if someone wished to look too closely at his life. And like a lurid gothic novel, it certainly couldn't have a happy ending. Yet as much as he told himself to accept this truth, his heart involved itself in the most dangerous sort of rebellion. It hoped.

He looked to the clock and noted the time. He'd said he would attend the Moorson rout tonight, and it was time to begin preparations. He swallowed hard, as if already feeling the excessively tight cravat he'd wear with his evening kit. Perhaps he'd wear something purple to match the color of his eye. Damn, it was going to be hell. All the questioning expressions with the infernal whispering the moment they saw his back.

How he missed Cambridge's social events and their casual requirements. He'd found his home among the Fellows and faculty, men more interested in ideas than in a person's pedigree. Renowned Fellows could be seen deep in thought as they crossed the lawn of Trinity College that only they were allowed to walk on, and, a few minutes later, shared their wealth of knowledge with their students. And the conversation focused on new ideas, shared experiences with a student, or something equally diverting and engaging. But the social events of London were created to display power and wealth and to fortify or create social alliances, he thought, shaking his head. Events there were painfully dull and equally disconcerting since those attempts at social alliances tended to be aimed at his bachelor self.

He rose and left his study, making his way to his room where his valet would be waiting to assist him. Lowson welcomed him with a bow. "Ah, I selected your ruby pin for this evening. Do you approve, Your Grace?"

"Indeed." Rowles nodded.

"Then, after you, Your Grace." Lowson gestured to the closet, and Rowles led the way.

Rowles was soon finished with his preparations and headed down to his carriage. His family crest decorated the side in a flash of gold. The ram with its head lowered appeared prepared to fight, its powerful hindquarters at the ready for battle. Rowles stepped into the well-sprung carriage and adjusted his coat.

Would Joan and Morgan have arrived already? More so, would Joan's dance card already be filled? He tapped his knee as he wondered if Morgan would be suspicious if he asked for another one of Joan's waltzes. The carriage rumbled along till it pulled into the queue behind the other party attendees. The footmen were quick in assisting each guest, and soon it was his turn to alight from his carriage. Torches lit the drive all the way up to the open door as ladies in feathered turbans and men in evening dress filtered into the grand house. Music welcomed each guest as they approached the house. Rowles took the steps and followed the music and the crowd down the hall toward the ballroom. The brightly lit room was buzzing with conversation as the string quartet finished the song. He scanned the room for Joan and, consequently, Morgan.

Already his cravat felt tight, but he quelled the urge to adjust it and moved forward, avoiding the observation of several young debutantes hiding behind their equally attentive mothers. The black eye wasn't much of a deterrent, apparently. He dared not show any interest, or he'd be preyed upon like a rabbit in the hunt.

As he turned to the left, he caught sight of a familiar face and smiled in response. His Grace, the Duke of Wesley, or Quin, as he was known to his close friends, was standing scandalously close to his wife, Catherine. Rowles started toward them, his smile growing wider when he noted that Morgan, with his own colorful eye, and Joan were also in their conversational circle. Perhaps luck was indeed on his side this night. The gossiping set would certainly notice the facers both he and Morgan sported and would no doubt concoct a story. But since the altercation had started at White's in front of God and everyone, it was better to display a mending of the friendship rather than let the gossipers spread rumors of a rift between the families.

"Ah, well, I didn't expect to see you here." Rowles extended his hand to Quin as he approached. His friend took his offered greeting. "I figured it was time to come out of hiding."

"Hiding. Is that what we call it?" Morgan chimed in. "I thought it was called being newly married."

Rowles snickered a little. "I think that ends a few weeks after the wedding. It's been more than six months. And I must say, I don't believe I've seen you in as much time."

Quin shrugged, utterly unrepentant. "I have no defense and do not care to have one. You're lucky I'm blessing you with my presence. Rather, the presence of my lovely wife." He beamed down at his equally enamored partner.

"I might have said something about being social, but I must admit I didn't miss this all that terribly." Catherine gave an apologetic shrug to Joan. "But we were out of the country for your come-out, and for that I'm sorry. It was quite the smashing success, if any gossip is to be believed." She reached out to squeeze Joan's hand.

"It was a lovely party, and I do believe it was a success. But being out of the country, your excuse is more than reasonable," Joan said cheekily. "I suppose I forgive you."

"You're all grace and charm," Catherine replied, a playful tone to her voice. "It's been an age, I'll call upon you soon. We need to talk, and I want to hear all about"—she paused, as if halting herself from revealing some secret—"the party."

Rowles wondered what she'd meant to say originally. Was there a suitor in Joan's life? Perhaps a gentleman she favored and had confided her interest in to her friend? It was well known that Joan was a close acquaintance of the Duchess of Wesley. His mind circled with curiosity, but he pushed it aside as Quin addressed him.

"And you, are you well?"

"As can be expected," Rowles answered. "I'll be doing better if I can ever get back to Cambridge. Tell me I am not the only one who desperately misses that place."

Quin shook his head. "Every day. Someday we'll be old and have sons to carry on the title and we shall return to teaching, you and I. We'll be the disagreeable old codgers who torment the new students."

Rowles chuckled at the thought. "Someday indeed." Quin was far ahead in that department. No doubt he'd be boasting several heirs in the next few years. However, Rowles didn't share that same optimistic outlook. To have heirs, one needed to have a wife, something he was without.

Thankfully.

Yet his traitorous eyes shot to Joan. Her expression was restrained, as if diligently working to be proper and not give in to the wide and dramatic smile that had so captivated him earlier that day. He was thankful for her restraint. The thought of other gentlemen being on the receiving end of one of her brilliant looks made his fists clench.

That smacked of jealousy.

And he had no right to such a strong emotion. Yet there it was, without invitation, and he suspected it wasn't leaving anytime soon. As if spurred on by the offending feeling, he approached Morgan. "And how are you this evening? Better?"

Morgan shot him a teasing glare. "About as good as you are."

"Ah, then you are excellent," Rowles replied with a smirk. He took in the room and noticed the furtive peeks cast at them. "If anything, I think our bruising makes us more dashing, maybe lending a dangerous air to our persons." He shrugged and turned to his friend.

"Speak for yourself. *I* am dashing and dangerous naturally."

"And humble and reserved," Rowles said with a hint of sarcasm.

"He's also surly and temperamental," Joan interjected, turning to include herself in their conversational circle.

"I don't remember asking you," Morgan said dryly.

"Since when have you needed to ask me for my opinion?" Joan matched his expression, battling him with her wit.

Rowles couldn't restrain his amusement and watched the two of them enjoying the dynamic. He missed that sort of good-natured sibling rivalry. He'd had a tumultuous relationship with Robert, largely due to his mother's favoritism, but they were still brothers and teased, fought, and enjoyed the bond of blood.

"Unfortunately, I do not need to ask you for your thoughts since you offer them so freely," Morgan chimed in, bringing Rowles back to the conversation.

"You're welcome." Joan hitched a shoulder and turned to Rowles. "You'll have to forgive his mood. I had a meeting this afternoon, one of which he doesn't necessarily approve, so he's brought that irritation with him like a dark storm cloud."

Morgan stepped closer. "I'd rather you not mention anything in a setting such as this," he corrected her, but with a gentler tone than Rowles expected.

"I didn't say anything specific," she murmured.

Morgan's expression was concerned, and Rowles

felt the urge to dissipate the tension. Thankfully, a waltz started, and without hesitation he turned to Joan. "Is this dance spoken for?"

Joan's answering expression was enough to set his heart pounding in anticipation of holding her close again. As she offered him her hand, he looked to Morgan, who gave a quick nod and stepped back to give them room to navigate to the dance floor.

Rowles grasped her hand, noticed how it fit snugly within his own, and then placed his other hand at her waist, drawing her close enough to smell the rosewater clinging to her skin. Her eyes sparkled with a fun twinkle, and she stepped into the waltz with him effortlessly, as if they'd danced together a thousand times and would dance together a thousand more.

"So, what shall we discuss this time? You've already won the first debate. I think I shall select the next. It's only fair that I get some advantage when discussing the finer points of morality and virtue with a professor of divinity." She sent him a cheeky grin.

"I'm happy to oblige you with any topic that you select," he answered, his lips spread wide. There would be talk tomorrow, for sure. One didn't smile so openly in a waltz without someone noticing, especially when one was a duke.

"Hmm." She angled her head in contemplation. Rowles watched with interest as her eyes narrowed and her lips pursed, drawing his attention to their fullness. Had she ever been kissed? Likely no; she was an innocent. Dear Lord, he wanted to christen her lips, break that delicious seal and taste her. But in the middle of the ballroom floor wasn't the time or place, he reminded himself.

"I know." Her expression turned devious.

"Should I be alarmed?" he teased, flirted really.

"Perhaps. It is a divisive topic."

"Ah, then I'll do my best to be worthy of such a question."

"Very well. Our society has constraints on women's rights. Which begs the question, which rights are gender-specific and which are humanity-specific?" she asked boldly.

Rowles frowned. It was indeed a question that took thought. "That is a very good question, and one that tells me you have a decisive opinion one way or the other."

"You assume correctly."

"You might not like my answer."

"That's possible," she answered with a nod, her stare intently searching his.

He nearly tripped on his steps as her eyes searched his, and he couldn't break the spell her gaze wove around him. When she turned away, he released his breath as if he'd been holding it. He thought back to her question.

"I would add to your question to give it further

clarity. Is the worth of a woman based on her rights or privileges?"

Joan's expression furrowed. "I'm not sure I understand."

"You said that our society has constraints on women. This is true. But you didn't ask about her value. You made the direct correlation that her rights and her value were related. Do you think that the worth of a woman is directly based on what society allows her for latitude in her rights or privileges?"

When she didn't answer, he continued, "Because a woman's value doesn't change based on what she is allowed or not allowed to do. Value should already be ascribed to her, but rights are separate. Not equal."

Joan nodded slowly. "So are they less important?"

"I'm not sure I fully understand the question," he countered.

"If they are not equal, which is most important? The value of the woman or her rights?"

His brows knit. "Well, of course the value of the person is more important."

She nodded. He could feel her posture stiffen as if his words had offended her, or she was expected to be offended.

"So you're saying that you can restrain a person's rights and validate that decision because it didn't affect the intrinsic value of that person? Well, then my question would be, what good is the value of a person if they have no right to live in a manner that expresses it? Then could one truly call it *value* or is it just a pretty word?" she asked pointedly.

The waltz ended, and with a stiff posture, she stepped from his hold and waited for him to escort her to Morgan. With the music ended and people milling about, it wasn't a proper time to finish or, rather, continue the conversation, but Rowles instinctively knew he had offended her greatly.

Yet he couldn't exactly figure out how.

Because everything he had said was true. A woman's value was God-given, not hindered by the law of a mere man or nation.

But something whispered that maybe, rather than hearing what he'd tried to say, she'd only heard an excuse.

However, he found no opportunity to talk privately with Joan because she avoided him the rest of the evening. And after the ball, as Rowles rode home in his carriage, all he could think about was history repeating itself.

Because tomorrow he'd pay another call to Penderdale House to give an apology, or at least clarification.

Only this time it would be to the other sibling.

He only hoped she would have the good grace to hear him out.

Ten

JOAN WOKE UP WITH A POUNDING HEADACHE and the lingering suspicion that maybe her temper had got the best of her...again. Maybe she had put too much faith in the duke too soon, or maybe she had completely misunderstood his meaning, but whatever the reason, she had retreated behind a wall and now she found herself stuck. Because it wasn't as if she could pay a social call to *him*. And if he didn't want to clarify or continue the discussion, they would be at a stalemate.

And she didn't want that.

Because, well, she liked the Duke of Westmore. He was intelligent and appreciated her keen mind—or at least she had thought he did. Maybe he enjoyed the novelty of discussing and debating with a woman occasionally, only to excuse society's social and law restrictions on women because it didn't affect their value. She closed her eyes and lay back on her pillow. As she thought over it, the point he'd made wasn't terrible.

But she'd, well, wanted him to champion the cause, not excuse the reason it needed to exist. But in truth, she could have misunderstood so much.

Yet it was too late now, and only time would decide if the rift between them was something that could be mended.

She glanced to the clock. The women's society would be meeting again in two hours, which meant she needed to get up, get dressed, and send a footman to hire a hack. The women's society met in Lady Sandra Bookman's parlor, nearly twenty minutes away. They had met yesterday as well, but since next week's meeting had to be canceled because Lady Sandra would be out of town, they had voted to do back-to-back meetings.

In short order, Joan had accomplished all that needed to be done and was stepping into her hired hack with the arranged chaperone. The mist and smoke swirled around Hyde Park as they passed by and went deeper into the center of London. The stone buildings blurred together till the carriage halted in front of Lady Sandra's home. The widow of a wealthy merchant, she had used her funds to establish a meeting place for women to discuss and act on possible ways to enrich and establish women's lives and freedoms.

They were finishing up their second read-through of Mary Wollstonecraft's *A Vindication of the Rights of Women*. And a lively discussion would indeed follow today's assigned chapters. Sure enough, as Joan entered into the house and started toward the parlor, she could already hear the raised and enthusiastic voices of her peers. The room was filled with familiar faces, save one. The room held chairs enough for all of them in a circle, and Joan selected a seat next to Lady Sandra.

"We are discussing the concept in the chapter regarding women's need for education reform," Lady Sandra whispered to her.

Joan nodded and turned her attention to Miss Sarah Clarke who was passionately stating a case for women's continued education.

"It's not enough to read and write and study embroidery. To hinder a woman's education while supporting and pressuring men to continue with the enrichment of their minds is unfair. To have a university for men that will not allow a woman entrance is the worst sort of biased behavior."

A murmur of agreement swelled among the group.

Joan listened to further talk, then after a brief pause added, "It is undermining to society as a whole to have women in a subordinate position to men and teaches future generations of women that it is acceptable to be told your value based on your education and societal rights. Women deserve the same fundamental rights as men."

This brought on a fresh discussion, and in too short a time, the meeting was adjourned.

"You did well today," Lady Sandra encouraged Joan as she stood.

"Thank you, yet I can't help but feel a little…

lacking?" Joan fought for the correct word. "We discuss, and yet nothing happens. I want...I want something to *come* from this."

Lady Sandra gave a sad nod. "I understand. It takes time. We stay the course, and eventually we will have more of a voice. But in the meantime, why don't you explore another way to make a difference in young girls' lives? I know your heart. Lady Joan, and it's restless to do good. Have you heard of Thomas Coram's Foundling Hospital? They contacted me asking for women volunteers. They have young girls who need to be educated, and this would be a fantastic opportunity for you to give young ladies—as you so passionately said earlier—a taste of a woman who knows her value and fights for greater influence."

Joan nodded. "I'll look into it today."

Sandra answered. "The woman who contacted me is Miss Corinne Vanderhaul. Mention my name when you meet her. She'll explain what is needed. You can reach her by sending a missive to the hospital. She's expecting some referrals."

"Thank you." Joan squeezed her friend's hand and moved to leave, but heard her name.

"Lady Joan?"

Joan turned toward the voice and noted the one new face in their meeting. She moved to offer a kind welcome, but the girl was quicker and extended her gloved hand as Joan approached.

"Forgive me for being so bold, but I wanted to

introduce myself. I'm Miss Bronson, my father is Baron Treyson. I believe I saw you last night at the Moorson rout."

Joan grasped her hand. "Yes, indeed, I was there. And it's a pleasure to make your acquaintance. Is this your first time attending? Or have you met with a different chapter before?"

Miss Bronson shook her head, her brunette curls swaying as her brown eyes widened. "This is my first time, and I'm quite certain my mother wouldn't approve, but my father is actually the one who suggested I attend. He's forward-thinking."

"How lovely! What a blessing. Does that put him at odds with your mother, however?"

Miss Bronson grinned. "Only if she finds out."

Joan giggled. "I see. Then I suppose it's best if she does not."

"Indeed." The young woman grasped her skirt nervously. "I overheard a little of the conversation between you and Mrs. Bookman. If I may be so bold, would you mind if I accompanied you? I'd love to help in any way I can."

"Of course, I'm sure they can use all the help they can get. I was planning on sending a missive to the contact Sandra gave me this afternoon. I can send a message to you when I find out what's needed. Or would that not be good since you're trying to keep this from your mother?"

Miss Bronson twisted her lips. "That could

be a problem. However, since it is the Foundling Hospital, I can say I'm volunteering, not how I came about volunteering. Perhaps that will solve the problem."

"Brilliant." Joan said her goodbyes to the rest of the ladies and proceeded to her carriage. But as she started on her way home, her chest grew tight and her mind uneasy as she considered her voiced opinions at the meeting and how they correlated with her earlier conversation with the Duke of Westmore.

The rain started to fall in gentle drips that slid down the glass of the carriage, adding to her melancholy mood. The next social event was on Friday, and thus several days away, and unless the duke paid a social visit, she would be carrying this troublesome burden of irritation along with her for the next few days. Assuming he'd even noticed, or cared, that she had been put out with his words.

Frustration clenched her belly as she realized how this was another constraint on women in society. If she were given the same social latitude as a man, she could direct her carriage to his residence, seek an audience with him, and have a civil conversation.

But because she was an unmarried woman, she had to wait on his leisure or inclination to remedy the rift.

Again, assuming he noticed or cared.

She wanted him to care.

She tipped her head to the side as she considered that truth. She wanted the Duke of Westmore to care, to think highly of her opinions and thoughts, to...favor them. It was a sobering realization, and in her current frame of mind, she further considered if this was also a societal constraint on women.

Or if this was something more.

Like falling in love.

And if so, that put her at a far greater disadvantage.

Because what if he didn't return the interest?

She thought back to the suitors who had paid her court the day after her come-out and would probably come to her at-home hours today as well. The duke had not participated in the courtship ritual of paying a social call. No, his social call had been directed at her brother.

She had seen him first and proceeded to have a conversation.

A conversation that she still carried with her.

Drat the man.

The carriage came to a halt in front of her home, and with a resigned huff, she straightened her gloves and stepped out onto the gravel of the driveway. Taking the stone steps, she made her way through the door and down the hall toward the grand staircase. What she wanted was to find a distraction from caring about the Duke of Westmore and wondering whether he happened to care about her. She was almost to the stairs when she heard her brother's voice.

"Ah, there you are." Morgan's boots clicked on the wooden floor at a quickened pace.

Joan paused in her steps and turned toward the sound. "Yes. I only this moment arrived," she replied, her tone clipped even as she tried to be polite. It wasn't her brother's fault she was in a sour mood.

Morgan slowed his progress and studied her. The lines on his forehead drew together as he frowned a moment, then nodded as if understanding dawned. "You've seen it, then."

It was Joan's turn to frown as confusion momentarily distracted her from irritation. "Seen what, exactly?"

"The papers? Well, the *Tattler*. Not sure I should call that by the same name as the *Times*." He shrugged.

"The society papers? Good mercy, what have they said this time?" She stopped a fraction shy of an eye roll. Her patience was wearing thinner by the moment.

Morgan rocked on his heels once. "So you haven't. Then why the devil are you acting like you're angry?"

"Turns out I have other concerns than the on-dit of the moment."

"Even if *you* are the on-dit of the moment?"

Joan paused her next breath. "Pardon?"

"Come, follow me." Morgan turned and headed toward his study. "I have the sheet on my desk."

Joan followed him down the hall and through the open door of his study. The cheerful light was the opposite of her mood. Morgan lifted a single sheet from his desk. The print was familiar, the same gossip publication that had been circulating for the past half a year. Joan plucked it from her brother's hands and began to read.

If the eyes are the window to the soul, then there was some soul reading that happened last night at the Moorson ball. This author suspects that more than one match will be made from the couples dancing last night, perhaps one in particular. Miss L was clearly enamored of a certain viscount. However, it wasn't only the spark of attraction that was lit last night. Apparently for another couple a quarrel, rather than attraction, was also ignited. This author may have to retract her earlier words regarding the affections of the Duke of W with a certain lady who recently had her debut. If last night's dance is an accurate representation of their true feelings, one might wonder if the line between affection and anger is closer than originally thought.

Joan slapped the page onto the desk with more force than necessary and growled low in her throat. "Of all the…" She wasn't sure how to finish the sentence. Nothing seemed an accurate representation of her anger toward the author.

Or herself.

Because it wasn't anything but the truth.

And, if anyone should approve of truth being told, it ought to be her, oughtn't it? How ironic and dreadful that she was on the receiving end of someone else's keen observation of truth.

Drat and drat again.

"If we are to look for a silver lining, at least now we needn't worry about society gleaning the wrong impression about your acquaintance with the duke," Morgan stated with far too much cheer for her taste.

Wrong impression. Too bad she was among the ranks of the poorly impressed. Or the misunderstood. It didn't matter which; her irritation didn't change.

Now everyone knew, or at least suspected, which added a deeper layer that was like an itchy chemise, rubbing her wrong. Because any of her true feelings of frustration or even attempts to address the situation with the duke couldn't happen, at least not in public. Society loved a feud more than romanticism, and she'd be watched more closely than ever if in his presence.

Which, she reminded herself, was a big *if*. H very well might not wish to dance with her anym or pay any visits that could potentially lead to deep and meaningful conversations.

Why did everything always come full circle? She'd already mused these thoughts, and yet they continued to surface.

"It is unfortunate, but it's not a total loss. It wasn't as if you had a great friendship or affection for him. Give him space in society, and this will all wash out in a week or less."

Joan worried her lip. "I see."

She sighed, then lifted the discarded page and reread it. Had she appeared that angry with him? Certainly, he had seen the same thing then. If so, wouldn't it be the gentlemanly thing to come and apologize?

Of course, that only worked under the assumption that he had done something wrong.

Which he hadn't. Technically, he hadn't done anything wrong other than offend her.

That was, unfortunately, subjective. Not set in stone.

She sighed again, then turned her attention to her brother.

Morgan's blue eyes were studying her with wary suspicion. He placed both hands on the desk and leaned over it, narrowing his eyes. "Joan."

"Yes?" Joan replied, swallowing.

"I must admit, I really wish you could lie right now. Because I don't think I want to know the truth," he said evenly.

Joan didn't look away; it would be useless regardless. She wouldn't lie, even if he'd rather she did. "What's your question."

"You don't... That is..." He huffed and closed his eyes for a moment, as if mustering his resolve to continue. "You haven't a tendre for Rowles."

Joan tipped her head. "That's not a question."

Morgan closed his eyes, then smacked the desk. "Blast it all, Joan."

She jumped at the sound, then scowled at her brother. "I'm not going to cower just because you are having a fit of temper."

"Believe me, I know you don't cower. You don't back down, and you don't lie. It's a disaster."

"How is that a disaster?" Joan threw her hands up in the air. "Do you want me to run and hide in a dark corner when you lose your temper and lie to your face about it later? What sort of man wishes for that?"

"Joan—"

"Answer me."

Morgan met her stare. "I wouldn't call a person like that much of a *man*, to answer your question. But you've put me in a dreadful position."

"Oh? In what way? Because last I checked your heart isn't invested in anything, so what do you possibly have to lose?"

"Is it?" Morgan asked, his stare boring through her.

"Is what?"

"Your heart invested."

Joan ran a finger along the wooden grain of the desktop. "Not enough to cause harm or regret. He likely doesn't know, and I was already chiding myself for it."

"Good, that's…good."

"Whyever is that good?" Joan's eyes flickered back to his.

"Because…" Morgan sighed, his shoulders caving ever so slightly. "Because he's London's most eligible bachelor with a mother fit for Bedlam, and when…if he found out about your education and how you use it freely, he wouldn't necessarily appreciate it for the gift that it is. Rather, he'd likely see it as a precursor to his mother's malady. She was… she was quite educated in her youth, and there were rumors of her working as a spy…" He paused. "All I know is that there are similarities, and enough of them that it's not a stretch. And…I want better for you than that, Joan. The last thing you want is for someone you have a tender affection for to think you're a bit unhinged."

Chest tight, Joan struggled to take a deep breath. "Do you?"

"Do I what?" Morgan asked, his tone soft and… defeated.

"Think I sound unhinged? That something is not right with me? Because I love to study handwriting and behavior and use that skill for my king and country?"

Morgan frowned, his jaw clenching. "Joan, you're my sister. I would fight the fires of hell for you. And I've seen firsthand from day one your abilities. But that is far different than someone coming to understand them right now. I know you're perfectly sound of mind and heart."

Joan released the breath she'd been holding. It was silly, she knew. Morgan had always been her champion, but she needed to hear it again.

Because sometimes she did feel a little different.

Like an outsider.

Even in her own family.

"But I also have eighteen years of your consistency to prove it. Others...do not. This is why we had that conversation before your debut," Morgan continued.

"I understand. Thank you," Joan replied honestly. "Maybe it was a mistake, the come-out."

Morgan shook his head. "No, you deserve to have a life, a future. Your come-out shouldn't define you, merely be a facet of your beauty, inside and out."

"Thank you." Joan sighed.

The butler stopped by the entrance to the study with a silver tray.

"Come in." Morgan called the older man into the room and lifted the card. "Speak of the devil," he muttered so softly Joan almost missed it. "Show him in."

Joan gave her brother a quizzical look as the butler departed.

"Well, it looks like perhaps we shall see how the land lies."

"Pardon?"

Morgan raised an eyebrow and nodded to the door.

Joan turned, her belly filling with fluttering butterflies at the sight of the Duke of Westmore. Then as he met her gaze, the fluttering stopped, replaced by a heavy feeling of disappointment.

He wasn't here to see her.

Eleven

Rowles's observation shifted from Joan to Morgan and back. Indecision gave him pause in how to proceed. In truth, he wished to talk to both of them, but separately.

After this morning's gossip pages, he knew something had to be done. And he wished to discuss that aspect with Morgan. But conversely, he'd prefer not to offer a heartfelt apology to Joan in front of her older brother. However, standing there in such an awkward manner wasn't helping with either task.

"Good afternoon." He bowed. "I, that is, would you mind terribly if I had a word with you, Morgan?" He flickered his attention to Joan, hoping she could read the apology in his expression.

But after last night, he wasn't sure she could read him as well as he'd thought.

"Of course. Joan and I were finishing our discussion." He gave his sister a nod and a *look*.

Rowles wasn't sure what it meant, but it certainly meant something.

"Of course." Joan curtsied in his direction and gave a silent nod of understanding to her brother.

Rowles missed the silent communication often

to be had with siblings. A wave of sadness tinted his heart for a moment at the memory of his brother. Pushing the thought aside, he bowed to Joan when she moved toward the door. A cold chill ran up his spine as she passed him without a pause.

Perhaps he should have asked to speak to her first.

Except he couldn't, not without her brother's permission.

Blast it all.

"Won't you sit?" Morgan waved to a pair of chairs opposite his desk.

"Thank you." Rowles selected a seat and noted the gossip page in the middle of the desk. "I see you've read it too." He gestured to the sheet.

"Indeed. Joan hadn't seen it yet. She left before it arrived this morning." Morgan sat behind his desk and folded his hands over the offending paper.

"I see." Rowles nodded, then said, "She was certainly out early this morning."

"Yes, well…" Morgan paused, then continued with a bit of a mournful expression. "I'm afraid she's fond of a women's society that champions women's rights. She was at her chapter meeting his morning. Bluestockings, the lot of them. I've tried to dissuade her, but she's stubborn." He shook his head. "Please keep this information to yourself though. Society can be unkind to ladies who favor social change."

"Yes, yes, of course. I wouldn't mention

anything." Rowles tapped his fingers against his thigh, a piece of the puzzle of last night's conversation falling into place.

No wonder she was unfriendly toward his answer. She'd be operating under the premise he didn't have sympathy for the cause.

Which couldn't be further from the truth.

But he could also see how his words could quite easily be misunderstood.

"I can't say I'm surprised. Such things were part of a conversation we shared," Rowles answered, using the topic to transition into his true intentions for paying the social call.

"Oh? Is that the nature of the argument mentioned in the article?" Morgan asked, appearing only half-interested. He was examining his fingernails, not seeming to pay attention to the conversation.

"Indeed. Which is part of the reason I decided to pay you a visit this morning."

"Oh?" Morgan asked, opening a ledger.

"Yes. I hoped to talk to your sister later and offer my apologies for what I hope is a misunderstanding. But I also recognize that because of the society papers, the effect could be unpleasant for her, so I wanted to ask you how I could best handle the situation."

Morgan nodded, then set the ledger aside. "Of course you should speak to her if you feel there was a miscommunication. I don't wish for the two of you to be at odds unnecessarily." He shrugged.

Rowles's forehead drew in at Morgan's last word: *unnecessarily*. What could he mean by that?

"As far as the society-paper article, as long as you maintain your distance but don't appear offended with her, I believe all will sort itself out. But don't dance with her, only offer polite conversation and take your leave. That way no one will get the wrong idea." Morgan nodded.

Rowles leaned back in the chair. "I see."

"She has several suitors, and I wouldn't want anything to jeopardize her season, you understand."

Rowles gave a silent nod.

"Thank you." Morgan met his eyes. "If you'll wait a moment, I'll send someone to fetch Joan for you so you may speak to her." Morgan stood without waiting for Rowles's response and quit the room.

So much for hoping to speak to her without an audience. But it wasn't done, and it was of the utmost importance to abide by societal rules, especially with a best friend's sister.

Morgan walked back into the study, returning to his seat behind his wide desk. "The housekeeper is finding her. Care for tea?"

"No, thank you." His stomach was tight with frustration, so even tea didn't sound appetizing.

"Very well," Morgan replied, lifting one ledger on top of another and flipping through the pages.

"Could I possibly offer to take her for a walk? Chaperoned, of course," Rowles added, his mind skipping ahead to expectation of Morgan's refusal. Morgan didn't even want him to dance with his sister to keep the talk at bay, so a walk would probably cause the suspicion that they were trying to avoid.

Correction: Morgan was trying to avoid.

Which led to a whole plethora of questions.

Did Morgan not approve of him? Not that he'd asked or even implied his interest in Joan, but...to be so clearly *not* considered a suitor was telling, was it not?

"A walk?" Morgan asked, perplexed.

"Chaperoned, of course," Rowles repeated himself.

"I don't see why not," Joan said as she walked into the room.

Rowles turned toward the door, watching with amusement as she gave her brother a challenging expression.

"Chaperoned, of course." Morgan repeated Rowles's declaration.

"I'll ask Mary to accompany me. I'll only need to fetch my pelisse, and I shall see you in a moment," Joan offered to Rowles, her expression unreadable.

Rowles answered, "Of course."

When Joan quit the room, Rowles turned back to Morgan, meeting his irritated stare.

"You realize this will cause more talk, do you not?"

"Talk happens with or without the situation to warrant it," Rowles returned.

"Indeed. However, consider your actions and be cautious." Morgan's words were clipped, and Rowles had the distinct feeling of being chastised.

"I will be circumspect in every way."

"See that you are, and don't be out long. Thankfully, it's not the social hour, far too early for the park to be busy."

"I'll avoid the commonly used paths, if you'd like."

"Which would only create greater suspicion, as if you didn't wish to be seen." Morgan's tone bordered on hostility.

"What would you have me do, Morgan?" Rowles asked in frustration.

"Make it quick and be about your business." He leaned forward on his desk. "Forgive me, I'm trying to protect my sister. Rowles, she's all I have, and I won't see her reputation or chances at a match hazarded by your misguided sense of chivalry and busybodies coming to the wrong conclusions."

"I understand." And he did. In this, Rowles couldn't fault his friend. He was doing what he should to protect his sister.

Rowles stood, studying his friend. "I'll be cautious, and no damage to her reputation will come at my hands."

"Thank you." Morgan's shoulders sagged as if bearing a weight he couldn't fully shake.

Rowles left the study and made his way to the front step of the house, awaiting Joan. A few minutes later, the door opened. Joan stepped into the sunshine with a maid close behind.

"Shall we?" Rowles gestured to the cobbled road before them.

Joan nodded and started down the stairs. He stepped quickly to catch up with her. The town houses lined the street with stone grandeur, silent sentinels with watchful eyes. One was never truly alone in London due to far too many windows and even more wagging tongues. Rowles turned from the scenery to study her.

Joan's eyes were fixed ahead, her hands grasping the fabric of her skirt tightly. Was she nervous? Whatever it was, she felt ill at ease if her posture were any indication. He wished to dispel any tension, but he was unsure how to begin.

Taking a breath, he started to speak only to find she had come to the same conclusion and tried to speak as well.

He gestured for her to go first.

"No, please," Joan replied.

"Very well," Rowles began. "I believe you're frustrated with me, and if you misunderstood my words last night, you'd have rightful cause." He turned his attention ahead.

When she didn't say anything, he turned and met her curious expression.

"I'm not sure if I was more frustrated with you or myself, Your Grace."

"Rowles," he said, almost instinctively. The title still didn't feel comfortable.

She nodded. "Rowles." Her lips dimpled. He was struck by the way his name sounded on her tongue, by how much it pleased him and how much he wished to hear her say it again.

"I never meant to imply that it was justifiable for society to be unfair in the constraints against women. For miscommunicating that, I apologize. It wasn't until later that I reconsidered how I made my point in our discussion and recognized how it could be interpreted."

"I jumped to a conclusion that was also unfair. For that, *I* apologize," Joan offered, meeting his look with a contrite expression. "It's a subject that's close to my heart, and I was probably oversensitive." She turned her attention to the ground.

"Oversensitive?" Rowles shook his head. "Not at all. It's a subject close to your heart, clearly, and also one that isn't given as much credit as deserved."

"Truly?" Her expression became painfully hopeful.

What would it be like to be at the mercy of society because of gender, he wondered. "Truly. Now, your brother tells me you're part of a women's society?" he asked, hoping she'd trust him enough to talk freely.

Joan studied him for a moment. "Indeed, and as my brother is the one who informed you, he also conveyed his displeasure."

"Possibly," Rowles answered.

Two shallow lines creased her brow as she grumbled, "He is afraid society will consider me a bluestocking not because of my position in the world but because of my beliefs."

"That is a possibility," Rowles pointed out.

"And another aspect of the unfairness of the system."

"Indeed," he answered, curious how she'd continue.

Releasing her fistful of skirt, she waved her hands. "Most only consider the aspects of the unfair constraints of culture on women in the societal aspects, but it's so much deeper," she said with feeling.

"Which aspect do you find the most important to consider?" he asked, leading them to the entrance of Hyde Park. Morgan's prophesy was correct and the park was mostly vacant. Rowles relaxed some, thankful they wouldn't be under watchful eyes.

He turned his attention back to Joan, noting the way her lips twisted to the side as she thought. Were her lips as full and soft as they appeared? He desperately wanted to find out.

"The education aspect," she replied with a firm nod.

"Formal or informal?" he asked, curious and intrigued at her keen mind.

She met his eyes. "Both, but formal foremost. No respected university will allow a woman student, which only hinders the potential of a woman without prospects. Women only have a few options for honest work, and those options could be expanded by offering education."

"A valid point. Now, allow me to challenge your thoughts." He glanced at her, waiting to see if she'd accept his words or grow irritated. He'd long ago learned that students fell into two categories: those who wanted to learn, and those who wanted to be right.

If they wanted to learn, they were disappointed if proven incorrect, but appreciated the aspect of personal and intellectual growth. If they wanted to be right, they would do whatever it took to prove their point correct, even if they were utterly wrong, because of pride.

It took a stronger intellect and more character to be the first sort of student, and he hoped and expected that Joan would be of that variety.

Except, she wasn't a student.

She was...something else entirely.

The sobering realization made him tread carefully as he watched her.

"Go ahead. I have realized my earlier error in jumping to conclusions. I'll not make the same mistake twice," she said in a challenging tone. "Do your worst, Professor." Her lips curved into a wide and delighted smile, a hint of mischief dancing in her eyes.

Rowles blinked once, twice, and forced his mind

to work properly rather than be distracted entirely by her calling him *Professor*.

Again.

Good Lord, how could something so innocent seem like a siren call?

"You were saying?" she encouraged.

Rowles nodded, swallowed, then collected his wayward thoughts. "Are intelligence and education directly correlated to success? Or, in a whole new question that likely borders on heretical for British society…" He paused a moment. "Should education be limited to the wealthy and powerful, and if it were available to all, what would be the result?"

Joan's brows knit together as she considered his question.

She sighed. "I see I'm going to have to organize my thoughts in a clearer fashion. Give me a moment." She held up a finger.

Rowles replied with amusement, "Take all the time you need. I am enjoying our conversation immensely, and I hope I'm not pressuring you."

"Not at all, I enjoy our discussions," she said good-naturedly, then abruptly sobered. "To answer your questions, yes, I believe that education is directly correlated to success, but not exclusively. There are always exceptions to every rule, for example, the family of your birth."

"But are there? Truly? Or are there justifications one wishes to exercise?"

"One question at a time." She held up a hand. "Education offers something that one didn't have previously. It's a blessing. And for that blessing to only be offered to a man is tragedy, because women should be allowed that same opportunity in learning."

"One would argue that a husband's skills take priority over the wife's," he added cautiously.

"Yes, if one is *married*." She emphasized the word. "But what if a woman is not? And has no prospect for marriage? What then? Is she relegated to work as a governess? Or working in a textile factory?"

"Aren't men relegated to working in factories or on the docks? In shops or in other labor?"

"Yes, but…they have options. More so than women."

"Indeed."

"What I'm asking is, shouldn't those options be universal?"

He nodded. "And what should be the qualifier?"

She met his eyes with an amused expression. "Intrinsic human value."

"Well done, using my words to prove your point." He offered a brief round of light applause.

"Thank you." She gave a hitch to her shoulder. "Unfortunately, convincing you isn't the same as creating a real change in our society." She tilted her head to the left and studied him. "And…I don't think I convinced you truly. You already believed what I was saying but helped me make a stronger argument for it."

"It was a very persuasive argument," he agreed. "But you are correct. It doesn't change the reality of it all."

Joan let out a small sigh. "The leader of my ladies' society suggested I contact the Thomas Coram's Foundling Hospital to help young ladies," she confided, turning her attention to the fat oaks lining the path.

"Oh? It sounds as if that is a possible avenue to be a catalyst for change."

"A small one." She shrugged. "Is it terrible that I wanted to make more of a difference?" She met his look, a frown puckering her forehead.

He paused, studying her silently for a moment before he spoke. "It is making a difference, a large one, in the person's life whom you assist."

She sighed. "I'm aware, but nothing changes, not really—"

"Except for the one whom you help. That person's life could change entirely." He tipped his head. "Is it better to create a small change for society, or a monumental change for one person?"

Joan remained silent, her observation of him piercing and true as she seemed to consider his words.

"What of exponential change?" he asked, breaking the silence. "Have you considered that?"

"I'm not familiar."

He motioned for them to walk again. "Follow me. I think it might be best if I showed you."

Joan nodded and followed his lead down the path to the water's edge. Rowles strode toward the still water, a duck quacking as it swam away from his presence, only to turn back a few feet away as if waiting for a bread crumb.

"I've nothing to offer you today," he called to the duck, who shook his tail and swam off after a moment.

Rowles bent down by the shore and lifted a small pebble. Turning, he offered his hand to Joan. The grass was still damp from the morning's dew, and he didn't wish for her to slip.

She grasped his hand firmly, her touch sending a shock of awareness through his arm and into his chest, his heartbeat picking up speed as a result. Her hands were dainty, yet capable and firm. They were the hands of a woman who would use them to benefit and bless others, hands that were unafraid of challenges and obstacles. Hands that would change the world.

Hands that could change his world.

"Rowles?" Joan's voice broke through his thoughts. Clearing his throat, he showed her the pebble in his hand.

"A pebble?"

"Indeed."

She raised a brow in query.

"One pebble is small, clearly, and seems insignificant, but it is not the pebble, but the pebble's effect that creates the change." He tossed the pebble into the water. "Count the ripples."

Joan lifted her other hand, the one not still holding his, and began to silently count.

He was careful not to adjust the pressure or move the hand still holding hers, lest she realize they were still attached, in however innocent a way. He wasn't yet ready to let go.

"Twenty," Joan answered.

"One pebble, twenty ripples. That is an exponential effect. Something small may initiate the reaction, but its effect continues outward, far beyond what the pebble could do on its own."

"So, you're saying that assisting one person could in turn create lasting change."

"Yes. Not that we should be small-minded and only help one person in our entire lives." He chuckled.

"Agreed."

"But it gives us perspective that our efforts go beyond. Have you ever heard a sermon on the sower and seeds?"

"I believe so," Joan replied.

"At the end of the parable, the seeds that fell on good soil produced fifty, seventy-five, and a hundredfold."

"It replicated itself, as seeds do."

"Yes, and are we so different? Our one seed of change can create a harvest later." He met her look, willing for her to see herself as more than one woman. But with the potential he knew whenever he saw her.

"Thank you." Joan's words were a mere whisper. Her forehead twitched as if reacting to the thoughts filtering through her mind. "I... That is..." She gave her head a little shake. "I am grateful for this conversation, for your perspective."

"It's my pleasure." And he meant it.

The sound of voices met his ears, and with a swift tug, Joan pulled her fingers free from his grasp and took a step backward, but it was too quick a movement. Her foot slid against the wet lawn.

Rowles reacted as quickly as possible, reaching out for her hand, arm, anything within reach. But it was too late.

And with a mighty crash, she slipped onto her backside. Her legs kicked out from beneath her and smacked into his, effectively knocking him off-balance.

With his abrupt submersion, the icy water instantly saturated his coat and breeches, stealing his breath. As he drifted down beneath the surface, the surge of water up his nose brought with it the taste of stale pond and rotting vegetation.

When he pushed to his feet and rose above the

pond's surface, utterly soaked, it was to a scene he'd not soon forget.

Joan, hand over her mouth in mortified shock. Her maid bumbling over, withdrawing a hanky. And Morgan, arms folded and watching without even trying to contain his laughter.

As Rowles sloshed to the edge of the pond, he cast an irritated glance to his friend, who didn't so much as offer his hand. Well, Rowles mused. This was not how he'd expected the morning to go. But as he glanced at Joan, who still seemed utterly flustered, he decided that it might not have gone as he expected. But it had gone better.

Even if his Hessian boots were likely ruined, again.

Twelve

JOAN WAS NOT ONE GIVEN TO HYSTERICS. No, she prided herself on being rational and even-tempered, not fainting easily or given to rash outbursts—but when the duke rose from the water with a strand of pond grass lying across his head, she came dangerously close to losing her composure.

Because it was her fault.

The sound of his boots squishing in the mud—her doing.

The scent of stale water—a result of her clumsiness.

And damn her brother, who stood there and laughed.

Never in her life had she been more mortified, more at a loss for what to do, or more willing to murder her own flesh and blood. She was not the violent sort, but she most certainly had a moment as Morgan circled the dripping duke once he rose from the water like some merman.

"I wasn't aware that swimming was a great passion of yours," Morgan noted, hand on chin, smug expression fixed to his face.

Joan clenched her fists. And why was he even

here? They had been obeying propriety, and nothing untoward had happened.

"It seems I was suddenly inspired to take a swim." Rowles displayed an ironic expression.

Joan wanted to sink into the ground and become invisible. Her bottom ached from the force with which she'd fallen. Her legs had slipped so quickly, it indeed felt as if someone had kicked her. Bothersome grass.

Yet, instead of *being* kicked, she had kicked someone else—and with enough force to send him flying into the drink.

A crowd began to gather despite the early hour.

"Are you well, Your Grace?" a gentleman asked. Joan didn't even glance over to take note of who it was. Her eyes were fixed on Rowles, on the way the water darkened his sandy-blond hair and his blue eyes flashed with tempered amusement.

"I'm very well and excessively refreshed," Rowles added with a jaunty bow.

The movement made his boots squeak, adding to the effect.

"If you'll excuse me, I'm going to take my leave." He turned to Morgan. "Shall we?"

"Oh, indeed," Morgan replied, his hand concealing his wide smile even as his words were little more than a chuckle.

Rowles turned to her, nodding once. "Lady Joan."

"Of course. I… That is…" She took hasty steps toward the retreating gentlemen. "I'm so terribly sorry, Your Grace," she whispered, her face heating with humiliation.

"Seeing as it was an accident, I do not think an apology is necessary."

"Regardless—"

"I do believe that was one of the rare occasions when I was caught completely off my guard." He chuckled softly. "I must say I'm impressed. This is a day that I will not soon forget, Joan."

"Oh, Your Grace—"

"Rowles," he whispered softly, so as not to draw Morgan's attention. Her brother had stepped quicker than they had, giving a few feet of privacy.

Joan met his eyes, only seeing amusement. There was no resentment, anger, or frustration; well, perhaps a little frustration but that was understandable. One never appreciated walking in wet boots.

Or breeches, for that matter.

"Again, I apologize."

"Are you hurt?"

His question caught her off guard. "Pardon?"

He nodded to her. "You fell. Are you hurt?"

She blinked, then nodded. "I'm quite well, certainly better than I dare say you are, Your… Rowles," she corrected herself.

He gave her a conspirator's smirk. "I dare say the

water was a gentler fall than the wet grass, but I'm glad you're none worse for it."

Joan grinned in spite of herself. "I'd say the water was a gentler fall. But perhaps with greater consequences."

Rowles chuckled, then motioned to his wet coat. "Indeed."

"What are you two murmuring about?" Morgan turned, then smirked at his friend as the fabric of his coat dripped onto the gravel path. "I don't believe I've ever seen you in such a state, Rowles. It's not a sight I'll soon forget."

"I wish I could say the same for you, but unfortunately, I've seen you in worse situations," Rowles added with a touch of sarcasm in his tone.

"Oh? I do believe I wish to hear this story," Joan chimed in, earning a glare from her brother. She was certain there were many stories of Morgan's escapades she hadn't been privy to, and she was all too enthusiastic to hear them. Any ammunition against one's brother was useful.

"Misery does love company, Morgan," Rowles threatened.

"Don't," Morgan answered, his eyes narrowing.

"Why?" Joan asked sweetly, thankful the conversational topic had shifted from her blunder to something else entirely.

The walk to their house in Grosvenor Square was indeed short enough, but she had the feeling that any length of walk would be too long in such conditions as the duke found himself. Any sort of diverting and distracting conversation would be most welcome, she assumed.

As well as entertaining, especially if it concerned her brother.

"Well, I do remember you were once sitting by the Cam behind one of the colleges in Cambridge. Which one was it?"

"Trinity," Morgan ground out. "And that wasn't my fault."

"Nor was this ours," Rowles replied, then shot an apologetic smirk to Joan. "It had rained that morning, and you were walking to St. John's Kitchen Bridge, but a bird… What was it again?"

"A swan." Morgan sighed.

"That's why you hate swans?" Joan asked, surprise raising the pitch of her voice.

Morgan glared at her. "It's reason enough."

Joan shrugged and turned back to Rowles. They had just exited the park and were heading toward the square.

Rowles looked to her, mirth making his blue eyes twinkle. "The poor creature was only trying to land."

"The bloody thing weighed at least two stone," Morgan all but shouted. He scanned the area about him and then turned to Joan. "Pardon me."

She waved off his offering. It wasn't as if she'd

never heard her brother use language like that before, nor would it be the last time. But they were in public, so she supposed that required some sort of contrition.

"Regardless, the swan must not have seen you. I do believe you were wearing a green coat. Maybe it thought you blended in with the grass?"

"Perhaps," Joan added playfully, earning an approving nod from Rowles.

Morgan gave the two of them a baleful glare.

"Anyway, the bird clipped your shoulder as it tried to land in the river and sent you sprawling into the water with it."

Joan held up one gloved hand to cover her wide smirk as she laughed at the image that created in her mind.

"I was a few steps behind your brother, luckily, and watched the whole sordid event transpire. I'm not sure who was more confused, Morgan or the swan."

Joan covered her mouth with both hands. It wasn't polite to laugh so boisterously in public, but the tale and the imagery being portrayed threatened her decorum. She breathed in through her nose and laughed, willing her body to calm but it was no use.

She snickered.

She held back a snort.

And then as if sensing her delicate balance of

self-control, Rowles arched a brow and squeezed a stream of water from his coat onto the path.

She lost her composure and laughed, her belly aching with the power of it. Tears welled in her eyes as she nearly bent over from mirth.

"I can imagine it all!" she said breathlessly between giggles.

"Joan," Morgan chided, standing beside her and pulling her close. "Gather yourself."

Joan straightened and breathed in through her nose and out through her mouth, her lungs burning with the need to burst into another fit of giggles, but she nodded once to her brother.

"Yes, of course," she whispered breathlessly.

A few steps ahead of them now, Rowles smirked over his shoulder, earning a glare from her as she tried to gather her wits.

"It's your fault," she said to his smug expression.

"And the world is better for it," he said. "The unrestrained laughter of a lady is a beautiful thing indeed, and I cannot help but congratulate myself for bringing it forth."

"You're no help," Morgan admonished his friend, but amusement threatened his features.

"I usually am not." Rowles shrugged and started onward, leaving Joan a fine view of his back.

Her merriment shifted into awareness as her observation took in the way his wet coat hugged his broad shoulders, the taper of his waist, and the length of his legs. Proportionate in every way, he was beautiful, even from the back. Especially from the back. One wasn't distracted by the green of his eyes or the brightness of his smile. She could appreciate his form, as wanton as it sounded to her own mind.

But it was the truth.

And if she was anything, it was honest.

And honestly, she was enamored. Fascinated and…hungry.

But she didn't exactly know for what, since it wasn't a hunger of her belly, but of her heart.

Her soul.

And she had the odd sensation that perhaps it wasn't a hunger as much as an appetite.

An awareness.

A need.

"Joan?" Her brother's voice cut through her greedy perusal.

Shifting her attention to the ground, then to her brother, she noted his curious expression. Understanding must have dawned because her brother's eyes darted from her to his friend, then back to her.

He gave his head a shake, as if scolding her. "Come. Let's get home."

Chastised, Joan kept her eyes from straying to Rowles's form, even as it pulled her like a magnet. It was an exercise in self-control, one she wasn't sure she was equal to. But as they crossed the square to their home, she breathed a sigh of relief as the duke's carriage waited out front.

"I'll take my leave, if you don't mind. I have grown uncomfortable on our trek here." Rowles gave a self-deprecating smirk.

"Understandable. Will I see you tonight? I believe it's the Rathbone fete. Though I imagine you'd wish to stay in after this afternoon's events," Morgan stated.

Rowles's eyes shifted to Joan, only for a split second, and then he turned back to her brother. "I'll see you tonight, then."

"Indeed." Morgan nodded, and then gestured for her to follow him up the steps and into their home.

Ivy climbed the stone face of the town house, adding life to the otherwise stark gray stone. As they entered the foyer, Morgan turned to her, then lowered his eyes and spoke in a soft but warning tone. "I meant what I said earlier. He is not..." He paused. "There are better options, and we shall find them. Do not let your attachment grow." He speared her with his unflinching stare, then stepped back, heading toward his study.

Joan released the breath she'd been holding.

What he asked was nearly impossible.

She climbed the stairs to the second floor. As she passed through the hall toward her rooms, she blew out an exasperated sigh. She went into her chamber and closed the door softly, leaning her back against it as she closed her eyes.

It wasn't as if she'd cultivated these feelings, this attachment.

It was involuntary.

But real, insistent, and growing.

How did one extinguish an attachment when she wasn't even sure how it had started?

She looked to the bed, noting the gown her maid had laid out for the Rathbone ball that evening, reminding her that she needed a change of clothing at present as well. After ringing for her maid, she was alone with her thoughts once more. With a lack of charity, she half suspected her brother would cancel their plans tonight since the duke planned to attend.

Her chest tightened as she considered her brother's earlier words.

Would the duke, in fact, count her among the ranks of his mother if he knew her true talents? Would he not believe her? Think her insane or of warped mind? Her heart fractured at the thought, a slight pinch, but nonetheless real. She couldn't imagine how it would pain her if it were real. If she were to walk that path only to find the most terrible of heartbreak at the end of it.

By his hand, no less.

Maybe her brother was right.

Maybe she should listen to him.

Maybe her heart should listen to the reason of her mind. Yet, wasn't that exactly the problem?

Distraction. She needed a distraction from all the heavy thoughts that plagued her mind. She noticed the window, spilling in the sunshine as it spread to her writing desk. Remembering the missive she was to send to Thomas Coram's Foundling Hospital and the new friend she'd made from interest in that facility, she squared her shoulders and strode to the desk. Withdrawing her quill and ink, she set about sending a message to both.

She sealed the letters with wax and rang for a maid. In short work, the missives were dispatched and she was once again at a loss for what to do to distract herself.

Because the moment her mind wasn't otherwise occupied, it drifted back to a certain duke.

Joan quit her rooms and took the stairs down to the first floor, seeking her brother. He was easily found behind his broad desk in the study and readily answered her insistent knock.

"Come in."

Joan took in the scattered missives, then frowned. "Is there something you need help with?"

Morgan answered, "No, no, only busy work, I'm afraid. The kind that is necessary but never truly feels important."

"I see," Joan replied, approaching the desk. She

lifted a small brass ball with a flat bottom from a wooden stand. The heaviness of the ball was a testament to its quality. She weighed it in her hand and then said to her brother, "I have need of the carriage."

He flicked a perfect cross to a *t* and looked up. "Oh? To go where?"

She set the brass ball back into place. "I want to visit the Thomas Coram's Foundling Hospital."

Morgan dropped the quill, ink splotching across the missive. "Drat," he muttered and blotted the stain. "Pardon, what did you say?" He met her look, and she read uncertainty and…fear.

Odd.

And unexpected.

Her mind quickly tried to understand the source of his tension at the mention of the hospital. It was in Bloomsbury and was a popular place for the fashionable set, oddly enough. To her mind, it wasn't kind for the more fortunate to observe and tour the orphanage of those so much less fortunate. But since those visitors provided generous donations for the place, she supposed the benefit outweighed the negative.

"It's perfectly safe, I assure you," she added.

Morgan tapped his finger and looked down, as if on purpose so as not to reveal the expression in his eyes.

"I… That is, there's been an increase in crime

recently, Sister, and I don't wish you to be one of the statistics."

"I doubt that is likely, considering the Governor's Hall is next to the hospital. Lady Farthingham had her tea party there not a month ago. If the area were crime-infested, I doubt the fashionable set would deign to darken the door or the roads to it."

"While that may be the case, you haven't the time today anyway."

"Whyever not?" Joan asked, irritated that he refused to meet her eyes. He sighed, then glanced up, finally.

"You have the Rathbone ball to dress for, and I'm sure you haven't had tea. Certainly you wish to be home for callers this afternoon as well." He pinched his lips as if knowing he'd won the argument with that last point.

Joan tilted her head. "Very well."

Her brother nodded, his lips twitching in what she was certain was an effort not to crow in victory.

"I'll go tomorrow, then."

He narrowed his eyes. "Why this sudden fascination with the orphanage?"

She shrugged. "I was told that they needed ladies to help train, teach, and mentor the young girls there."

He studied her. "Is this information gleaned from your women's society?"

"Yes, it is."

"I see." He nodded. "Very well. I know I won't

be able to hinder you in an effort you see as worthy and serving, so go. But be cautious."

"Because orphans are so dangerous."

He signed the bottom of a missive. "Nevertheless, use caution."

"Always," she added cheekily, and then took her leave of the study, her mind tickling with something she couldn't name.

It felt like suspicion.

But it was more.

Her brother wouldn't lie to her.

He couldn't.

Could he?

Thirteen

ROWLES HAD NEVER BEEN SO GRATEFUL TO DON dry clothing in all his life. By the time he'd arrived at his residence, his breeches had chafed something awful and his wool coat had shrunk tight to his shoulders. Blisters were forming on his feet, and he sent longing looks to his now-ruined boots.

But if the loss of a jacket and boots were the cost of Joan's unrestricted laughter, he would pay the price gladly.

Again and again.

His lips tugged into a bemused expression as he remembered the way her gray eyes narrowed into slits when she lost the battle of her amusement, her laughter like chiming bells on Christmas Day and every bit as spectacular.

Of all the restrictions of society on women, he was especially irritated with the fact that a lady couldn't do more than simper and giggle behind a fan without being considered impolite.

Laughter, laughter like Joan's, was music, and should be shared, explored.

It wasn't an impolite action.

It was a reward.

To the reason for its unleashing.

"Your Grace."

Rowles turned to face the voice, his merriment fading as he noted the butler bringing news of his mother.

"Yes." Rowles stood, taking a deep breath.

The butler bowed, then straightened. "The doctor has finished situating your mother's new staff and is ready to move her, upon Your Grace's command, to her new situation."

Rowles nodded. "Begin at once."

"As you wish, Your Grace." The butler bowed. "I'll inform the servants, and I will inform you when your mother is situated in her new environs."

"Excellent," Rowles answered.

The butler quit the room, taking with him all the earlier amusement that had filled Rowles's spirit.

The doctor had procured what he considered the greatest and most able nurses in London as well as a staff capable of managing his mother, should she fly into a violent rage once again.

Rowles wiped a hand down his face. It had been necessary to keep her sedated on laudanum for the interim. He couldn't risk her harming his staff any further, or himself. It broke his heart, but what other recourse did he have? None.

He strode over to the wide window overlooking the back garden of his home. The stone steps led down to a small hedgerow with roses and lilies, all blooming, all boasting life and color. But he felt none of it, at least not anymore.

He wanted to hear her laugh again, Joan. It would certainly be balm to his aching heart and plagued mind. But was that fair to her? He thought not. Furthermore, would it be fair to subject any woman to a mother-in-law such as his mother would be? He knew his answer to that as well. At least not now, not when he had to restrain his mother to keep her from attacking others. If he were to become engaged, the woman would want to meet her future mother-in-law. Which, under the circumstances, was impossible and would only lead to questions and result in answers he really didn't wish to give.

While London knew his mother was ill, that knowledge was far different from telling his future wife that same blood ran through his veins and could run through any future progeny's veins. Who would want to be saddled with that, title or not? Dukedom or not? He knew the answer: only those truly only concerned with the title. Which meant he wasn't interested in them at all.

It was an equation in which there was no winner: only losers. He would rather lose alone than make someone else lose along with him.

A carriage pulled up into the drive and he recognized the crest.

Penderdale.

Why in heaven's name was Morgan seeing him

again after so recent a visit? A cold chill ran down his back as a suspicion grew in his mind. And it was no less than what he'd concluded himself only a moment ago. Rowles quit his rooms and took the stairs to the main floor as the butler answered the door.

"Let him in," Rowles called, earning a bow from his butler and a nearby footman.

"I assume this isn't purely social, is it, old friend?" Rowles asked, taking in the grim line of his friend's countenance.

Morgan nodded.

"Come with me." Rowles turned and led his friend to the study, then closed the door behind them. "Brandy?"

"No, thank you," Morgan replied, his tone subdued, tired even.

"What plagues your mind?" Rowles asked, taking a seat on the couch beside the wide window. He gestured to another chair beside the fire.

Morgan nodded, sat, and leaned forward. "I... sense an attachment on Joan's part and...I wish your assistance in severing it."

Rowles had expected the words. However, the searing pain to his chest as those words settled in was utterly unexpected.

Was he already so invested himself? How had it gotten so far? And only to meet such a tragic fate.

"Your words are nothing but an echo of my own convictions." Rowles sighed. "My mother is being moved, as we speak, to a separate house with a full and competent staff, but even that doesn't give me peace of mind that she won't harm herself or others. I... It would not be fair... to subject anyone to such a family as mine, at least currently."

Morgan released a tense breath. "Your family is not my concern—"

"I know, and you're a better friend for it, but it is my concern." Rowles leaned back in his chair.

Morgan studied him, then gave a curt nod. "I thank you."

"It is a difficult position, shepherding one's sister in the season."

Morgan looked heavenward. "Tell me about it. I don't resent it, but I do feel unequal to the task at times."

"You're doing well, and I do not resent that you are having this conversation with me."

"You're a better friend than I deserve, Rowles." Morgan stood. "And I'm grateful for that."

"As am I grateful for you." Rowles stood as well. "It goes without saying that I'll be giving my regrets to Lady Rathbone concerning tonight's event."

"A loss."

"It is always a boon to have a duke in attendance, but I think she shall recover." He gave a chuckle, but it was sad, mournful in nature. "Give my apologies to Joan. Please, I've already had one miscommunication with her, and I do not wish for this to be an additional one."

"I'll take care of it," Morgan promised. "Until later." He bowed and took his leave.

Rowles watched his friend's retreat and sighed deeply, his bones weary as if sensing a hopelessness that threatened to overtake him.

It was for the best.

He knew it.

Didn't he?

Fourteen

The poor folk gladly came to me, for I did them no unkindness, but helped them as much as I could.

—Joan of Arc, from The Trial of Joan of Arc by W.S. Scott

JOAN HAD RECEIVED NO FEWER THAN FIVE CALLers that afternoon, but the one caller she sought did not appear. Lord Goodman was attentive, and his light-blond hair was combed in the utmost fashion, but as she conversed with him, he kept reminding her of someone else.

Only lacking the conversational skills of said person.

One could only talk about the weather and hounds for so long.

And her disappointment continued when her brother conveyed the news that the duke wouldn't attend the evening's ball. He assured her it was nothing to do with their escapade that afternoon at the park.

Yet she couldn't help but wonder if perhaps it did.

The evening at the ball was lovely, perfect, if one viewed it from the outside. But appearances were often deceiving, so while she danced the cotillion, she appeared cheerful and serene on the outside, but her heart was heavy.

While she sipped orgeat and admired the flowers along the refreshment table, she was reliving the earlier events of the day and berating herself for her blunders.

And while she waltzed with Lord Goodman, she wished another's arms held her.

It wasn't till the carriage ride home that Morgan questioned her silence.

"It was a lovely evening, was it not?" he asked, clearly probing for information.

Joan's contemplation strayed from the window. "It was as expected, yes."

When she didn't elaborate, Morgan continued. "I saw you waltzed with Goodman."

Joan nodded. "He called this afternoon as well."

"Then I shall check my sources to ensure he is as good a man as his name suggests."

"If you wish," Joan replied, uninterested. She twisted her lips and met her brother's eyes. "Did the duke mention anything that would give you reason to think he was angry with me?"

Morgan sighed. "Joan, this hasn't anything to do with you."

"It feels as if it does," she muttered.

Morgan chuckled. "Why does that not surprise me?" He reached across the carriage and patted her hand. "Leave it be. You have to focus your efforts on a match… You said so yourself at the beginning of the season. I thought we agreed that you'd release this…attachment…to the duke."

"Easier said than done, I'm afraid."

Morgan sighed. "I don't know what more to say, Joan."

"Has he truly not said anything about me?"

Morgan shifted his attention to the window. "I don't know what to tell you. Sometimes things aren't meant to be, Sister."

Joan leaned back on the velvet cushion of the carriage and bit her lip. "I understand."

It wasn't until they arrived home and she was readying herself for bed that she questioned Morgan's behavior.

That was twice in one day he wouldn't look at her when he spoke.

It might be a coincidence.

But it might not be, either.

As she lay in bed that night, she formulated a plan. Morgan knew that if he lied to her, face-to-face, she'd likely see through it. So, she'd have to converse with him where he couldn't exploit her weakness.

It was a blessing to have family, but it was a curse when they knew how to use her weakness—her willingness to always believe them—against her.

Even when they thought they were doing it in her best interest.

After a fitful night's sleep and no small effort on her maid's part to help her not appear as weary, she went to break her fast, intent on finding her brother.

Only to discover he'd already left and wouldn't return till evening.

Joan scraped some marmalade across her toast, her frustration compounded by her lack of decent sleep. She was sipping her tea slowly, allowing the sweetness of the sugar to improve her disposition, when the butler came into the breakfast room carrying his silver tray.

Two missives addressed to her awaited her perusal. "Thank you." She took the letters and broke the seal of the first.

It was from the contact Lady Sandra had given her, Miss Corinne Vanderhaul. Joan read through the letter, noting the invitation for her to visit at her leisure. When she finished, she lifted the next letter.

Miss Emily Bronson.

Joan opened the seal and read the reply to the letter she had sent yesterday. Miss Bronson restated her interest in the Foundling Hospital, and before Joan read the rest of the letter, she stood from the breakfast table.

Miss Vanderhaul had invited her to the Foundling Hospital at her leisure.

Miss Bronson wished to help.

And clearly there were no other pressing matters on her schedule for the day, not with her brother absent on business. So, there was no time like the present.

With a quick stride down the hall, she turned into the blue parlor and sat behind the writing desk. Addressing a letter to each woman, she accepted Miss Vanderhaul's invitation, notifying her she'd be by around noon. She then sent a letter informing Emily of her plans and inviting her to come along.

After sealing the letters, she called for a maid and handed them off to be dispatched.

Joan's chest unwound a little, satisfaction taking its place as she considered her plans for the day. Determined to have a better disposition, she quit the parlor to head for her room. She'd need to change into a sturdier dress if she were to assist Miss Vanderhaul.

As she made her way to the staircase, a maid intercepted her. "My lady, this arrived, and I thought you'd wish to read it, as your usual." She curtsied and offered a printed leaflet.

Joan immediately recognized the typescript of the *Tattler* and thanked the maid, holding the leaflet carefully to prevent the ink from smudging her fingers. As she reached the top of the stairs, she started to read through the news.

It wasn't until the last paragraph that she paused,

rereading the words that immediately reversed any progress her disposition had made thus far.

And finally, it would seem that even the best qualities of a lady, or her pedigree, cannot compensate for a blunder as monumental as what transpired yesterday at Hyde Park.

Joan let out a groan. It wasn't as if the park had been completely vacant, but it wasn't as if the incident had happened during the fashionable hour.

Someone had seen and talked, and word must have spread like wildfire.

Great. Just brilliant. Joan closed her eyes, not wanting to read the rest, but helpless to ignore her curiosity.

She opened one eye, then the other, and read the rest.

A duke was baptized in the Serpentine. A lady was the cause, and I dare say, either the water caused a chill to keep the duke from attending the Rathbone ball or it was Lady J who abruptly caught the chill due to the lack of attention from the once-friendly duke.

Joan crumpled up the paper, no longer caring about ink stains. Growling low in her throat, she went into her room and hurled the offensive ball of nonsense against the wall in a fit of temper. The bit of gossip wasn't anything that she hadn't thought herself. But having someone else say it, notice it— well, that was an entirely different thing. And much more painful.

Maybe Morgan was right.

She flopped onto the bed in a most unlady-like manner and blew out an exasperated breath. Maybe she was trying for something that wasn't meant to be, forcing it, really. And maybe that was why it hurt. Because it wasn't meant to happen, like a square block trying to fit through a round hole.

Shouldn't love be easier?

Love should be sacrificing, true, noble, and pure…but surely it was also simple.

This felt anything but simple. Perhaps that was her answer. Closing her eyes, she took a moment to gather herself, then stood. She wouldn't spend any more effort on this pointless attachment. She had a purpose, she had plans, and she wasn't going to let them be hindered by herself.

So she rang for her maid and changed into a blue muslin day dress with a pelisse. An hour before she was to depart, Miss Bronson was shown into the parlor.

"I was so thankful to receive your kind letter! To think, you heard back so soon and we will be able to be of true assistance. It's delightful!" Miss Bronson said after greeting Joan.

"My thoughts exactly."

"I brought along Betsey. She's to chaperone me. I'm sure Miss Vanderhaul is most proper, but my father didn't wish for me to take any risks with my reputation." Miss Bronson waved to the plump maid in the corner, who offered a curtsy as she was mentioned.

"Of course. I'll be bringing along Mary as well, until we know what exactly is expected of us at the hospital." Joan walked to the bell and rang for a maid.

"One can never be too cautious." Miss Bronson nodded sagely.

"Agreed."

The maid came in and curtsied.

"Please bring in tea for me and my guest," Joan told her.

"Of course, my lady." The maid quickly left to do her bidding, and Joan turned back to her friend. "Why don't we get to know each other a little better while we wait? Won't you sit?" Joan motioned to a chair.

"Thank you." Miss Bronson sat demurely. "I'm not sure there's much that's interesting about me."

"I doubt that. Everyone has their own individual talents and character traits. Tell me, what do you like to do in your leisure time?"

Miss Bronson's dark brows pinched. "I enjoy reading, and when my family quits London for the season, we stay in Bath. I love the old Roman ruins. I miss it dreadfully when we're in town."

"Do you swim?"

Miss Bronson gave a delicate laugh. "Yes, as often as I can. It's a delightful refreshment for the heat of the summer."

"At least you can swim. I confess I've never learned."

"Truly?" Miss Bronson leaned forward. "I suppose there's not much opportunity in London."

"Not unless you wish to brave the Serpentine or the Thames." Joan giggled, but then sobered. She shoved all thoughts of the duke into the back of her mind and forced a controlled appearance. "I suppose if I lived near the sea it would be more prudent to learn, but I don't think I'll be needing to swim anytime soon."

"You're quite safe in London from swimming," Miss Bronson agreed. "What of you? What are some of your favorite things to do?"

Joan was starting to form words when the maid came in with the tea service. "Thank you." She stood and lifted a teacup. "How do you take your tea, Miss Bronson?"

"Cream, no sugar, please."

Joan served her the tea and then indicated to the butter biscuit plate. "Our cook has a fantastic biscuit recipe."

"You've convinced me," Miss Bronson replied cheerfully and took a biscuit.

Joan served herself tea and then sat back down. Biting into a flaky, sweet biscuit, she thought over Miss Bronson's question. "I suppose I enjoy reading; I also love riding and utterly hate needlepoint."

This confession earned a snicker from Miss Bronson. "On that we are agreed."

"Odious and time-consuming activity," Joan added.

"And what does it accomplish? Another frilly decoration? Or napkin, or handkerchief? As if we do not have enough already."

"Exactly!" Joan lifted her teacup in approval.

The clock chimed half past, and Joan nodded to her new friend. "I suppose we should start our journey if we are to be there by noon."

"Indeed."

"We can take my carriage. Will that work?" Joan asked.

"Perfectly." Miss Bronson rose from her seat and placed the empty teacup and saucer by the tray. "Betsey?" She turned to her maid.

"I'll send word to Mary, and she will meet us in the front."

Soon Joan sat beside Miss Bronson and across from their two maids as they started toward the Foundling Hospital in Bloomsbury.

In short order, they approached the stone building, clearly built for efficiency rather than beauty. As they alighted from the carriage, Joan studied the stone-and-iron gate that led to the courtyard. Ladies and gentlemen milled about, coming and going. And a row of children in white uniforms with blue sashes crossing their chests stood in a straight line, following their leader across the gravel yard.

A star with arrows decorated the front alongside the main gate. Joan nodded to Miss Bronson, waiting for her to catch up before they entered. The gravel crunched under their feet as they crossed the wide courtyard, lined by obelisks. Another courtyard could be seen to the left behind another stone wall with an arched entrance, but Joan made her way to the front of the stone building, where Miss Vanderhaul had said she'd be waiting.

As they approached, a woman in a nurse's uniform stepped into the sunshine from the doorway, smiling a welcome. "You must be Lady Joan and Miss Bronson."

Joan nodded. "Indeed, and are you Miss Vanderhaul?"

"I am, and it's a pleasure to meet you both. Sandra Bookman is a dear friend, and I've heard nothing but good things about you, Lady Joan. And I'm looking forward to getting to know you, Miss Bronson."

"It's our pleasure, and we're honored to be of any assistance," Joan answered, immediately liking the woman. Her thick black hair was swept into a tight knot, but the severity of her hairstyle was counteracted by the kindness in brown eyes full of compassion and hope. Joan read a deep well of hope beneath her look, one that was cool and peaceful, unwavering. It refreshed her very soul to see it.

"Yes, however we may help, you will find our hands equal to the task," Miss Bronson added.

Miss Vanderhaul nodded, clasping her hands in

front of her wide waist. "We can use the help. Come. If you'll follow me, we shall begin with a tour."

She started through the gate to the left and walked into the back courtyard. "There are two separate wings, east and west, so that we may keep the boys separate from the girls."

Gesturing to the left, she led them through a narrow door into a wing. "This is the girls' wing. You'll see that everything is nice and orderly. It's vastly important to keep everything tidy with this number of children," she said wryly. "And this way, as we pass down this hall and to the left…"

Joan glanced at Miss Bronson, sharing a smile as they worked to keep up with the energetic woman.

"This is the nursery where we take in the surrendered babies." She waved to a row of cribs. "And of course every mother is interviewed, making sure their child is a proper fit for the orphanage."

"Miss Vanderhaul," Joan asked, "what criteria do you use to decide if a baby is taken in or not?"

"Call me Corinne, please." She lowered her voice. "Unfortunately, the majority of them are either true orphans or by-blows. It's no fault of the babe, so we take in as many as possible. We'll keep some here, foster some to other families, and some go to stay with foster families in the countryside, but all will return here by the age of five."

"Do you name them? Or does the mother?" Miss Bronson asked.

"Every child is baptized and given a new name," Corinne responded, nodding to a row of cribs.

Joan noted that some of the cribs held tokens of various sorts tied to the wood. "And what are those?" She studied a faded blue handkerchief.

"Ah." Corinne nodded. "That is a token left by the mother. In case she were to return and collect her child, she would know which one belonged to her."

"But wouldn't a mother recognize her own child?" Miss Bronson asked.

Corinne shrugged. "Sometimes it's months later, and babes tend to change quickly."

"Ah, I see. Do…do the mothers usually come back for their children?" Miss Bronson asked.

Corinne gave her head a slow shake. "No. Oh, on rare occasions it happens, but if a woman has given her baby to the Foundling Hospital, she's in dire straits. Those don't often change."

Joan's heart pinched at the thought of the sacrifice of the mothers.

"We have fewer orphans than we used to, I'm told. Back seventy-five years ago or so, they had an 'indiscriminate admission' policy, and babies and children were taken in by droves. Though I can't say if fewer admissions are a pity or a blessing. So many often end up as thieves on the streets if they don't wind up here." Corinne sighed. "We help as many as we can."

"It's the Lord's work." Miss Bronson nodded, her words empathic.

"Indeed it is," Corinne agreed. "If you'll follow me, I'll show you the chapel where famous George Frideric Handel held a concert to raise money for the hospital."

Joan's brows rose. "I wasn't aware."

"It was a while ago…before you were born, I'd wager," Corinne replied. "After you've seen the chapel, I'll introduce you to the older girls, the ones you'll be assisting."

Miss Bronson and Joan shared a look of excitement, and Joan couldn't suppress her amusement. They traveled through the other courtyard and into a modest chapel, with its glass windows and wooden pews lining the stone aisle. Corinne's voice echoed softly, and Joan imagined the sound of voices raised in chorus to one of Handel's masterpieces. It would be heavenly to experience.

Shortly after that, Corinne led them to a small parlor-like room on the other side of the interior courtyard. Joan noted the way the young ladies, all several years younger than her, sat up straighter upon their entrance. Their keen expressions collectively darted between Corinne and herself, then took in Miss Bronson.

"Ladies, we have the great blessing of having two gentlewomen paying us a visit. Please stand and introduce yourselves."

By turns, each young lady curtsied prettily and lowered her eyes while giving her Christian name. Joan noted that the names were all Biblical in origin.

She stepped forward and nodded her approval. "It's a pleasure to make your acquaintance, all of you."

"Indeed," Miss Bronson chimed in.

"We are happy to be here and hope to be of assistance to you in any way you need."

"These are proper ladies who will be coaching you on proper etiquette and helping you perfect the attributes that may lead you to a position in a household."

A few anxious stares darted to Joan, and she read the hope, the desperation in them. A weight settled on her at the realization that *she* was the one offering hope; hope that they could find a way of supporting themselves by being a scullery maid or housemaid. That was their great hope. She, by birth, was afforded so much.

And they, by birth, were afforded so little.

"I will not only help, but if you strive to learn well and take my instruction to heart, I'll also give my personal recommendation to whomever needs it for a potential employer," Joan said with feeling.

A few of the girls gasped, then burst into giggles as if given a great gift.

"As will I," Miss Bronson added.

"Now, are we going to work hard for these generous ladies?" Corinne asked.

"Yes, ma'am." The young ladies nodded in unison and gave hearty affirmations.

Corinne's expression was one of approval as she turned to Joan. "Then, where shall we begin?"

Fifteen

THE TRANSITION OF HIS MOTHER TO HER NEW lodgings went seamlessly, according to the nurse's report. Rowles couldn't resist a deep sigh of relief and resolved to pay her a visit that evening. As he took the stairs to the second floor, he paused at the top and turned toward the hall that had, for so many years, led to his mother's chambers. The house was quieter now, with fewer servants bustling about or nurses quietly moving up and down the hall in efforts to care for their patient. It was sobering, and the house felt empty in a way he hadn't anticipated. It wasn't as if he'd spent much time with his mother on her sickbed, and for obvious reasons; however, he had *known* she was near. And that made a difference.

One that he hadn't noticed till it was startlingly absent.

All the more reason to visit her in her new lodgings. With a quick prayer for assistance from the Almighty with his planned visit, Rowles quickly washed up in his rooms, then called for his carriage to be brought around. The arranged house wasn't a far drive, and he could take in the air and walk, but he decided the privacy of a carriage was most apt.

In case things did go badly.

One never knew.

Which was all the more reason to take precautions.

Soon he stepped into his carriage and leaned back against the plush velvet while his two bays led the way to the new lodgings where his mother resided. They left the square and moved past the park, then turned left for a few blocks till the carriage paused in front of a perfectly respectable stone town house with lovely hedgerows lining the walk. A vine of some sort climbed up the front of the house and lent a welcome atmosphere, but Rowles's heart pounded in his chest. Before he knocked, the door opened wide, revealing a sturdy man with bushy eyebrows. "Your Grace." He bowed, his accent decidedly country. "An honor. I am Waitsberry, the butler, among other things."

"Thank you, Waitsberry." Rowles studied the man, deciding that he was quite likable; there was something sincere about his demeanor.

"Allow me to show you to the parlor, or would you like a tour of the home? How may I assist you, Your Grace?" the butler asked, clearly eager to please.

Rowles turned to the expectant man. "I believe I'll confer with the nurses first."

"Of course. Right this way, Your Grace." The stout man bustled down the hall, a limp to his walk.

The house was pleasing. It wasn't opulent or stylish, but held a well-built quality that made it feel secure and safe. The wooden floor was worn but polished, and the plaster on the walls was freshly painted. A parlor to the right held windows that spilled cheery light into the otherwise dim hall, and as they took the stairs, Rowles noted they squeaked only slightly—admirable for a home of this age.

Waitsberry led him down the hall on the second floor and paused as he came to a woman in nurse's garb. "Mrs. Leyton." He nodded.

Her eyes lowered and she curtsied upon seeing Rowles. "Your Grace. How may I assist you?"

Waitsberry gave a generous bow and started back down the hall, allowing Rowles some much-appreciated privacy. "I have been informed that the transition went well, and I want to see her condition for myself."

"Of course," the nurse quickly agreed. "And yes, the move went smoothly, though I will add that we did not lighten her dosage until recently. She's starting to wake, so she may not have understood what took place, Your Grace."

"I appreciate your insight." Rowles followed the nurse as she led him to the nearby door and slowly turned the brass knob. The scent of laudanum and soap permeated the air as the door swung open without a sound. The drapes were closed tightly, so the light from the hall was all that luminated the otherwise dark room.

"She may be asleep," Miss Leyton whispered.

"I'm not," came a clipped reply from the bed. "I am, however, quite confused and in a fit of temper." The words were abrasive but the tone lacked the energy the words should have conveyed.

Rowles's heart pounded painfully as he stepped closer to the bed. "Hello, Mother." Holding his breath, he waited for her reply, wondering if she'd see him or his dead brother—or no one at all.

"What is this place?" she asked, her tone warning that the wrong answer could prove ill-advised.

"It's a lovely soft bed and finely furnished room," Rowles answered cautiously, glancing about at the sumptuous furniture, taken from his mother's rooms and placed in her new accommodations. The decor was oddly out of place for the rest of the home, but in the dim light, Rowles wondered how she even noticed that she was in a different place. The staff had done wonders in placing her furniture in exactly the same arrangement as it had been at home. The only difference in the room was possibly the color—it was too dim for him to be sure—and the size. The room was a bit smaller, but not dramatically.

"It is not my home." She spoke softly, her tone on a boiling point. "It smells odd."

'"It is only temporary." Rowles decided to add some honesty but not fully disclose any information, to prevent a bad reaction. "You've been sick, Mother."

"I'm dying." His mother sighed the words. "And not soon enough, clearly, if my son is moving me from my own home to be rid of me even before I'm ready for my grave."

Guilt punched Rowles in the gut. "It's not—"

"It is. And this place… It's…" She choked on a sob. "It's not home."

Rowles moved to her bedside, his hand shaking as he reached out to tentatively grasp her fingers, attempting to sooth her.

She jerked her hand away at first touch. "What have you done?" she spat out, then hiccupped a sob.

"Cared for you, hoping it will restore your health."

"You want to be rid of me," she murmured, then rolled over, giving him her back.

Rowles gave a silent sigh, then turned to the nurse who had her attention lowered to the floor.

He turned back to his mother. "If you improve in the next week or so, we can move you home—"

"I'll die here," she vowed. "And you'll have no one to blame but yourself. I could have died at home, in my own bed, surrounded by my sons, but you've taken that away from me. I'm only surrounded by strangers, my own family having abandoned me."

"Mother—"

"Don't call me that." She bit the words, sending

an arrow through his heart as the words sliced through him. "Even Robert doesn't visit." She sobbed. "Robert would love me. It's you... You're keeping him away!"

Rowles turned to the nurse, waving his hand a little as if imploring help. The nurse saw his motion and met his expression with her own filled with sorrow and pity.

Damn, he hated pity.

He hated feeling as if he'd betrayed his mother more, however.

"Duchess, it's teatime. I have some lovely biscuits as well." The nurse changed the subject, offering a cheery alternative.

"The tea here is terrible."

"It's the same tea as from your very own kitchens, Duchess. I made sure of it. And your cook made the biscuits. That's how I know they are the best—a duchess of your caliber would have the best cook."

"Cook is talented," his mother admitted, almost against her will it sounded. She even rolled over and sat up. "It isn't a proper day without tea, I suppose."

"No, my lady, it is not," the nurse agreed emphatically. "I'll have it brought up directly. Did you wish for anything else to accompany it? Cake perhaps?"

"Yes. I do want cake."

"Of course." The nurse gave a delicate curtsy and

then quit the room. She conveyed the duchess's desires to a maid and dispatched her directly to the kitchens.

"Tea will be here soon. Do you wish to sit by the window?" the nurse asked, a bright expression on her face, as if the power of her will could lift the spirits of the entire room.

Her efforts failed.

"No. I'm ill." She glared at Rowles. "Or so I'm told. I must stay in bed, I assume."

"You may do whatever you wish, Mother."

"Except go home," she added, casting a dark look his direction.

"Perhaps soon, if you recover."

"Or I'll die. But at least I'll die having tea. It's more than *you* offered." She glared at him and made a small effort to sit up in her bed.

Rowles reached out to assist her, but she batted his hands away. "I thought I told you not to touch me."

Raising his hands in surrender, he backed up and allowed the nurse to assist his mother instead.

"There you go, easy now." The nurse stepped in quickly and effortlessly, adjusting a few pillows and even straightening his mother's mobcap. "Are you sure you don't wish to have tea by the window? There's a lovely view of the courtyard."

"Tomorrow, maybe, if I'm alone and not bothered by anyone." She nodded toward Rowles.

"I'll let you enjoy your tea then." Rowles took a

step back, earning an apologetic expression from the nurse. A maid came into the room carrying a tray set up with tea and biscuits, the scent inviting.

"Don't come back unless you're taking me home," his mother called out as he started toward the door.

Rowles opened his mouth, but to say what, he was unsure. How did a son respond? Agree? Heavens no, but to disagree would bring more harm than good. So with a bow, he bid her good day.

Bloody pity, it would be the death of him.

The carriage swaying as it conveyed him home, he was assaulted by another black thought. Because rather than have some sort of anticipation for the evening, he had none.

In a perfect world, he would arrive at the Rathbone rout, secure a waltz from Joan, and delight in her dazzling company, sure in his confidence in a pursuit for her hand. Yet, it was far from a perfect world, so he would do the right thing, the harder thing, and stay away. If anything, the afternoon with his mother proved his earlier assessments, and those of Morgan, correct.

Who would subject a potential wife to such a mother-in-law?

To such a bloodline?

Not him. Never him.

Which meant he could never pursue Joan.

And that thought, that realization, was far more painful than any of the words his mother had said.

And every bit as condemning.

Because loneliness was a wicked master, and he had no option but to surrender to it.

Sixteen

JOAN OFFERED A WELCOME TO THE APPROACH-
ing Lord Blackwood. More than a few years her
senior, he bowed with a stiff movement and asked
for her next available dance.

"Of course, Lord Blackwood. I have a reel available," she offered, wondering if he'd be up to the
challenge of such a spirited dance.

"Allow me." He took her card and signed his
name, his attention shifting from the card to her
décolletage and then back to the card, clearly
assuming she wouldn't notice.

Her opinion of him wasn't favorable and had not
improved. He gave another bow and left, promising to return for his dance.

"That one is all mouth and trousers." Morgan's
amused chuckle broke through her distaste.

Joan choked on a laugh of surprise as she
turned to study her brother. He was sipping
claret and staring straight ahead, dodging her
scrutiny.

"If you don't stop staring at me, people will guess
I delivered a witty remark about your visitor," he
challenged.

Joan turned away. "It was a very well-placed barb, I must say."

"And true."

"Indeed," Joan replied. She scanned the room once more, searching the faces for one in particular. "I thought the duke said he'd be in attendance tonight."

Morgan gave a cough. "He sent his apologies earlier. I thought I had mentioned it."

Joan turned to him, but he shifted away, lifting his hand to greet another gentleman.

"No, you didn't mention it," Joan replied, and then a chill went up her spine. "He's not ill, is he?" She moved to meet her brother's scrutiny, placing a hand on his arm.

Morgan's expression was open and surprised as he quickly answered her. "No, no. He said nothing of the sort. I'm sure he's right as rain, Joan. Just wasn't going to attend tonight." He gave her hand a pat. "Do not fret."

That would be far easier said than done. But if the duke wasn't ill, why did he not attend? She had learned her lesson and wasn't going to ascribe intentions to him without first being certain, but she couldn't help but wonder if she'd perhaps offended him.

Or if he truly was ill but didn't want to tell Morgan, in an effort to protect her. That was certainly something he would do, was it not?

"Joan?" A familiar feminine voice cut through

her worried musings, and she turned to see the welcome face of a friend.

"Miss Bronson! I was hoping to see you tonight." She offered her friend's hand a squeeze.

"I thought you'd be in attendance, but one never can tell and I quite forgot to ask you earlier," Miss Bronson said, her observation shifting behind Joan and then back.

"Oh, dear me. Allow me to introduce you. This is my brother, Lord Penderdale." Joan still struggled with the title for Morgan, knowing that it only reminded her of the loss she'd worked so hard to heal from.

"Ah, yes." Miss Bronson curtsied prettily, her dark lashes brushing against her cheeks. "A pleasure, my lord."

Morgan bowed crisply.

"All me to introduce you to Miss Bronson. She is a dear friend of mine." Joan stepped back to allow the introductions.

"A pleasure, Miss Bronson," Morgan said with a nod.

"Miss Bronson and I volunteered at the Foundling Hospital today."

"Ah, so this is the new friend my sister has been talking so much about. It truly is a pleasure."

Miss Bronson blushed and cast her eyes down. "I'm grateful to have made her acquaintance. I think we have much in common."

"I'm sure."

After a moment, Joan turned to Morgan and widened her eyes while touching her dance card. Morgan studied her for a second before turning to her friend.

"Miss Bronson, I'd be honored to have a dance. Do you have any available?" Morgan asked.

Joan couldn't help the satisfied look that spread across her face when she noted Miss Bronson's clear pleasure at being asked.

"Yes, of course. I only recently arrived so my card is quite open, my lord."

Joan covered her mouth with a gloved hand.

"A reel, then." Morgan selected the dance and gave a swift bow. "I'll let you two ladies converse." He turned and walked toward a circle of gentlemen, and Joan gave a finger wave to the Duchess of Wesley, who was standing nearby.

"I must say I'm very much looking forward to the reel," Miss Bronson said with excitement in her tone. "It was very kind of your brother to ask me."

"Of course, and he's a lovely dancer," Joan added, watching the spark in Miss Bronson's eyes grow.

Did she perhaps have a tendre for Morgan? A matchmaking intrigue flashed through Joan's mind before she pushed it away. "And how was the rest of your afternoon?" she asked Miss Bronson.

"A little dull. We arrived late to the season so our at-home hours have been a little lean, if you gather my meaning."

"I'm sorry." Joan patted her hand.

"It will get better. Sometimes you only need a little attention," Miss Bronson said bravely. "And a dance with your brother certainly won't hinder prospects. Rather, it could very well increase them. Don't men always want something they think others already found valuable? It's not the most poetic and romantic gesture, but if it draws attention, it can't be too terrible. We must use what we can." Miss Bronson gave a firm nod.

Joan's brows rose. "Indeed. But remember that worth is so much more than a mere man's opinion."

"Of course, of course," Miss Bronson replied emphatically. "But if I'm to find a husband this season, I won't discount any help."

"I understand."

"Have you found any suitor exceptional so far?" Miss Bronson asked, her tone low.

Joan bit her lip, her mind immediately conjuring up an image of Rowles, but the picture was colored in shades of confusion. She was well aware of her own feelings, but trying to decipher his was utterly disorienting.

Joan decided to give the truth but to a broader scope. "I've had several callers, most of whom are agreeable, but I find I can only talk of hounds and horses for so long before I wish for more enticing conversation." She shrugged. "But I do not mean to complain; I'm only making an observation."

"I understand. Though I don't have the same problem currently, I can imagine how it would be dull to discuss things that you find less than interesting," Miss Bronson replied. "So no offers of yet?"

"No. But the season is still very new."

"Indeed. Anything could happen, and I'm quite thrilled to be a part of it, rather than hear about it from the *Tattler* or gossip. It's much more exciting to see it with your own eyes, don't you think?"

"Yes, I agree," Joan replied. "What about you? I know you've only recently arrived, but has any gentleman caught your eye?" she asked.

Miss Bronson blushed. "I thought your brother excessively handsome, but I am not pinning my hopes on a mere introduction," she said demurely. "I hope to fill my dance card with gentlemen who will hopefully call tomorrow, and perhaps I'll have an answer to your question by next week." She giggled, a soft and delicate sound. "Much can happen in a week, can it not?"

"True." Joan was caught up in Miss Bronson's enthusiasm. The music for the reel started up, and Miss Bronson turned expectantly toward Morgan, who was still conversing. Joan watched as he excused himself and came to collect Miss Bronson for the dance. As Joan watched them depart, her delight was dampened by the arrival of her own dance partner, Lord Blackwood.

He offered his hand. "May I?"

"Of course." She forced a welcoming expression and followed his lead onto the dance floor. The music picked up the pace, and she started the steps. Thankfully, he hadn't requested a waltz; the reel offered little time for conversation and even less time for touching, which was a boon. As she circled and came back to the line, she peeked over to where Morgan and Miss Bronson were lined up. Miss Bronson's expression brightened the room, and Joan thought that perhaps Morgan was enjoying himself more than he'd expected, if his face were any indication.

Her attention shifted back to her partner as she continued in the dance.

When it ended, Lord Blackwood escorted her back to the edge of the ballroom. "May I offer you something to drink, Lady Joan?" he asked.

Morgan and Miss Bronson came to stand beside her. "No, I thank you, Lord Blackwood, but my brother already had promised to procure me some lemonade."

"Very well. Until later, Lady Joan." He bowed and took his leave, but not before Joan caught sight of his gaze as it raked over her body from head to toe in a quick assessment.

A shudder ran through her.

"He won't be welcome in our home, Joan." Morgan's soft voice was silk over steel. "Not with that certain lack of manners. I didn't miss that last look."

Joan released a pent-up breath. "Thank you," she murmured.

"And this is why we are in the ladies' society and want reform," Miss Bronson whispered for Joan's ear's only. "So we are not subject to such men."

"I'll return shortly with the lemonade I somehow promised without my knowledge," Morgan said to Joan. "Would you like some as well, Miss Bronson?"

"Indeed." Miss Bronson was quick to accept.

"I'll be back directly." Morgan disappeared in the crowd, leaving Joan with Miss Bronson.

"After we get our lemonade, we should take a turn about the room and see if we can gather a few more dance invitations," Miss Bronson plotted, her eyes slightly narrowed as if concentrating.

"A good plan. And much more fun to execute when not doing it alone or with one's big brother tagging along."

"I, for one, wouldn't mind if your big brother tagged along, but I can understand how it might hinder you," Miss Bronson said cheekily. "So, we may have to abandon him."

"Abandon whom?" Morgan asked as he offered each a glass of lemonade.

Joan took a sip of the cool refreshment and bit back a laugh at Miss Bronson's wicked expression.

"You, my lord," she quipped before she took a sip of lemonade.

Morgan paused and blinked twice. "Pardon?"

Miss Bronson angled her head and studied him with a teasing glint in her eyes. "If we are to collect a few more names for our dance cards, we need to abandon you."

"And here I thought I was an asset rather than a liability." He narrowed his eyes playfully at Miss Bronson.

Was he flirting? Joan watched him. She'd never seen her brother flirt. She was certain he knew how, of course, but…knowing and actually witnessing were two separate things.

"To some you are an asset and to others a liability, and I must defer to my friend's judgment here, so I'll bid you adieu." Miss Bronson locked arms with Joan, smiling cheerfully.

Joan hitched a shoulder. "She's right, and since it is the season and this is the goal…"

"Very well. I'd hate to be a hindrance to the progress of women, especially on the marriage mart." He raised his glass as if toasting them. "I'll be over here, in case you change your mind and decide you require my presence."

"Understood," Miss Bronson replied, nearly saluting with her words.

Joan all but rolled her eyes, and Miss Bronson pulled her away. When Joan looked back to her brother, she noticed that he wasn't watching her, but was curiously watching Miss Bronson's retreat.

Which she found excessively intriguing.

And interesting.

Fascinating enough, actually, that it distracted her from her own feelings of interest in the very person she wished had attended.

The person she'd found fascinating.

But as she endeavored to fill her dance card, she had a thought.

Perhaps he didn't find her fascinating enough in return.

Seventeen

It HAD BEEN A WEEK.

Seven days since he'd seen both Morgan and Joan, and it had bloody well felt like a year.

Rowles had stayed true to his word and kept away from the social scene, which had somehow led to further speculation about his mother, as was evident in a recent *Tattler* article.

What once was simmering has now cold, and this is most regrettable. It was excessively diverting to watch the Lady J with the duke, but alas, the duke has once again retreated into seclusion. One has to wonder why. Could it be because his mother's condition has worsened? Or perhaps it's because the duke follows her path as well…

Rowles reread the article and then crumpled the sheet in his hands. He tossed it into the fire, watching it catch and then burn to ashes. It was symbolic in so many ways.

How much of his life had been reduced to ash because of his mother? And like the article he'd burned, he had no way to stop the progression of the fire's hunger as it continued to consume parts of his life.

He returned to his study and lifted the gold letter opener, sliding a finger along the edge, flirting with the point. He sighed and put it down.

"Your Grace, Lord Penderdale is here to see you," the butler announced with a bow.

Rowles nodded, unsurprised he hadn't heard the butler's arrival; he'd been far too caught up in his thoughts of late to pay attention to small things like the comings and goings of servants.

"Show him in," Rowles directed, his curiosity piqued, followed by a slow dread that crept through his bones.

Was Morgan coming to release him from exile, and if so, was it because Joan had found a suitor?

Rowles swallowed tightly and waited as his friend strode into the room, his mouth set in a grim line.

"Good morning," Morgan said by way of greeting.

"Is it?" Rowles asked, then pointed to a chair.

Morgan took a seat and watched him. "You look like hell."

"I feel like it, too. Thanks for noticing," Rowles answered, his tone dripping with sarcasm. "To what do I owe the pleasure?"

Morgan studied him, his posture relaxing. "Have things not improved with your mother?"

Rowles let out a long sigh. "Indeed not. And as far as she is concerned, I'm dead to her. A lovely thing, that."

"I'm sorry, old chap."

"It seems there is nothing I can do about that, so it is what it is." He shrugged and leaned back in his chair. He wanted to ask about Joan, but doing such would only feed his insatiable appetite for her. Better to leave it, unless Morgan brought it up.

And if he brought her up in conversation, would it mean she was spoken for?

Rowles suppressed a physical reaction to such a thought.

He was protecting her by staying away, by keeping himself from being an option. This was the mantra he had rehearsed and recited over and over, a litany and a prayer that kept him rooted at home.

Away from her.

Because the only thing that could be stronger than his pull toward her was his drive to protect her.

Even if it meant from himself.

"I…" Morgan wiped a hand down his face. "I need help."

Rowles studied his friend. "Are you in trouble?"

"Yes, but not in the way you're likely imagining." Morgan's words were tight. "I need help because my little sister could be the death of me, and I've exhausted all options but one, which brings me to you."

Rowles leaned forward, his forehead wrinkling in confusion and concern. "Whatever do you mean?"

"I mean my sister will no longer take my word

that you are not sick, dying, or excessively angry with her. I've tried all I know, and this is the final option I can think of. I hate to ask this of you, but I am at a loss for any other option."

Rowles nodded. "I'll help however I may, but you'll have to be a little more specific."

"I'm talking in circles, I know. I apologize." Morgan sighed. "Would you, perhaps, mind making an appearance at some social event to prove to my sister you haven't given up the ghost and are not harboring some grudge against her?" Morgan closed his eyes in defeat.

Rowles released the breath he'd been holding. So…she wasn't spoken for. Relief pumped through him only to be deflated by understanding that he was being asked to play a part in pushing her away.

Further. Pushing her *further* away.

"I understand. She's a persistent sort," Rowles remarked, forcing a level tone while his heart reacted to the words with a mix of approval of her persistence, hope that she indeed cared—even a little—and desperation to see her, even if it meant he had to push her away.

"That, my friend, is an understatement." Morgan's voice was clipped, irritation with his sister clear in his tone.

Rowles's lips tipped upward with a ghost of merriment. "I'll do what you ask."

Morgan leaned back in the chair, his shoulders

sagging in what appeared to be acute relief. "I apologize for troubling you, but I truly have run out of options."

"It is of no consequence," Rowles said bravely. Deep within, he knew the cost, but it was outweighed by the salve of seeing her.

"We're attending Almack's this evening," Morgan informed him.

"Ah, watered-down lemonade and dandies. Lovely," Rowles said with a hint of sarcasm.

"And the most eligible place to be to court young ladies, so young ladies attend in droves—if allowed a voucher."

"Which I'm sure you've procured for your sister." Rowles nodded.

"Indeed. She'll be presented to Lady Jersey tonight."

"She'll approve of her, I'm sure."

"I wish I could convey that certainty to Joan." Morgan's tone was weary. "She's a little flummoxed."

"It's an important introduction." Rowles shrugged. "All those dowagers think quite highly of their opinion, but since the *ton* echoes whatever they say with near-Biblical obedience, it's not an introduction one wishes to meet with anything other than fear and trembling."

"Indeed, and the fear and trembling are present." Morgan turned his face heavenward, as if petitioning the Almighty for help.

"Also, I should tell you…" Rowles leaned forward. "I'm leaving town next week for Cambridge."

"Pressing business at the university? Did your replacement not work out?" Morgan asked.

"No, nothing to do with the university. As far as I'm aware, my replacement is doing well. It's for me to get away, you understand."

"Of course, a safe journey then. How long will you be staying?"

"A week or two. I haven't decided, but I thought you should know since your sister may ask questions and that way you shall have answers, should you need them."

Morgan gave a dry chuckle. "I'm hoping that all questions will soon cease."

"To aid you, I'll brave Almack's tonight."

"I'd be most grateful, and so would my lack of patience."

Rowles chuckled. "I'll see you there then." He stood and shook Morgan's hand when he did the same. "It was good to see you."

"You as well, old friend."

Morgan left, leaving Rowles once again alone with his thoughts.

Tonight.

He would see Joan tonight.

And it might be the last time for a while, which was bittersweet.

He'd drink in the sight of her and hold it close,

and then he would remind himself that she was worthy of a far better man.

One that wasn't chased by shadows.

Rowles considered the clock, his mind doing some quick calculations. He had more than enough time to go to the Burlington Arcade and stop by Hoby's for another pair of boots. His hadn't been replaced since he'd fallen in the Serpentine. He had his Hessians for this evening, but suddenly getting out of the house held great appeal.

He called for his carriage, and shortly went on his way to the arcade. The traffic grew more congested as they approached the new top-lit walkway. Boasting more than seventy small shops, the arcade was the new place to promenade and find whatever necessary—and unnecessary—items anyone might need. As he alighted from his carriage, he nodded to Lord and Lady Berkram, who were stepping out of Rundell and Bridge's jewelry shop. The air was crisp with freshly washed air from the light rain earlier, and Rowles could feel his spirits lifting, much like the vapor rising from the earth to the sky. The bell rang as he stepped through the door into Hoby's. Boots lined the pedestals and along the walls, and the scent of leather permeated the air. A younger man asked to assist him, and soon he was placing an order for a new pair of boots to replace the ones that had shrunk. They were to be delivered the following week.

Next, Rowles strolled under the glass ceiling of the arcade, studying the displays of the various shops lining the walkway. The door to Mrs. Bean's, the modiste, opened, and several young ladies stepped out from within. Rowles quickly looked away, lest they consider him interested, and moved along rapidly. The combination of acrid and sweet scents wafted on the air from a tobacco shop before the establishment came into view. Lock's shop for hats was next, and Rowles went in, a tall hat on display catching his eye. He ordered one to be delivered the next day and continued on to the next few shops. The window displays were impressive, should he ever wish to redecorate. His mother had always loved the shops that specialized in decor, along with the silver shops or Chappell's musical instruments.

If she wasn't so volatile, he'd consider bringing her down to shop. She would love it, if she were in the right mood or frame of mind. But the problem was that he could never be certain, and if he chose the wrong day or the wrong mood, she could easily destroy both merchandise and more of her reputation.

It wasn't worth it.

As much as he wished he could bring her here, the dangers outweighed the benefits.

Rowles gave one last look down the walkway and turned to stroll back to his carriage. The newly married Lord and Lady Winters walked by, a love match from last season. Rowles watched their animated expressions, deeply engaged in conversation and smiling—beaming—at each other. It pinched his heart to make the hard decision of choosing to reject such a life.

They passed him by, and he mused over his future as he stepped into his waiting carriage. On a whim, he had half an inclination to visit his mother, but she had been decisive in not wishing to see him. To go against her wishes never proved to be a good idea, so he directed the coachman to take him home.

He'd take tea and then prepare for Almack's. Dressing would be the simple part.

The difficult part? Preparing his heart.

To say one final goodbye to Joan.

Eighteen

I will not tell you all; I have not leave.

—Joan of Arc

IT WASN'T UNTIL HER BROTHER'S HAND COVERED hers that Joan realized she'd been incessantly tapping her fingers for who knew how long. Morgan squeezed her hand and released it.

"It will be well. You needn't worry," he offered kindly.

Joan gave an apologetic wince. "Pardon me. I'm a little nervous."

"A little?"

"A lot," she corrected.

Morgan nodded. "You'll do well, and it's not as though you're being presented to the queen."

"I dare say the Ladies Jersey, Cowper, and Sefton and Countess Lieven carry far more sway."

Morgan shrugged. "While that may be true, it's still only a Wednesday night, and tomorrow it will be Thursday, and this will be over with and you'll wait a full week before you attend again."

"True. It's the first time that will be difficult, I'm sure."

"You're not sure what to expect. That's understandable."

"I've heard the lemonade is terrible," Joan muttered.

Morgan chuckled. "Yes, that's well known. But thankfully there's ratafia as well."

"I dislike ratafia."

"You're going to have to make do with the watered-down lemonade then, I'm afraid."

Joan was about to make a comment when the carriage stopped. She gaped at her brother. Had he been distracting her with the mundane conversation about lemonade to help her? Bless him. Sisterly affection welled up within her, and it was much needed. She had been at odds with her brother for the past few days. There was this nagging feeling that he was keeping something from her. Not necessarily lying; no, he knew he couldn't get away with lying to her, for she'd see through it. But withholding information, which wasn't exactly lying. She's been quite a pest, but there was never a decisive answer from him concerning her questions.

Questions that all revolved around Rowles.

"Allow me." Morgan stepped from the carriage and offered her his hand. She relied on his strength for balance as she stepped down to face the white stone building. Footmen dressed in smart livery verified the vouchers of each person before they were allowed inside. The strict dress code was enforced without discrimination; Joan double-checked her brother's appearance. Satisfied, she waited for their turn.

Morgan handed the footmen their vouchers, and with a nod, they were allowed entrance. The air was warm, stuffy almost, as they walked through the hall toward the ballroom where a reel was being played. From the hall, Joan could see the dancers lining up.

"Did you know that the Duke of Wellington was once rejected from Almack's?" Morgan whispered.

"No." Joan turned to him, shocked.

"Indeed, he hadn't followed the dress code."

"What happened? What did he do?" Joan asked, her eyes wide. Dear Lord, she couldn't imagine a footman deigning to reject the entrance of the Duke of Wellington.

"Well, he understood and obeyed. When he returned on a different day, he was dressed properly."

"I'd be terrified to be the porter who rejected his entrance."

"I think the porter was more worried about the displeasure of the Almack's patronesses than that of the duke," Morgan answered.

Joan nodded sagely, agreeing with her brother's astute assessment.

"Ah, and here we go. Head high," Morgan whispered as they walked into the ballroom. The Almack's patronesses were holding court at the middle of the far wall, their elaborate dresses all of the highest fashion as they scanned the room, their gazes like a force to be reckoned with.

Lady Jersey met Joan's eyes, and Joan immediately lowered them and nodded her head, even from the distance of across the room. When she dared look up, Lady Jersey gave a curt nod, then Joan turned her attention back to her brother.

She released her breath and followed him along the side of the dance floor.

"Would you like some lemonade?" he asked, mirth in his tone.

Joan gave a soft laugh, making sure to follow every inch of protocol in such a hallowed hall. "Yes, thank you."

"I'll return directly." He bowed and headed toward the refreshment table. Joan studied the dancers and then scanned the room for familiar faces. Was Miss Bronson in attendance? Or was she not able to secure vouchers?

"Here you go," Morgan said upon his return and offered her a glass.

"Thank you." She took a small sip and held back a wince at the tart flavor. "Assessments were correct," she whispered, earning a conspiratorial grin from her brother.

"Lord Penderdale." Someone spoke from behind Joan. She turned and noted the smart bow of one of Almack's footmen.

"Yes?"

"Lady Jersey has requested a word with you and your sister."

Morgan nodded. "Of course, it would be our honor." Morgan waited till the footman turned to lead the way back to his mistress, then gave Joan an encouraging nod.

She took a slow and deep breath, as deep as her corset would allow, and followed her brother's lead along the dance floor toward the Almack's royalty.

The Countess Lieven, who was married to the Russian ambassador, watched their approach with interest. Princess Esterhazy, who was married to the Austrian ambassador, leaned over to whisper a soft word to her companion, Lady Castlereagh.

Morgan bowed, low and proper. "Lady Jersey, allow me to introduce my sister, Lady Joan Morgan."

Joan executed her most perfect curtsy. She waited an extra moment, then rose, meeting the formidable woman's eyes.

Lady Jersey inclined her head, a sign of approval. "And how are you finding this season, Lady Joan?"

Joan bit the inside of her lip to keep from smiling too widely as she considered how much of a burden she had been to her brother this season, rather than her own pleasure at the social events. "It's been an enchanting experience, my lady."

"Did you wish to add something else?" Lady Jersey's keen eye hadn't missed her slight hesitation.

Joan debated but refused to be anything less than honest. "I was considering my brother's enjoyment of the season. I'm aware it's been an experience for him as well, shepherding me through it."

At her honest words, Lady Jersey gave a delicate chuckle. "Indeed, it is a testament to your brother's character."

Morgan bowed again, accepting the compliment with a twitch to his lips.

"See that you make it worth his efforts," Lady Jersey commanded.

Joan sobered and nodded in assent. "Yes, my lady."

Lady Jersey lifted her glass of lemonade to take a sip, signaling their dismissal.

Morgan bowed in understanding, and Joan curtsied as well. Then they took their leave, winding back around the edge of the ballroom.

"Well done," Morgan murmured. "Everyone will be talking about how you made Lady Jersey smile. She showed you great favor."

Joan's heart pounded with excitement; she hadn't made a cake of herself. Relief soared through her. "I'm so thankful that's finished."

"Now you can enjoy the evening while everyone talks about your introduction." Morgan replied. "The gossip mill will be working hard, I'm sure."

"How delightful," Joan replied in mock enthusiasm.

"Careful," Morgan chided gently. "This is not the place to practice too much honesty. Some candor will single you out, but too much will earn you a cut."

"Yes, you're right, of course." Joan gathered her wits and scanned the room as her brother led them to stand along a row of empty chairs.

Just as her heart calmed, it stumbled, then raced as she picked out a familiar face directly beyond the entrance to the ballroom. Either her eyes deceived her, or the Duke of Westmore had graced Almack's with his presence.

She blinked, her greedy stare drinking in the sight of him. She couldn't see his blue eyes from across the room, but she imagined their color from memory. His knee breeches and white cravat were dignified, less dandy and more masculine. The air whooshed from her lungs when he turned, as if feeling her attention from across the room.

He paused, his head tipped ever so slightly before he took a step in their direction.

"Did you know?" Joan asked, then turned to her brother.

Morgan frowned, then as her eyes shifted from the duke, then back to her brother, he followed and then nodded. "Yes."

He wasn't lying. She could see that, but there was still something deeper he wasn't disclosing. She could feel it like an itchy undergarment, driving her mad.

The duke skirted the dance floor and paused before them, bowing in greeting.

"Penderdale, Lady Joan."

The sound of his voice melted though her, and it was embarrassingly painful to realize how much she'd missed the sound of it. His eyes met hers, and whatever truth lay there flashed and changed so quickly she couldn't capture its meaning before he turned to Morgan.

"Don't you look dandy with your chapeau bras."

"No more so than you," Morgan countered.

The air buzzed around them, and Joan glanced about, noticing the whispers and attention their little party was drawing.

Blast the *Tattler* for making such a story concerning her friendship with the duke.

Or at least she hoped they still had a friendship. It seemed so…strained at the moment.

The duke had regarded her once and then kept his attention on her brother, as if choosing to be near her but not engage her in conversation.

Oh, how she missed their conversations.

"Tell me, Your Grace, how have you been?" she asked, wanting his attention, needing to see his expression and know what lurked in its depths.

"I'm afraid I've been terribly busy. We've made some adjustments in the estate and I'm to travel soon, so it's consumed much of my time." He met her eyes unflinchingly.

"I hope nothing is amiss?" Joan inquired, then regretted her invasive question. But rather than apologize, she waited to see how he would answer.

"Well, I think the best answer is to say it's all being addressed, Lady Joan."

Joan almost corrected him playfully, but then remembered their setting and nodded.

Someone approached from her side, and she turned, curtsying to a bowing Lord Archby. "Lady Joan, may I have the next dance?"

Joan nodded and offered her dance card. She noted his selection of the cotillion. Archby had been one of her first callers, and she studied him with curious interest as he bowed to the duke and her brother, then took his leave.

"Archby is still scratching at the door," Morgan whispered softly.

Joan's face heated as her look flashed to the duke. Rowles was engaged in conversation with another gentlemen beside him and had apparently missed the entire interaction.

Disappointment filtered through her.

He truly wasn't interested in her, then.

She didn't wish for such an answer, but the unknown was far worse than the known.

With renewed interest, she offered shy looks to several other gentlemen, all of whom approached her and asked for dances as well. As the music for the cotillion began, she departed for the dance floor on the arm of Lord Archby.

Joan didn't need to force a delighted expression as she enjoyed the dance, since Archby was an excellent dancer. He even offered to procure her some lemonade after the dance.

"It's awful, but if it will allow me one more moment to stand by your side, I'll do what I must," he said with a flirtatious smile.

"When offered in such a way, how could I refuse?" she flirted back, thankful for the distraction.

The evening progressed, and she danced, ate, and chatted, all with the duke nearby but never truly engaging her unless absolutely necessary.

It was awkward, stilted, and dreadful.

The final dance was a waltz, and no one had requested it, likely because her brother stood nearby, a silent sentinel of protection.

"I don't believe this dance is spoken for?"

Joan turned to the duke, her brow furrowing in confusion. He'd hardly spoken to her, and now he wanted the most intimate dance? What sense did this make?

She had the inclination to refuse him, but in truth, she didn't *want* to say no. She wanted to feel his hand at her waist. Her fingers itched to rest upon his shoulder, and her ears burned to hear his voice.

"Of course," she whispered.

He offered his arm, and she placed her hand on his jacket, welcoming the warmth radiating from him. The strings led the rhythm as he pulled her in close, his hand branding her waist as he held her gloved hand. He met her eyes, and she was powerless to turn away, even for a moment, as he led them into the swirling dancers. Her heart sang, her body hummed with pleasure as if a missing piece was suddenly put back in place. Eyes drifting closed, she gave herself over to the moment, living for it, knowing it was all one-sided, all on her side.

But that mattered not. She would savor the moment, the dance, and then she would move on.

What other option did she have?

"I'm sorry."

Her eyes fluttered open, and she met his look with a confused one of her own. "Pardon?"

"Forgive me." His words were raw, and at once, she saw the truth of them, of the words he wasn't saying.

It wasn't one-sided after all.

But then…why? And why the apology?

She voiced her query. "For?"

He glanced away.

Anger simmered within her. "Sorry for…ignoring me all evening? Or perhaps pretending to be my friend only to have that friendship when convenient for you. Or maybe—"

"All the above. But it's necessary."

"Enlighten me as to why, Your Grace," she said with a clipped tone, then gathered her wits as she noted the attention on their conversation. "Never mind. I used to wish for those conversations we shared, to enjoy that...friendship we had. But I can see that it was my...naivete that kept me hopeful. You have more pressing matters than a friend's younger sister. And while I imagined myself your friend, perhaps the truth was I was a convenient extension of the true friendship you have with my brother. So allow me to relieve you of putting forth any more effort."

The waltz ended, she stepped back, and slowly walked to find her brother, lest anyone think she was storming from the dance floor. As soon as she found Morgan, she silently released a pent-up breath.

"I wish to go home."

Morgan studied her, his look hesitant, before he agreed. "Very well, I'll call for the carriage."

Joan nodded and raised her chin, keeping a brave and graceful expression on her face.

Lord Archby nodded from across the room, and she waved back. Then as she saw a flicker of the duke, she turned and walked toward the hall.

The crowd was still conversing, unwilling to disperse because of the last dance, and Joan was thankful the hallway was mostly vacant, save for a few footmen lining the wall with perfect posture.

She took in deep breaths through her nose and went to stand outside the entrance, waiting for her brother. Feeling rather than hearing him, she glanced over her shoulder to see the duke standing a few feet from her. She looked away, angling her body in the opposite direction. It might be childish, but she wasn't in the mood for more of his apologies or excuses.

As he stepped closer to her, she could hear his foot on the stone, feel his presence.

She refused to turn.

Keeping her eye on the far-off horizon, she caved slightly, allowing her other senses to take over as she breathed his presence in like air. The slight breeze carried a peppermint and spice scent that clung to his clothes. The air was warmer, his body heat radiating toward her in welcome. She closed her eyes.

"Joan," he whispered.

She squeezed her eyes shut, her traitorous body turning.

"Joan." Her name was a song.

The barest hint of a touch slid up her forearm, and she gasped, then looked to where her skin had caught fire. His gloved finger brushed lightly up her arm, his eyes following the movement before he glanced up and met her gaze.

"Rowles…" Joan breathed his name.

So much regret, need, and love swirled in his

eyes, and she drank it in like a thirsty deer at a stream, desperate for more. The sound of a carriage approaching shook her from her trance, and as her attention wavered to the coach, she felt and saw Rowles take a step away.

When Morgan alighted from the carriage, her eyes shifted from her brother to Rowles and back. Watching as the duke swallowed and turned away, nodding once.

No.

She turned to her brother, watching him as he refused to meet her scrutiny and only offered his hand.

"Morgan." She spoke his name in a clipped tone.

"Allow me, it's a bit chilly but we should be home soon," he offered. As quickly as his met hers, they slithered away.

But it was enough to confirm her suspicions. She stepped into the carriage and waited for her brother, knowing all hell would break loose as she asked the one question she suspected she knew the answer to.

"Did you refuse the duke permission to court me?"

Nineteen

ROWLES DELAYED THE TRIP TO CAMBRIDGE. Running away had never solved any problems, and currently he had more than his share of them to deal with in London. First and foremost, Joan.

He'd tried.

He'd kept his distance.

He'd utterly failed.

Because the moment Joan beamed at Archby, something in his soul had snapped. Because seeing her court another was entirely different than understanding the concept of it, and all his good intentions evaporated. While she'd danced with Archby, he'd forced himself to unclench his fists.

During every dance when she swirled away with another suitor, he'd forced a calm he didn't feel till all his patience was spent and all that was left was desperation.

So he'd asked for a waltz, praying she'd agree.

And when he'd held her, the familiar scent of rosewater clung to her skin and erased any other thoughts. Her luminous green eyes captivated him, and he'd been powerless to look away, to do anything but drown in her gaze, drink it in, pretend for a moment that it was where he belonged—while in her arms.

He'd tried to apologize, but the effort was weak even to his own ears, and the attempt had only made matters worse, which was why he followed her to the front of Almack's. He couldn't, wouldn't let her leave when she was so clearly angry with him, and rightfully so.

He'd taken away any choice she'd had to choose him by taking himself from the running.

And wasn't that exactly the sort of thing they'd talked about? Women having little say in the matter of their futures? And here, after all his spouting about the intrinsic value of a person, man or woman, he'd made such a grave error.

He'd decided to make the choice for her.

Rather than trust her judgment.

In his efforts to be self-sacrificing, he'd overstepped and sacrificed that which wasn't his: a choice.

He'd wanted to say so much to her, but words failed him. So instead he'd acted. He had whispered her name, a prayer and litany on his lips. When she had refused to turn, he'd stepped closer, careful and cautious—making sure he wouldn't put her in a compromising position and thus take away another choice. Carefully, and so softly it was hardly a touch at all, he'd reached out and traced a light finger up her gloved hand to her elbow, his body catching fire at the innocent touch.

She'd turned, and in a moment, he was sure she'd read his soul—only to have the carriage arrive. And if the eyes were indeed a window to the soul, he was certain hers went from affection to anger in a flash.

Affection for him.

Anger for her brother.

Because in Rowles's unguarded moment, he'd shifted his attention to Morgan as well and nodded his understanding. Because he shouldn't be so close, and he shouldn't be following her; but Joan saw. And worse, Joan understood, if that fire in her eyes was an indication.

And so, reason number two for staying in London was to be around for Morgan's sake. He'd likely gotten a tongue-lashing he'd not soon forget, and it was all Rowles's fault.

He was not one to run from responsibility. The proof of that was in his mother's situation.

Rowles half expected to see Morgan that day, and he was fully prepared to defend himself and ask for permission to court Joan—but Morgan didn't come to call.

It was growing closer to evening when Rowles faced a decision: participate in the social calendar and hope to see Joan, or try to honor Morgan's initial request.

After a moment of debate, he called for his valet to prepare his evening kit. Lady Garrison was having a birthday fete, and it was sure to be well attended. With the decision made, Rowles couldn't restrain the lighthearted feeling in his chest. The gray clouds that seemed to constrict his soul had lifted, making way for sunshine and warmth.

Certainly, that indicated he'd made the right choice, did it not?

He arrived fashionably late to the fete, the majority of the London *ton* already engaged in full celebratory fanfare. Ivy climbed the front of the Garrison home, and torches lined the short walkway to the front. Rowles walked in, scanning the crowded hall as it echoed with buzzing conversation. Ladies nodded in greeting, their feathered hats swaying with the motion. Gentlemen gave him room as he navigated the hall and then entered the ballroom. Lilacs filled crystal vases on every table, and footmen walked about with silver trays of champagne. Candles twinkled in sconces along the walls, and the scent of beeswax melded perfectly with the lilac, filling the room with a heavenly scent. A string quartet broke into a reel, and Rowles quickly scanned the dancers, looking for a familiar face.

When he didn't see Joan among the dancers, he turned to survey the rest of the room.

"Interesting seeing you here." Morgan's voice interrupted his perusal of the crowd, and Rowles turned to the left to regard his friend.

"Morgan." Rowles greeted his friend cautiously.

Morgan stood stiffly, as if chaffing at being so near him. "Rowles," he replied. "What brings you to this evening's event?"

Rowles hesitated, then answered, "You. I was expecting a visit earlier, and when you didn't show up, I began to worry for your safety." He cast his friend a slight grin.

Morgan studied him, and then his lip twitched. "It was a rough day."

"I'm sure."

"You have no idea." Morgan sighed. "And I'd be worried she'd lay into me once again, *if* she were talking to me, which she isn't." His eye twitched. "Odd, that. I usually resent her constant chattering but now that I'm absolved of it, I miss it. I tell you, life is unfair."

"Of that, we can utterly agree," Rowles added, then forced the question he needed to ask, knowing it could potentially make matters worse. "I...should call on you tomorrow to discuss something important."

Morgan blinked, then tipped his head slightly. "Of what nature?" he asked with heavy suspicion.

"Tomorrow," Rowles stated firmly.

Morgan didn't relax his stare as he nodded once. "Very well."

In for a penny, in for a pound. "I'm assuming your sister is in attendance tonight?" Rowles scanned the room for her.

When Morgan didn't answer, Rowles turned to him.

Morgan nodded once. "She's with her new friend, Miss Bronson. They've bonded over their mutual interest in the Foundling Hospital."

"A worthy endeavor to be sure," Rowles suggested.

Morgan shrugged.

As if the waters parted, the reel dancers lined up, and through the divided humanity, Rowles caught a glimpse of Joan across the room.

Splendid in a pale-blue dress, her skin peaches and cream. Her lips parted in a perfect O when she caught sight of him, which led to a lovely blush tinting her cheeks.

"Pardon me." Rowles didn't spare a glance for his friend, but sidestepped and started to navigate the perimeter of the dance floor, flicking attention from his path to the person at the end of it.

As he neared, the lady beside Joan whispered something softly, earning a nod from Joan, even though her attention never wavered from his.

"Good evening, Lady Joan." He bowed crisply.

"Your Grace." Joan curtsied, followed by another greeting and curtsy by her friend.

"Allow me to introduce my friend, Miss Bronson." She stepped to the side and gestured to the other lady. She was a classic English beauty with curly brunette hair, dark-brown eyes, and porcelain skin, but she didn't compare with Joan, in Rowles's opinion.

Of course, Rowles was fascinated with far more than Joan's feminine beauty; he was also captivated by the mind it harbored.

"A pleasure, Miss Bronson." Rowles bowed to her as well.

"The honor is mine, Your Grace," Miss Bronson added, all politeness and refinement.

"And how are you this evening?" Joan asked, her expression curious and still slightly suspicious.

It was nothing less than what was his due.

"I'm well, but I shall be decidedly better if you allow me a dance, Lady Joan," he requested, flirting boldly.

Joan's expression softened. "It would be an honor, Your Grace." She offered her dance card, and he quickly selected two, not caring that would likely lead to talk.

Let them talk, speculate, and gossip.

Tomorrow he'd be talking with her brother about securing her hand. Until then, let the others assume all they liked.

"And you, of course, Miss Bronson," Rowles offered. At her pleased nod, he selected the cotillion for his dance with her. "May I offer either of you lemonade, or something else to drink?" he asked.

Joan covered her mouth with her gloved hand,

as if the pleasure in her expression was too much for polite society. "Yes, indeed. Thank you, Your Grace."

Miss Bronson replied, "Yes, thank you, Your Grace."

Rowles turned and made his way to the refreshment table, selecting two glasses before returning. As he handed the glass cups to the ladies, the quadrille's music began to play.

"Ah, Lady Joan, I do believe this is our first dance." He offered his hand.

Joan handed her cup to Miss Bronson and took his offered hand as he led them to the dance floor.

Grasping her hand, he swung them in a turn and released her, switching partners with the couple beside them. Belatedly, he noted they were partnered with Lord Archby and a young lady he'd not yet met. Archby beamed at Joan, familiar and warm. Rowles's chest tightened with jealousy, but he tamped down his rather uncivilized emotion and as Joan returned to him, he pulled her in slightly closer for their turn, earning a dancing look from her, one that held a hint of daring and understanding.

She took another turn with Treyson, and Rowles danced the steps with Treyson's partner, and they all repeated the steps. Each time Joan returned to his arms, Rowles's chest released its tension.

Never before had he experienced jealousy of such force.

When the quadrille ended, he bowed to Joan and was about to escort her off the dance floor when they were interrupted.

"Ah, Lady Joan, I believe this is my dance?" Archby bowed and offered his hand as a country dance started up.

"Indeed," she answered, then turned to Rowles. "Thank you," she said softly, her expression warm and inviting.

He released her to Archby and took a place on the edge of the ballroom. He knew that eyes were on him, watching for his reaction or lack thereof, so he engaged Lord Brookmoor in conversation until the song ended.

As luck would have it, rather than finding a reason to engage Joan in conversation once more, it was the cotillion's music that began. He sought out Miss Bronson and engaged her for his requested dance. Grasping her hand, he led her to the dance floor and bowed. She offered him a reserved expression as they circled up with the other couples and danced in the opening circle of the cotillion.

As they moved in the circle, he searched for Joan. Finding her standing beside her brother, he returned his attention to the dance. Turning to spin with Miss Bronson, when he faced the direction where Joan stood, he studied her again. The distance between her and her brother wasn't obvious, unless one knew them well. Their bodies were angled away, even though they stood close, as if neither one were inclined to speak to the other.

The ladies circled up in a pinwheel movement in the middle, and Rowles grasped Lady Greerheart's hand and turned with her, then took a turn with Miss Lynn. Returning his attention to Miss Bronson as they started the next movement, he caught her curious expression. "Distracted, Your Grace?"

He regarded her and answered softly, "My apologies."

Her lips pursed in an amused smirk.

As the dance continued, Rowles kept his attention more disciplined and on his partner rather than allowing his focus to wander in Joan's direction. If Miss Bronson noticed his distraction, then others would too. Talk surrounding his interest in Joan was acceptable; for the *ton* to call him desperate was entirely another matter.

He bowed to Miss Bronson as the dance ended and escorted her back to Joan's side.

Morgan turned toward them as they approached.

"Lord Penderdale." Miss Bronson curtsied and offered a flirtatious smile.

"Miss Bronson." Morgan nodded, then turned his attention from her to Rowles.

"Thank you for the dance, Miss Bronson," Rowles offered, then gave an encouraging smile to Morgan.

Morgan regarded him coolly, then turned to

Miss Bronson. "Would you favor me with a dance, Miss Bronson?"

She quickly offered her dance card.

Rowles turned to Joan and offered a reserved nod. More than anything, he'd love to secret her away on some balcony and talk, but even a trespass so innocent would ruin her reputation. So he settled for the next best option.

"Care to take a turn about the room?" he asked, then offered his arm.

"I'd be delighted," Joan answered, her eyes darting to her brother, as if challenging him to forbid it.

Rowles swallowed hard, knowing that the road ahead wouldn't be an easy one.

But worth it.

Entirely worth it.

They took a few steps and Rowles turned to her, his watchful eyes drinking in the sight of her so near. "And how are you enjoying your evening?"

She looked to him. "It is improving as it progresses."

"I hope that's not because Archby asked for a dance." Rowles playfully growled the words, earning a soft laugh and a delighted grin from Joan.

"And what if it was?" she flirted, her eyes sparkling with merriment.

"I suppose it's your choice, even if it would be a poor one." He shrugged one shoulder, playing along.

"Oh? And do you think you can persuade me otherwise?"

Rowles turned her, pausing in their progress along the room. "I'd certainly be up the challenge, my lady."

She frowned slightly, then sighed. "Explain yourself." She started forward again, and he moved to keep pace with her. "Your swiftly changing decisions concerning myself are quite opposing, so much so I feel like the rope in a game of tug-of-war."

Rowles chuckled, but without mirth.

She halted and watched him.

"It was an apt metaphor, Lady Joan," he admitted. "And much kinder than I deserve."

"On that we are in agreement," she said, and then her expression softened. "I dislike games, Your Grace. So please, do not use me as a pawn in one of them. Be honest. And tell me with your words, rather than a look."

Rowles's forehead knit as he considered her words. Was he so easily read?

He regretted the populated ballroom, the listening ears and gossiping lips that were only a polite foot away. "There's much to say, but in the correct setting, Lady Joan. And I promise you," he vowed, waiting till she met his eyes, "your questions will be answered till you are satisfied."

She took a deep breath, then nodded. "Thank you."

Rowles wanted to give her something, though, some honesty to hold to while she waited; it was the least he could do.

"I suppose it would be wise to give you the time to consider not how I feel about you, Lady Joan, but how you could potentially feel about me. And in answering that question, you might find more of the answers you seek. Because while we spoke of women, rights, value, and futures, I want you to know that as far as I am able, you will decide yours."

He turned and lifted her hand, then kissed it softly.

She parted her lips and gave a slight gasp at his words. And as if heaven were listening and writing the narrative, the strains of the waltz began to play, signaling his dance with her.

"May I?" He inclined his head toward the dance floor.

She nodded, wordlessly agreeing as he escorted her among the swirling dancers. Again, his body unwound from any earlier tension as he pulled her close, a feeling of home centering him.

"You needn't worry," she said as they danced.

He tipped his chin in query.

"You're a brilliant man. You'll figure it out." Her lips bent secretively and she inched closer, as if giving a hint at the meaning of her words.

Rowles's hands memorized the feel of her frame, while his mind studied the pressure of her hand on his shoulder, the loving look of her eyes, and the upturned bow of her lips as they danced.

He wanted to say something but restrained himself, not wishing to break the spell of the moment. So, remembering what she'd said earlier about reading the honesty in his eyes, he unshuttered his soul and met hers unflinchingly.

And rather than turn away from the rawness of it, she looked back like she loved what she saw. As if it answered questions she hadn't asked.

As if it soothed her soul the same way it soothed his.

And he wondered what she saw there, deep within him.

And for the first time, he wondered if maybe… maybe it was enough.

He might not be the best man.

But perhaps, his love might be the best love.

Twenty

Sometimes people believe in little or nothing, nonetheless they give their lives to that little or nothing. One life is all we have, and we live it as we believe in living it, and then it's gone. But to surrender what you are and live without belief—that's more terrible than dying—more terrible than dying young.

—Joan of Arc, from Joan of Lorraine by
Maxwell Anderson

STANDING AT THE FRONT GATE OF THE Foundling Hospital, Joan waved at Miss Bronson's coach as it pulled to a stop. Miss Bronson stepped down from the carriage and adjusted her skirt. With an amused smirk tipping her lips, she made her way to where Joan waited.

Joan waved, her mind alight with curiosity. What was Miss Bronson thinking?

"Interesting evening, was it not?" Miss Bronson said by way of greeting as she looped arms with Joan and they started toward the front entrance.

"And what exactly is that supposed to mean?" Joan asked playfully.

Miss Bronson gave her a look. "Only that I'm friends with the future Duchess of Westmore." She gave her brows a wiggle.

"Miss Bronson!" Joan hushed her, even as her heart pounded at the thought—rather the hope—that she'd scarcely let herself dwell on. "That's gossip."

"That's what anyone with eyes saw last night. Do you know, when he danced with me…" She lowered her voice and Joan leaned in. "I actually asked him if he was distracted."

"No, you did not," Joan said, shock rocking her to her core.

"Yes, because while he is an excellent dancer, I thought he might run into me because his eyes weren't on anything but *you*."

"I was on the edge of the ballroom."

"I know," Miss Bronson said with gleeful emphasis. "And beside your brother, who, I might also add, is a delightful dancer. It was very kind of him to ask. Is he attached?"

Joan's forehead pinched at the sudden shift in topic. "Er, no. He's not… Well, it will be some time till he takes a wife, I'd imagine." Joan thought over his work, work that could be of the dangerous sort, and thought Morgan was disinclined to add any woman to that equation.

"That's a pity." Miss Bronson sighed. "He's enchanting and quite handsome."

"He has his moments," Joan allowed, still not fully ready to forgive him.

"You're his sister. That's quite a different perspective, I'd imagine."

"Yes," Joan said, her focus on the opening door as Corinne stepped out and welcomed them.

"Good morning, ladies! I'm so pleased you could come today. We had several new arrivals and two ladies who will meet with prospective employers later this week, so it's quite an eventful day."

Joan answered with confidence. "I'm sure you'll find us equal to any task, Corinne."

"Yes. How shall we begin?" Miss Bronson inquired.

Corinne led them into the building and paused at the hall. "I'll need one lady to work with the girls who have interviews, and I have some research to do on a potential family member for a young lady."

"I'm happy to do any research," Joan offered.

"Then I shall help with the interview preparations," Miss Bronson volunteered.

"Excellent." Corinne clapped once. "Joan, could you meet me in the library? I'll first take Miss Bronson to the parlor where the young ladies are waiting. I'll meet with you shortly."

"Of course." Joan answered as the other two made their way down the hall toward one of the hospital's parlors.

Joan started toward the library. The doors were open and welcoming, so she stepped through and studied the shelves of registers, ledgers, maps, and a section with books on various topics. She took a seat at a circular table and looked to the tomes lining the shelves beside her.

The names were all in alphabetic order, listing all the shires of England: Bedfordshire, Berkshire, Buckinghamshire, Cambridgeshire…

"Thank you for waiting," Corinne said as she entered.

"Of course," Joan replied. "I was looking at the shire registry. Is that geographical?"

Corinne shook her head. "No, we keep a record of the foundlings taken in from each location, should a next of kin come looking."

"Oh, I see."

"That's why we have some registries smaller than others. Bath, for example, is small, but if you were to look at the one for Middlesex, it is several volumes." She moved to point to the middle of the bookshelf. "In fact, we started to divide it into the town areas of London rather than the shire."

"Makes sense." Joan nodded. "How far back to your records go?"

"To the very beginning. Our organization is something we've worked hard to keep and continue." Corinne's expression reflected humble pride.

"And one of the foundlings might have a

connection to another in the registry?" Joan asked, referring to what Corinne had said initially.

"Yes. It's a simple task but it can be time-consuming. I need to check the name of each new foundling, making sure it's not connected to another. If the name is that of a younger sibling to a current foundling, we want to know that. If there's a family connection, we'd like to make it known."

"I understand." Joan's appreciation for the hospital's work grew as she regarded the scope of books carefully maintained to keep record of each orphan's origin.

"Here's the name. I believe you should start by looking in the Bath registry, beginning about fifteen to twenty years back."

Joan took the scrap of paper Corinne handed her. "L. Agneau."

"I'll be back to check on your progress a little later. If you need anything, send a nurse or maid in search of me. I truly appreciate your help."

"Of course." Joan stood, watching Corinne leave.

Then she turned to the high and fat bookshelves and ran her fingers along the leatherbound spines, reading the names till she came to "Somerset."

She took the first ledger and set it on the table, carefully unwinding the leather strap. She opened the book to read the first date listed.

Too old.

She rewound the leather strap, took it back to its original place, and selected the next book.

Following the same procedure, she opened the first page and beamed in triumph. She read through the dates till she neared twenty or so years ago and began looking at the names. Organized by year, not by last name. Now she understood why Corinne said it would be a time-consuming project. Each line carried a name, a year, and a date, followed by a new name and the date accepted by the hospital. Most names carried a small-print family name in the margin. Joan assumed that was because orphans were sent out to live with families in the country till they were older. The small-print name must be that of the family the orphan lived with.

A half hour later, she stretched and blinked, giving her strained eyes a moment to adjust. Taking a deep breath, she returned to reading.

An hour later, she found the name.

Agneau, West Sussex.

But unlike the names above and below it, it didn't have any other information except a scratched-out name that was no longer readable.

She marked the page and went to find Corinne or someone who could be sent after her.

As Joan was walking into the hall, the woman found her instead. Corinne lifted a hand in greeting. "I was coming to check in on you. Have you found anything?"

Joan nodded. "Yes, I located the name you gave me but there's nothing helpful, I'm afraid. I'll show you."

Corinne followed her into the library and stood over the circular table as Joan opened the ledger. "See? It's only a last name, location, and year. Nothing else is included like in the other registries." Joan indicated the name with a sweep of her hand.

"I see. Well, you're correct, that doesn't help us much."

"What does it mean when there's so little information? Did the baby die?" Joan asked, frowning to mourn a baby she'd never known.

"No, it means the child was adopted, actually," Corinne answered with warmth. "It happens quite often, and when there's this little information, it usually means the child was adopted by someone who wished to remain anonymous. Likely someone unrelated to the child, or it could mean that the child was reclaimed by its mother soon after being left at the hospital or church." She shrugged. "It means we have a dead end on finding a next of kin, however, and that answered the question we needed to answer, so thank you." Corinne studied Joan. "It wasn't the answer we were searching for, but it will help us to do what is best for the young one."

"Indeed," Joan replied.

"And I think Miss Bronson is finished as well. If you two wish to have tea, you're welcome," Corinne invited.

"I'd love some tea," Joan replied, following

Corinne out into the hall. Miss Bronson waved as she approached. "Will you join us for tea?" Corinne asked.

"I'd love to, but I really must be on my way. Perhaps next time?"

"Certainly."

"I'll remain," Joan told Corinne, and said good-bye to her friend. She wasn't exactly in a rush to return home, not while still angry with her brother. The Foundling Hospital had a peaceful atmosphere that called to her, so she stayed an extra hour for tea before reluctantly calling for her carriage.

Her disinclined attitude shifted to anticipation and curiosity as she approached her home, only to see the Duke of Westmore's carriage departing.

Rowles had called? On her? Her brother? What was the nature of the visit? Her mind spun with questions and possible answers.

When the carriage came to a stop in front of her home, she stepped out quickly and all but rushed inside to seek her brother.

"Himes, where is my brother?" she asked the butler, handing a maid her reticule.

"I believe he's in his study, my lady."

Joan strode down the hall toward her brother's office, and rather than greeting her as she walked in, he held up two letters.

She paused.

"Can you assist me?" Morgan asked.

Realizing it was War Office business, Joan nodded, pushing her own personal questions into the back of her mind for the moment. "Of course."

"One is a forgery; one is the real document. Can you tell me which one is the falsified one?" He laid out the linen papers with their wax seals, then leaned back in his chair, steepling his fingers as he waited.

Joan studied them each, reading through the sentencing document from a magistrate in Wessex. One carried a much harsher sentence than the other.

"My inclination is to believe the papers with the heavier sentence," Morgan stated.

"I disagree." Joan's attention shifted between the two documents. "They are both sentencing papers for a criminal, but see this, here." She pointed to a small spot of ink beside a word. "Compare with this." She pulled the other document closer and traced her finger over the paper. "No spots."

"I don't follow." Morgan's replied.

Sighing, she explained. "Magistrates aren't usually known for perfect penmanship on a document that they tend to fill out multiple times a day. In the second document, great care was taken to make it *seem* authentic. The first one *is* authentic because it's written in the common way, with the lack of attention a magistrate would take to complete it and send it on its way. This one"—she pointed to it again—"is perfect. Not one dot of ink or flick of a *t* out of place. It was carefully completed. Carefully cultivated."

"Well then." Morgan cleared his throat.

"Yes, but that's strange, don't you think? Why would someone wish to make a sentence heavier rather than lighter?"

"That's exactly the question, dear sister."

"Who carried the sentencing papers?"

"A constable's messenger."

Joan looked at the papers again. "Someone wants him dead, whoever he is. Rotting way in the London Tower isn't a light sentence."

"House arrest is quite different," Morgan agreed. "Someone wants him to be killed by another prisoner of the London Tower. Easier to accomplish than with someone on house arrest."

"He must know something? Have seen something?" Joan inquired.

"I'm going to find out." Morgan stood.

"Wait." Joan held out her hand and sighed. "As I arrived, I saw the duke's carriage departing." She swallowed. "What was the nature of his visit?"

Morgan twisted his lips and cast his attention to the top of the desk and the papers still resting there. "May we speak of it later?" He returned his attentiveness to her.

Joan shook her head once. "I truly wish to know. Even a quick answer will suffice for the moment."

"You," Morgan replied. "It was concerning you, and now I have a choice I never wished to make." He sighed.

"In what way?" Joan asked, frowning as she sensed her brother's distress.

"I'll explain later." Morgan rolled up the papers and watched her. "This is important, and it shouldn't wait. There's a prisoner headed to the London Tower who shouldn't be admitted." He sighed. "We'll speak at dinner. The duke will attend as well."

Joan gasped, then nodded. "Of course. Dinner. Be safe." She gave her brother a long look.

He nodded, then quit the room like the fires of hell were licking at his heels.

Joan wondered if it was his job that caused his haste.

Or putting distance between the two of them.

Twenty-one

IT WAS HARDLY THE ANSWER HE WAS HOPING for, but as the dinner hour approached and Rowles prepared to depart for his engagement at the Penderdale residence, he thought that anything rather than a flat refusal was hopeful.

Morgan hadn't been surprised by his query.

But neither had he been pleased.

As Rowles stepped into his awaiting carriage, he thought back over the conversation.

"I'll be direct. You're my greatest friend, and you deserve no less. I've attempted to honor your request concerning your sister and my own convictions, but I can no longer."

Morgan watched him coolly, nodding once. "You wish for her hand."

"Yes," Rowles answered. His heart pounded fiercely at the sound of his affirmation.

"And you believe that she returns your interest?" Morgan asked, his lips twitching as if withholding his true feelings on the subject.

"I'm hopeful that if she doesn't currently, we have a...friendship that will only lend to a promising future," Rowles said. He didn't wish to speak for Joan.

He was certain she'd make her own wishes known to both of them.

"I'll discuss the matter with her."

Rowles wanted to say more, to plead his case, but he kept his peace. It was only as he was about to leave that Morgan had invited him for dinner, an invitation which he readily accepted.

The coach hit a hole in the cobbles and brought Rowles's mind back from its woolgathering. The driver took a right onto the square and slowed before Penderdale House. Heart solidly hammering against his ribs, Rowles drew a fortifying breath and whispered a prayer.

So much could be decided within a short period.

Odd how so much time could lead up to such little defining moments.

He stepped from the carriage and straightened his coat, then walked to the front steps. After a brisk knock, he waited for an answer.

In short order, the door swung inward.

"Your Grace." The butler bowed and stepped aside to allow him entrance. "If you'll follow me?" He indicated in the direction of the parlor down the hall and Rowles stepped after him.

In a few moments, he paused at the threshold of the parlor, his gaze taking in the scene. His heart deflated slightly as he noted that Joan wasn't present. Morgan stood and greeted him, however.

"Rowles." Morgan waved to a chair. "Would

you like some whiskey?" He lifted his own glass of amber liquid.

"Yes, thank you." Rowles took a seat on a settee and studied Morgan. Never had he been so ill at ease with his best friend. It was like sitting on pins or needles rather than a seat cushion.

The one question that continued to plague his mind was *why?* What did Morgan find so lacking in him that he didn't consider him a suitable match for his sister? Was it, despite his words, the fear that Rowles's mother's malady was at work within him as well? Or was it that Morgan didn't trust him enough to cherish Joan?

He wasn't a monk, but he hadn't kept a mistress nor had he dallied with the merry widows.

He was a professor of divinity; he knew the parameters God had set up for men, and he'd honored them.

He wasn't one to teach and not implement the same facts in his own life, knowing that to do such was the greatest hypocrisy.

But all this reflection didn't answer the pressing question.

Morgan handed him a crystal glass filled with whiskey, not meeting his eyes. It was on the tip of Rowles's tongue to ask him, to speak the burning question aloud, but soft footsteps distracted him.

Turning his head, he noted the understated entrance of Joan.

The whiskey glass balanced in his hand, he

stood and bowed at her entrance, drinking in the sight of her.

She was resplendent in a pale lemon-yellow dress, her skin glowing, but her eyes and smile were what captivated him.

His lips burned to feel hers, to taste the soft velvet of her mouth and know her flavor.

Blinking back the tempting thought, he greeted her. "Lady Joan."

"Your Grace." She curtsied and turned to her brother.

Rowles noted the way her brows puckered ever so slightly, as if concerned. "Morgan."

"Joan." He nodded his greeting.

The tension was thick, and Rowles was uncertain if he should try to dissipate it or allow it to run its course between the siblings.

It turned his stomach sour to think that he was the reason for the rift between them.

Perhaps it was because he'd lost his brother, but the unity of family was of the utmost importance in his opinion, and he hated that he was causing trouble.

But Joan…

His eyes studied her. Every nuance, curve, and breath spoke to him. Called his name like a siren he couldn't ignore, and regardless of how he felt about the tension between the siblings, he wouldn't regret speaking the truth.

He wanted her for his wife.

Simple.

True.

Real.

And if there was one thing he'd learned from his studying divinity and the Bible, it was the power of the truth.

It set you free.

Joan's eyes shifted to his, a myriad of emotions shifting through their mossy green depths before her lips bent into a welcoming expression. "I arrived home earlier only in time to see your carriage depart, Your Grace."

"Ah, a disappointing revelation." His own lips lifted in an answering grin.

"And my brother"—her eyes shifted toward him, then back to Rowles—"was exceedingly tight-lipped about your social call. A pity, that."

"Joan, do you think it possible to get through dinner before you begin raking me over the coals? It's harder to endure with an empty stomach," Morgan drawled, shooting his sister a warning glare.

"Rake you over the coals? And they say women are the ones who exhibit theatrics." She shook her head, a teasing glint in her eyes.

"We all have our moments," Morgan replied with a heavily sarcastic tone.

Rowles bit his lip to keep from chuckling at

their interaction. Regardless of Joan's frank question, it had served a purpose, breaking the tension. Morgan's posture was far more relaxed, and a ghost of a smile, wry as it was, appeared on his lips.

Joan turned to him, her eyes dancing with amusement. Her lips parted, but before she could speak, the butler arrived to announce dinner.

It wasn't till they were seated at the table that Joan turned back to him. "And how was your day, Your Grace?"

Rowles waited for the footman to set a bowl of soup in front of him before he answered. "It wasn't nearly as exciting as this evening has turned out to be," he replied. "How was your day, Lady Joan?"

She took a delicate sip of soup. "I was assisting at the Foundling Hospital today. It was research on a child who possibly had kin associated with the hospital nearly two decades ago, so I was looking through the archives. It was an interesting name, Agneau. French, I believe. I think it was a baby girl."

"Lamb," Rowles translated.

Morgan's spoon dropped into his soup with a splash. Muttering a curse under his breath, he made a quick apology while the footmen cleaned the splattered soup. "Slipped," Morgan said to Rowles, then to Joan before lifting the new spoon given by a footman and beginning to take another bite.

Joan studied him, not disregarding his quick words but staring, as if willing for him to meet her waiting eyes.

And Morgan studiously avoided doing so.

It was a tense moment, and Rowles waited to let it play out between the siblings.

Joan spoke clearly, her attention still fixed on her brother. "Is the name familiar?"

Morgan gave his head a shake and wiped his mouth with a napkin. "No." But still he didn't meet his sister's inquiring look.

"Did you find her?" Rowles asked after another tense moment.

"No, she wasn't ever admitted into the Foundling Hospital. Miss Vanderhaul believes her mother or kin took her in. And it's possible there was no familial connection to begin with, but they always check. They are very thorough, which I find is very honorable."

"Indeed. In that we are in agreement. I hope it wasn't too much trouble to research."

"No, it was quite fascinating, but I can see why they wished for a volunteer to assist them. It took some time." There was tension that belied her relaxed expression.

The footmen removed the soup and replaced it with the next course.

"Are you enjoying your time at the Foundling Hospital?" Rowles asked.

Joan's tone was answer enough as she enthusiastically described the way the hospital operated and provided information concerning the building and its patrons. "It's quite fascinating and they truly have the children's best interests at heart."

"And you started with the Foundling Hospital because of your friend who leads the women's group, correct?"

"Yes. You're correct. It's also where I met my new friend, Miss Bronson," Joan answered.

"And are you still reading Mary Wollstonecraft?"

"Yes, but we won't meet again till next month. Lady Sandra is away from town so we've postponed."

"That's surely a welcome diversion," Rowles added.

"Yes, she will be in Bath."

"It can be quite healthy, I've heard."

"Indeed. I wouldn't mind visiting Bath as well. It's been at least five years since we've been to our estate there." She turned to her brother. "Hasn't it?"

Morgan was watching the two of them cautiously. "At least five years, but it's a small estate and doesn't need much hands-on management. My steward is the best in the shire."

"Murtaug is quite capable, but it would be fun to return, even for a few days," Joan suggested hopefully.

"We shall see, perhaps after the season." Morgan's scrutiny shifted to Rowles, then back to his meal.

If all went as Rowles hoped, the decision to visit Bath would rest upon his shoulders. By the end of the season, Joan could be his wife. But Morgan could have been conveying his disapproval by sending the message that he would still be in control of Joan's future come the end of the season.

Which meant a refusal.

All the nuances of the social scene wore on Rowles, and with a soft sigh, he turned his attention to Joan.

"Bath is lovely. My family has an estate not far from there as well. You're more than welcome to visit, with Morgan, of course," Rowles qualified, giving a curt nod to Morgan.

His friend didn't return the gesture, and Rowles considered his demeanor. After all, he'd seen Morgan in a fit of temper. He'd seen Morgan broken with the loss of his own brother. And he'd seen Morgan at a loss for how to address a difficult situation. But never had he encountered this full concealment of emotion from his friend, and he couldn't help but wonder what it meant exactly.

For him.

For Joan.

For their future.

Or, worse yet, for the lack thereof.

Dinner passed with the same sort of tension, and as the final plates were cleared, Morgan waved a hand toward the door. "Care to join me for a snifter of brandy?" He rose from the table and started toward his study without a backward glance.

Rowles gave a bow to Joan, offered the most reassuring look he could, and followed his friend, wondering if the defining moment had finally arrived.

As Rowles stepped into the study, Morgan called to him. "Close the door, if you will?"

The door clicked shut, and Rowles turned to his friend.

Morgan held out a snifter of brandy and took a generous sip of his own. "If Joan will accept you, I will not hinder your marriage. In fact, I'll give you my blessing, but…" He took a deep breath and regarded Rowles with a piercing look. "There are a few things you should know. I will tell you one, and Joan will have to tell you the others."

Rowles nodded, his heart racing with the revelation that his suit was accepted. Relief washed over him, only to give rise to new tension. Joan would accept him, wouldn't she?

"Take a seat." Morgan sat as well, waiting for Rowles to settle. He drew a deep breath, paused, then took a long swallow of brandy. He inhaled another slow breath and then leaned forward.

Rowles's shoulders tightened with tension at his friend's actions. What secrets could he be harboring? Certainly nothing that would change the way Rowles felt about Joan. Yet the tension remained.

"Joan is my sister in every way...save blood," Morgan confessed softly, as if the walls had ears and were waiting for the secret as well.

Rowles blinked, frowned, and then tipped his chin. "But—"

"My mother couldn't have any more children after she gave birth to me and my twin brother..." Morgan shifted in his seat. "They wanted more children, and one summer while we were at our estate in West Sussex near Chichester, an infant was left on the steps to the Cathedral Church of the Holy Trinity. The vicar intended to send the child to Thomas Coram's Foundling Hospital, but he knew how long my mother had been praying for a child and sent word to my family." Morgan paused, taking another sip.

"I was only four, but I remember when they brought her to our home. My mother was in raptures, and my father immediately agreed that the babe was to be a Morgan. The rest of the process was simple, and as fate or God would have it, we had skipped the London season the year before and traveled, so it wasn't a far stretch for everyone to believe she was born of my mother, my true sister."

Rowles's heart pounded as he listened to Morgan, one question ringing in his ears. "She doesn't know?"

"No. She has no idea."

"And...you do not plan to tell her?" Rowles

asked, his whole body bristling at the idea of keeping such a secret from Joan.

"As her likely future husband, I will leave the decision to you."

Rowles's chest tightened at the weight of the decision. "Me? Doesn't she deserve to hear the truth from her brother? The one who knows the details? Can affirm to her your parents' love and care for her? What can I possibly offer other than information?" Rowles asked, his heart still thundering.

"Then don't tell her." Morgan shrugged. "It's not necessary. My parents never wanted her to know, so I've honored their request."

Rowles wiped his hand down his face. "Wouldn't you wish to know, if the situation were reversed?"

Morgan scowled. "No, ignorance is underappreciated in circumstances like this one."

Rowles could hardly believe his ears or his eyes as Morgan swirled what was left of his brandy coolly.

"Anything else you wish to disclose?" Rowles asked, irritated with the blasé reaction of his friend to the secrets he'd kept from his sister.

"No, the rest are for her to tell you when she's ready. I won't interfere with secrets that aren't mine to tell."

Or with the secrets that are *yours to tell.* "Did you think that this revelation about Joan would change my mind?" Rowles asked, watching his friend with a sharp eye.

"I wasn't sure. I didn't think so, but I'd prefer to tell you before you officially propose."

"It doesn't change anything," Rowles affirmed, in case his friend could use the acknowledgment.

"Good. Then, without further ado, why don't we call for Joan to join us? I believe you may have a question to ask her." Morgan stood and strode to the door, presumably to fetch his sister.

"May I have a moment with her?" Rowles asked, standing as well.

Morgan turned to him, nodded once, and disappeared.

Rowles took a short sip of his brandy and set the snifter on the side table, then breathed deeply through his nose.

So much weighed on him, especially after that conversation with Morgan. But he pushed it all out of his mind. This was the defining moment he was waiting for.

Joan walked into the room, her gaze finding his.

His body warmed with anticipation.

He walked toward her, his eyes fixed on hers, willing calm as he reached out a hand toward her.

A question.

One that would start the most important conversation of his life.

Twenty-two

ONCE MORGAN HAD INVITED ROWLES INTO THE study for brandy, Joan was at loss as to how to pass the time till she was called upon. Frankly, she was irritated at the custom that excluded her from their company after dinner, even if it was only for a short time. Yet her irritation solved nothing. She'd retired to the library to wait upon her brother's leisure, her mind evaluating the dinner conversation. As she sank into a soft wing-backed chair, her irritation softened. Rowles was down the hall, and there was some reason her brother had invited him to dinner. The tension was too high, and Morgan was in too foul of a humor for it to be anything less than significant. When she'd asked her brother why the duke had called earlier, he'd said, "You." That conveyed volumes.

And yet, nothing specific.

She rose from the chair and began to pace. Was it foolish to hope that Rowles could offer for her? Proposals were given for far less than they had already shared in conversation. What plagued her mind was her brother's resistance. Did he truly question his friend's acceptance of Joan's work for the War Office? Yet for her brother to be so reluctant gave her pause, made her wonder if perhaps rather than her brother making too much of it, she was making too little.

"The carpet is showing signs of wear." Her brother nodded to where she paused her pacing. He was leaning against the doorframe of the library, watching her with an expression that wavered from concern to sorrow to something she couldn't see before he turned away quickly.

"An excuse to buy a new rug," Joan suggested with a teasing tone. "Unless it's a secret favorite of yours."

"It's no such thing, and I will happily trod on whatever you choose for its replacement." He straightened from the doorframe. "The duke would like a word with you," he said, then stepped toward her. "Consider your heart and your future before you make any decisions. Be honest with him, and uncover all that needs to be known before you run headlong into…anything," he finished, awkwardly pulled her into a rare hug.

"And if you wish to tell him nothing, your secret will always be safe with me," he murmured, then released her as quickly as he had embraced her. "Go." He nodded, taking a step back.

Joan blinked, her heart pounding with the implication of his words yet also the serious nature of their meaning. She tipped her chin, studying him before giving a single, solemn nod.

Wordlessly she left the library and walked on silent feet to the door leading to the study, the absence of her brother following behind a telling indication of what waited within the doors.

Her hand trembled as she pushed the slightly ajar door open. Nervous anticipation filled her as she raised her eyes to meet Rowles, who stood abruptly as she entered. His Adam's apple bobbed as he swallowed hard, then bowed.

"Joan."

Her heart raced at the sound of her name on his lips, and a smile slipped through her tension, softening the moment.

"Rowles," she murmured, tasting his name on her tongue, reveling in the weight of it, owning it. Praying it was only the beginning of the millions of times she'd speak his name.

He took a few steps toward her, then paused, his lips parting, then closing as if searching for the perfect words. With a self-deprecating expression, he rubbed the back of his neck and looked up to her from his lowered chin, which gave him an almost shy expression. "Now that I have the moment I've wished for, I have no idea where to begin."

"I suppose the most important part would be a good place to begin." Joan traced a finger along the back of a settee as she took a step toward him.

"That is the heart of the matter. All of it is important." Rowles's intensely observant eyes followed her every movement as if he was captivated. "Because it's all about you, and not one aspect is less grand than the other," he confessed, his blue eyes trapping her with their hope, intensity, and love.

Good Lord, she'd never seen anything like it.

It enveloped her, as if she was jumping off a rocky shore into an ocean that immediately swallowed her, only to realize she was at home in the depths even more than on the land. It wove a spell around her, called to her, soul to soul. It named her beautiful, loved, cherished, and wanted all with one glance, filling her soul in ways she had never known it was empty.

"If you want my heart, I'm not going to second-guess your choice. I've spent my life second-guessing myself, my worthiness, and even my sanity." He gave a humorless laugh. "But I need your love more than anything, and I refuse." He stepped forward and closed the distance between them. Reaching out, he grasped her hands and pulled her in so that their toes touched. The scent of peppermint and clove clung to his skin, spicing the air around them. "I refuse to choose for you, and I confess that I was. I had made the choice to remove myself from your life, as much as was possible, so that you could find someone better, more worthy. Yet, with every conversation, every look..." He met her eyes, his tormented soul laid bare in his expression. "It haunted me, called to me, and eventually I realized that by removing myself, I'd also made the choice for you, which was unfair. After all our conversations about the place and position of women in our country, I fell into one of the oldest traps of thinking I knew better than you."

Joan reached up and touched his jaw, sliding her fingers till she cupped his face. Her heart was breaking at his confession, at the bareness of his soul that didn't see all the wonderful things she saw when she looked at him, talked with him, thought about him. How could someone be so blind to their own glory? She opened her mouth to speak the truth, but he continued.

"And then I had a thought, and it pierced me like an arrow." He took a deep breath and leaned into her hand's caress. "I might not be the best man available, but I swear to you, Joan Morgan," he whispered, "my love for you will be the best love."

Tears welled in her eyes as she smiled through them. "Yes, yes, it is," she murmured, reaching up her other hand and cupping his face.

He leaned down, resting his forehead against hers, setting her heart to hammering with the touch. Her blood pounded in her veins with the power of the moment, an she could feel his heart thudding as it echoed hers.

Two hearts.

One soul.

She'd never understood the concept she had read in books until that moment.

"Often the hero is the savior, but Joan…rescue me. You're the only one who holds my heart. Marry me?" He leaned back, and with a reverent bow, he took a knee and laced his fingers through hers, gazing up at her.

Warm love surrounded her like a song as she nodded through the tears that fell freely down her cheeks. "I can't imagine loving anyone more than I love you," she whispered, hiccupping on a mix between a laugh and sob.

He bowed his head as if saying a prayer of thanks, then quickly rose and in one swift movement pulled her into his arms, holding her tight. Joan closed her eyes and melted into his embrace, memorizing it, finding it felt like home.

Leaning back slightly, he reached up and touched her chin, lifting it a bit. "May I?" he asked.

Joan's heart melted a little more. He always asked, never assumed, his will at the mercy of hers, and not realizing it was the very same with her. Her will was at the mercy of his.

That's what love was about, selfless.

Yielding to the other.

Thinking of the other before oneself.

"Yes, always yes." She leaned forward, brushing his lips with hers. The light touch took her breath away, her body reacting with heat and need. He met her lips once more, lingering there, nibbling her lower lips softly, playfully, another request. She mimicked his movement, and as if her body already knew what to do, her arms reached up and wrapped around his neck. Her fingers tentatively slid into the soft hair at the nape of his neck, caressing up as she pulled him closer.

How was it possible to be so close to someone and still feel like they were too far away? Her thoughts scattered as his hands splayed across her hips and branded her with his warm touch. His mouth captured hers, teaching—ever the teacher—and caressing her. A flicker of his tongue against her lips made them part in shock. She could feel his smile rather than see it, as it spread across his lips before he flicked his tongue against hers softly, invitingly, a request.

His flavor enveloped her, sang a love song as she gingerly kissed him back. New and untried, she gave every drop of affection and love in her kiss, speaking through her actions rather than her words.

"Five seconds before I come through the door," Morgan called, his voice shattering the fragile moment like a firework in a glass greenhouse.

Rowles pulled back reluctantly, then raised his voice in answer, "Fifteen." He kissed her again, and he lingered a moment longer against her lips.

"Two," Morgan countered from the hall.

Joan blinked, the spell dissipating as she met Rowles's exuberant expression.

"One," Morgan said.

"Zero?" Rowles replied, his tone teasing. He grasped Joan's hand and held it tightly, moving to stand beside her.

Morgan walked in, watched them cautiously, and then relaxed. "I suppose there's news you wish to impart?" He rocked on his heels, and while he still looked less than thrilled, the edge to his tone and demeanor was absent.

"It turns out you will be stuck with me for quite some time, but now as a brother-in-law." Rowles gave Joan's hand a squeeze as he turned to her and grinned.

"I see. I suspect you'll next ask to procure a special license?"

Rowles chuckled. "No, I can survive three weeks for the banns, and it will keep the gossipmongers at bay. No need to raise suspicions by a hasty marriage." He paused a moment, then held up a finger. "But I would like the banns to be read this week, so that we can marry sooner rather than wait an extra week."

Joan couldn't hinder the wide smile that stretched across her face. "And I have plenty of preparations to see to before the wedding. Besides, I think it might be helpful for my poor brother to have some time to adjust to the idea of my absence. I think he misses me already." She turned to Morgan, giving him a playful smile.

He narrowed his eyes. "Would you prefer that I be happy to be rid of your annoying presence?"

"You can say all you want about it, but I know the truth," she sang out. "You'll miss me."

"I see him often enough, so I imagine I'll see you every bit as often." But Morgan's expression softened. "I am happy for you."

"That means much to me." Rowles nodded, his expression sobering. "Truly, it does. And I will—"

Morgan held up a hand. "I know. You needn't affirm your affections. You've proven them."

Rowles gave a nod.

"Now the question is, can I stomach being around the two of you long enough to win at whist? Or are you not up to the challenge?" Morgan replied.

"Since you lost the five games I challenged you to the other night, I don't see you as much of a threat," Joan replied as she turned to meet Rowles's playful expression. Her heart danced with a happy cadence. Could a person be too happy? Was it possible? Yet as she considered it, a slight tension bloomed in her chest. She needed to talk with Rowles, explain how she helped at the War Office, and what the study and application of that knowledge that allowed her to do so. But as her brother set up the whist table, she turned to her betrothed and decided that tonight was not the night.

No. For now, she would celebrate the joy of returned love.

Tomorrow, or maybe the day after, she'd offer new love's first potential challenge: the truth.

Twenty-three

ROWLES AWOKE BEFORE DAWN. FILLED WITH anticipation and purpose, he set out to begin all the preparations for his upcoming wedding. The thought had a physical reaction of joy so powerful, it almost hurt. The sheer force of his emotions was unlike anything he'd ever experienced.

She had accepted him.

Joan would bear his name, his title, their children.

A smile tripped across his lips, refusing to be restrained as he made his way to the study to begin sending out the proper notifications.

He took a seat behind his desk, a cheery fire already glowing in the hearth to ward off the morning chill. Withdrawing a quill, he began to draft a notice for the *Times* and the *Courier* to be published after their wedding. And as soon as it was a reasonable hour, he'd take his carriage to Hanover Square, to St. George's to talk to a curate about the ceremony.

Certainly after that they would return to his home for the wedding breakfast, which reminded him that it was pertinent to confer with his housekeeper posthaste.

Rowles rang for his housekeeper, his mind reviewing all the necessary tasks to complete.

Next, he sent a missive to his solicitor to request a meeting later today. Marriage articles would need to be drawn up and agreed upon. He had no concerns that his terms would be satisfactory. A wry grin tipped his lips. Rather, he had the suspicion that Joan would object to such a large settlement, but he refused to anything less. No, he had already given her his heart, so worldly goods seemed trivial in comparison.

"Your Grace?" Mrs. Adams curtsied as she entered his study.

Rowles nodded. "Yes, thank you, Mrs. Adams. I have news that will require some attention from our staff, and I thought it best to meet with you first."

"I'm honored, Your Grace. How may I be of service?" she inquired, her mobcap barely restraining her wiry gray curls as she nodded.

"Won't you sit?" Rowles signaled to a chair.

She said her thanks and took a seat, her keen eyes watchful and waiting. It was a blessing to have such a competent staff.

"Last night, Lady Joan Morgan accepted my offer of marriage."

Gasping, Mrs. Adams clapped her hands together. "What wonderful news, Your Grace!"

"Thank you," Rowles returned. "And I'm sure you understand the upcoming events that need your attention."

"Of course, Your Grace. I'll notify the staff to prepare the duchess's rooms—" She paused, and then met his look with a hesitant one of her own. "Forgive me, Your Grace. But, which rooms would you like to prepare for the new duchess? I admit I'm not certain if you'd wish me to ready your mother's previous rooms or others?" she asked with a cautious tone.

Rowles nodded. His mother had moved from the original suite that connected with the duke's rooms. But she'd modified her new rooms to be even grander than her former ones. Since then, the staff had referred to her rooms as those worthy of the title. "Thank you for your considerate insight. My mother will not be returning for some time. Prepare the one that adjoins mine. I suspect it will need some attention."

"Of course, Your Grace. We will begin immediately," she agreed. "And a wedding breakfast, I assume?"

"Yes. I suspect the new duchess will wish to have some input on the festivities, so I shall introduce you later this week."

"I look forward to meeting her, Your Grace," Mrs. Adams said with a tone of reverence. "I will see that the new duchess is put at ease as much as I am able. The staff will make every effort to please her, Your Grace."

"I believe you, Mrs. Adams. For now, that will be

all." He looked to the clock. "Please have a footman bring my carriage around. I need to go to Hanover Square."

"Of course. Yes, Your Grace." She stood and curtsied again, then took her leave.

Rowles nodded to himself, pleased with all the tasks he had addressed. He set his quill to the side and stood. Next would be the securing of a date, finding a curate to oversee the marriage, and arranging for the banns to be read.

As he strode to the front of his home, he calculated when the wedding would take place. He stepped into the carriage and leaned back against the soft velvet upholstery. It was Thursday, so the first banns would be read in three days' time. The reading was a mere formality, but an important one. It was an announcement, a declaration of intent. He shook his head in wonder. The gossip mill would certainly get word out before Sunday, but when the banns were declared to the whole parish, asking for any impediments to their marriage, such a statement made the couple as official as they could be without an actual wedding.

The banns would need to be read two more times before they could marry, so that would mean the wedding could take place the Monday after the final reading, at eight in the morning if they wished.

And he did wish.

If it didn't seem suspect to have a hasty marriage,

he would direct his driver to Doctors' Commons to procure a special license so they could be married tomorrow. But as much as his impatient heart wished for it, he would gladly wait the weeks needed to make her officially his wife, because in the end that kept her reputation as clean as possible.

He could do that for her.

He would do that for her.

The carriage rolled to a stop before St. George's Church, and due to the early hour, the square was quite empty and the church reverently silent as he walked through the open doors. Stained glass filtered the sunlight into prisms of color.

"May I be of assistance?" An older man in a curate's robes approached him with a kind expression.

"Indeed you may," Rowles answered, and in short work, he'd arranged for the banns to be read and for the wedding time on the first Monday after the final reading. He thanked the curate and returned to his carriage, the most important errand of the day accomplished.

Unfortunately, the time of the wedding was at ten in the morning, instead of eight as he'd originally hoped. But as the carriage took him home, he considered that Joan might appreciate a few extra hours of preparation.

Yet his lighthearted and joyful mood had one damper—the news Morgan had disclosed last night concerning Joan's birth.

He took a deep breath and leaned forward, his elbows resting on his knees as he considered the quandary. It mattered not to him that she was not titled by blood, but it did put pressure on him that made him consider the best option for her.

Unlike the proposal, information about her birth wasn't a question he could pose to her. Once he spoke the truth of it, there was no taking it back—no unrevealing what had been revealed.

He considered his own reactions if the situation were reversed. Would he want to know? Yes. Likely he would. Did the truth change anything? No. It didn't.

He twisted his lips as he considered anything that could be gained from telling her the news. He couldn't think of any benefits from knowing. However…the one thought that plagued him was the truth that in knowing something but keeping his silence, he was in a way choosing to be dishonest. And should the truth ever come to light, and she discovered that he *knew* and *didn't* tell her, that would be far more damaging than any other aspect. It could cripple their friendship, their relationship. And that possibility was a risk too great.

It was settled; he would tell her. The only question left was when? He was still mulling that over when he stepped from the carriage once it stopped in front of his house.

"Your Grace." His butler met him at the bottom of the stairs leading to the front door. "The doctor is waiting for you in your study," he stated softly, but with purpose and intention.

Rowles met his stare, nodded once, and entered the house, his steps purposeful as he turned to the study door.

"Doctor," Rowles greeted his visitor, his earlier elation evaporating at the haggard appearance of the man.

"Your Grace." The doctor bowed, then paused.

"Did something happen?" Rowles asked, his impatience gnawing at his mind.

The doctor nodded. "Your Grace, I think it is best for you to come and see your mother. There was…an event this morning that—"

"What happened?" Rowles asked with a clipped tone, needing more information than was being offered.

"She overdosed on laudanum," the doctor admitted quietly, as if whispering of the news would soften the blow.

"How?" Rowles asked, his heart pounding with understanding. Laudanum in any excessive dose was lethal.

The doctor took a deep breath. "This morning, when the nurse was administering the usual dose, your mother…took the bottle quite forcefully. We were able to…stop her… She swallowed enough that we are uncertain she will survive, Your Grace." The doctor let out a tense breath.

"I'll leave directly." Rowles turned on his heel and left the room. His carriage was still in front, and he directed the driver to his mother's residence.

As the carriage lurched forward, he rested his head in his hands, taking deep breaths through his nose and easing them out through pursed lips. It wasn't the fault of the staff, he reasoned. But anger welled within him regardless. Anger at the staff, anger at his mother, and anger at himself. He couldn't shake the nagging feeling that if he had been there, or had not removed her from her home, or any of other various things, she would not have taken such measures.

And did she even know?

Had it been intentional?

She'd said she would die there… Was that prophetic or was it a choice? Laudanum overdose had been a plague and scourge across England, with many succumbing to the opiate's power and allure, overdosing both intentionally and unintentionally. Wretched stuff, both medicine and poison in the same bottle, able to help life and take it.

Even though the distance wasn't far, time passed slowly. When the carriage slowed in front of the house, Rowles quickly stepped out, straightened his coat, and walked to the already opening door. The footman's expression was crestfallen with a tinge of fear lurking below the surface.

The house was deathly silent.

As if every servant, every nurse was holding their collective breath.

As if he were the judge, jury, and executioner.

Something broke in him, in that moment.

They were not at fault.

No.

His shoulders slumped under the weight of it, and he took the stairs to the second floor toward his mother's rooms. The cinnamon and clove scent of laudanum was strong in the hall, reaching his nose before he got to the door.

As if sensing a question, a stout older nurse whispered, "When we tried to take it away, it spilled on the floors…and us, Your Grace."

Rowles turned to the woman, noting her stained clothing. They hadn't even changed before they'd sent word to him to notify him of the events.

Never before had he felt so helpless, so responsible and unable to do anything about it.

"I'm sorry," he whispered to the nurse. The words seemed so empty, but it was all he had the strength to say.

She blinked, as if unable to understand why he would apologize to her, but he was already moving on, opening the door and stepping into the faint light of his mother's rooms.

Her form was still.

Her breathing shallow.

And as he knelt by her bedside, he looked for any semblance of the woman who had borne and loved him…

And found none.

Twenty-four

You say that you are my judge. I do not know if you are! But I tell you that you must take good care not to judge me wrongly, because you will put yourself in great danger.

—Joan of Arc

JOAN TAPPED HER FINGER ON HER BOOK, NOT seeing the words. Happiness coursed through her like waves on the shore, and she was certain she even slept with a smile on her face.

The only damper on the joy that filled her was the question of if and when she should tell Rowles about her involvement with the War Office, and why. It was a simple conversation, no need to make it drawn out…but fear threatened to linger there.

What if he didn't understand?

What if he was unwilling to let her continue?

So many possibilities, yet not telling him… She couldn't. It would be dishonest and that was not a way she could live, having that between them.

"The Duke of Westmore," the butler announced,

and Joan stood, her book slipping through her fingers and hitting the floor with a thud. She quickly retrieved it and was setting it on the sofa as the duke entered.

She was expecting a joyful expression, a secretive glance.

What she received was a frown, worried eyes, and a distressed countenance. Immediately she strode to him. "What is it?"

He met her eyes, his body relaxing slightly, as if her very presence calmed his soul.

"My mother." He spoke softly. "She...isn't healthy."

"I'm terribly sorry." Her brow puckered with empathy as she waited for the rest of the story. It was widely understood among the *ton* that his mother wasn't in good health, but Joan suspected there had been a turn of events.

"And I have a request for you." He reached down and grasped her hands. His fingers were chilled; even through the kid leather of her gloves she could feel it. "My mother may not survive the night, Joan. And I am torn between wanting to protect you from what her illness has made her become and wanting you to at least have met her...even if she will not respond. And I don't know the right answer, or what to ask..." He closed his eyes.

"Let's go." Joan tugged on his hand, leading him toward the open door of the library. "For better or worse, I want to know the woman who bore you, and thank her. Even if she doesn't know me or respond or even hear me. It's a gift I wish to give to *you*."

His expression softened as if her words had lifted a weight off his very soul. "Truly?"

"I'm not one to lie," Joan replied, the truth of her words echoing deep in her soul.

"My carriage is out front." Rowles escorted her from the room. "Where is Morgan?"

Joan turned back. "He's attending to some business. Allow me a moment to call a maid to accompany me, and we shall be off."

Only a few minutes later, Joan sat beside Mary in the duke's luxurious carriage as it made haste toward his mother's lodgings.

"She…" His attention wavered to the maid and back to Joan.

"She is trustworthy," Joan said, answering the unspoken question. Often the help were greater gossipmongers than the *ton* themselves, but Mary was soft-spoken and had her own secrets to keep, so she honored the confidences of others with more discretion than most. It was for that reason Joan had asked her instead of her lady's maid to accompany them.

Rowles nodded in acceptance of her judgment. "My mother isn't well, as you are fully aware. All of London is aware," he added softly. "But the extent isn't known. It's all speculation. A few weeks ago there was an incident that required me to move her to separate lodgings. The staff at the house are fully competent, but I fear my mother's malady is beyond even their capabilities." He hesitated. "I'll explain more when we arrive."

Joan nodded once. There was much she wished to say, but she kept her peace, waiting for the right moment.

It wasn't a long trip to his mother's lodgings, and soon they were halted in front of a gray stone town house outside of Mayfair. Rowles stepped from the carriage and immediately turned to assist her.

The door to the house opened as they approached, a footman clearly awaiting the master's return. As they entered, Rowles nodded to the footman and waved toward the stairs, leading her upward. "There are nurses aplenty. Your maid can wait in the parlor, if you wish."

"Thank you," Joan replied, then turned to her maid. "Mary?" Joan nodded to the servant, who curtsied and followed another footman to the door on the left of the staircase, which displayed a small but lavishly furnished parlor.

Joan followed Rowles up the stairs, her nose tingling with the scent of something familiar yet not. The sweet scent of cloves and licorice with a hint of cinnamon filtered through the air, permeating it. She took a deeper breath, and Rowles turned slightly toward her as they strode down the second-floor hall. "Laudanum."

It was one word that conveyed volumes.

"She grabbed the bottle from the nurse who was giving her the usual evening dose. My mother made quick work of ingesting as much as possible before they were able to stop her. It spilled everywhere as they…fought her for it."

Joan's heart sank, myriad emotions swirling through her: empathy, pity, despair, mourning, and understanding.

"I'm very sorry," she whispered, not knowing what else to say, and knowing it wasn't nearly enough.

Rowles answered, "As am I. But what's done is done." Two nurses and a footman bowed and curtsied as they approached a wooden door.

"Your Grace," the footman said, echoed by the nurses.

Rowles nodded. "Has there been any change?"

"No, Your Grace," the older of the two nurses replied, her expression sad. They were good people, Joan noted. No hint of malice in their eyes or demeanor that made her suspicious; rather, they cared deeply for the duke. It reassured her.

"She's still asleep, if you'd wish to see her, Your Grace," the other nurse added, hand on the doorknob to open the room for them.

"Yes, thank you," he said sadly as he made his way through the door.

Joan followed behind, the aroma of cinnamon

and clove, sweet and bitter all at once, intensifying as she entered the darkened room. The warmth of the room made the scent overpowering, and she fought to breath steadily. It was choking, as if death hovered above them, weighing down the air.

As her eyes adjusted to the dim candlelight, she made out the furnishings of the room as well as the bed where Rowles led them.

Joan's heart ached at the sight of the duchess. Small, frail, and still; it was hard to imagine this woman had fought anyone, let alone two nurses and a footman. Under the bedcovers, her chest rose slowly. Each breath held a long pause between. Joan was no stranger to death. Her mother had died when she was ten, and her father five years after; most recently, her brother. No, death was a companion at this point, an unwanted but very real one. However, this was different. Rather than the ripping of a loved one's life from a family's hands and heart, this was a slow, methodical descent into the grave. As if the duchess was taking one step with each breath, bringing herself closer and closer.

Joan had seen the result of death, but never the process, and it was a sobering experience.

"Mother?" Rowles whispered softly. Gently, he traced the line of her forehead, swiping a wayward gray curl from her mobcap. "Can you hear me?"

Joan silently counted his efforts as futile, only to

be surprised by the stirring of the woman's hand as her fingers twitched. Joan looked to her face, but saw no change in the woman's expression. More than anything, she wished to see the duchess open her eyes. So much could be read there.

Joan looked down to her own fisted hands. How she hated feeling powerless! It was an accompaniment to death, she supposed. Feeling unable to mourn enough, or to comfort those who mourned as well—it was never adequate. A constant emptiness that would never again be filled, and her heart ached for Rowles. He stood so close beside her that his hands nearly brushed her dress. Joan's fingers twitched, then slowly arched toward his, touching him slightly, then finding home as her hand was surrounded by his. Warmth seeped through her, and she squeezed softly, communicating with action what words couldn't convey.

Rowles addressed her with a small, sorrowful nod of thanks.

She returned it with a tip of her lips, and glanced back to his mother.

"What…" Joan started, then hesitated.

"Go on," Rowles urged.

"What would you wish to tell her, if she could hear you right now?" Joan finished, her voice soft and tender.

Rowles exhaled a mirthless laugh as he turned to Joan. "So much, but…" He looked to his mother.

"I'd want to tell her I love her, and regardless of her condition, I've always loved her. But...I think even more, I'd wish to tell her about you." His voice was barely more than a whisper. "She always wanted Robert to marry, but he didn't, and now he's gone. When she was healthy, she always wanted grandchildren and it is painful to think that now, when it's too late, she would have had that possible future to look forward to." He breathed deeply.

"Go on," Joan encouraged.

He turned to her, then back to his mother. Kneeling beside the bed, he withdrew his hand from Joan and placed both on his mother's frail one. "Mother, I want you to meet Joan. She's to be my wife."

Joan blinked back tears.

Rowles continued. "She is the loveliest, kindest, most honest and intelligent woman I've ever met, and through some miracle she has accepted me." He gave a low chuckle of disbelief. "We talk for hours, and she continues to challenge my thinking, my opinions, and I'm a better man for it. She is good, Mother. Her heart is benevolent and selfless, and so much more. I...wish you could meet her. Yet maybe this is for the best. You're not well. So I pray to God that you can hear my words even as you sleep, and that they comfort you."

Joan reached up to wipe a tear from her cheek as Rowles stood and reached for her hand. She gripped it tightly. "What beautiful words."

"It was nothing but the truth," he answered and turned to meet her eye to eye.

She read the honesty in his expression, and it fed her soul. "I know. Yet another reason I am grateful to be yours."

Rowles swallowed as if tamping down his emotions before speaking. "Thank you for suggesting I talk to her."

Joan nodded. "I...did the same for my father when he passed. My mother as well."

"Experience can be a painful teacher."

"Indeed it can be," Joan agreed.

With a soft sigh, Rowles nodded once and gestured to the door. "I think it's time to leave her in peace."

Joan followed him out into the hall. He studied the nurses. "Please notify me at once if there is any change. Any at all."

"Of course, Your Grace." The younger nurse curtsied.

Rowles thanked them and led Joan back down the hall. Her maid met them at the front door as they all climbed into the carriage.

"Penderdale House," Rowles instructed the driver, and they were soon off and down the street heading toward Grosvenor Square. The carriage was quiet, the sound of the horseshoes on cobbles and breathing the only sounds. Joan was deep in thought, debating on whether to speak to Rowles concerning the last revelation she needed to divulge, or whether she should wait.

Turning her focus to his face, she read the tension there, but it was less than before, as if speaking to his mother had lifted some of the burden. Indecision followed her as they slowed before her house and all exited from the carriage.

"Will you have tea?" Joan offered.

Rowles gave her a nod. "Yes, thank you. I need to speak to your brother as well."

"Of course," Joan agreed, and as they entered her home, she handed a footman her reticule and sent a maid off to procure tea for the green salon.

"Morgan is likely in his study. He should be finished with his business in town," Joan said over her shoulder as Rowles followed. The first to enter through the open door, she noticed three letters on the top of the desk. Curious, she went over to the desk and scanned them quickly.

Three letters.

Three different messages.

Irritated, she wondered whose brilliant plan it was to constantly send false messages along with valid ones to confuse the recipient. It hadn't worked so far, so why would they keep trying? She'd rather thought criminals were more inventive than that.

She read the third letter and paused.

Rounding the desk, she lifted all three letters and

compared them, her heart racing as she checked, then double-checked her suspicions.

"Joan? Is something amiss?" Rowles's voice interrupted her scattered thoughts.

"Good God, they're setting a trap," she whispered, her eyes shifting from one page, to the next, then back. "They want to find out…" She paused, then glanced to Rowles, then back to the pages.

Well, she had been wondering if today was the day to reveal her truth.

It looked like there wasn't any other option.

"Rowles…there's something I need to tell you," she said with an unsteady voice, even as her hands quickly rolled up the parchments and tucked them under her arm. "But I'll have to tell you in the carriage. No. Wait." She paused, regarding him critically, then said, "I *will* explain later, but…I need you to trust me." Heart pounding, she breathed deeply, trying to slow the wild galloping of her heart.

"Whatever you need."

Joan nodded. "I need you to hire a hack and pick me up at the park, east gate. And I need you to run."

"A hack?" Rowles frowned. "Why, when we can—"

"I promise to explain," Joan cut in. "But we haven't the time now. Morgan is in danger."

Then Rowles said the most beautiful words she'd ever heard. "I'll be there in fifteen minutes," he said. And all but ran out the study door.

He trusted her.

Her heart swelled with the power of it.

Only to sink.

Because he trusted her now.

Would he trust her when he found out the truth?

That was a question she wished she could already answer.

Twenty-five

ROWLES RUSHED DOWN THE HALL AND OUT THE door, only to take a leisurely pace to his carriage— should anyone be watching. And it was Mayfair, so it was to be assumed that someone was, indeed, always watching. He took his carriage out of Grosvenor Square far enough to find a street that had several hacks lining the side, all awaiting fares. Instructing the driver to stop on the next street, he stepped from his own carriage and quickly found a hack to hire.

In less than fifteen minutes, he was arriving by the designated gate. A woman dressed in widow's garb was waiting. As the horses stopped, the woman slowly approached the hack.

Rowles considered the woman with some suspicion, since he couldn't see her face with the dark veil in place. She approached the driver and spoke an address, not hesitating when the driver questioned her command.

Rowles instantly recognized Joan's voice and opened the carriage door for her, helping her in. As the carriage door closed, the hack moved onward, apparently realizing the current occupant was acquainted with the new one.

He wasn't sure where to start because there were so many questions. First, she seemed to address this situation so easily. Had she done this before? Was it a usual occurrence for her to hire a hack and traipse about London all alone? Or with someone else? And if so, whom?

Jealousy over a phantom challenger ate at his soul.

Joan slid the veil from her head and observed him with a hesitant expression. The veil made a rustling sound as she set it beside her, worrying her lip with her teeth as she did so. Taking a deep breath, she spoke. "You have questions."

"That's an understatement," Rowles replied, careful to keep his tone even.

Joan sighed, having expected this but feeling unequal to the task. "When I was a little girl, I watched my father work." She smoothed the veil as if needing something to do, as if the story made her restless. "He would lay out parchments and linen paper and study them, comparing various things with this immense stack of reference books that never left his desk. Always curious, I would ask what he was doing, and eventually, he showed me."

Rowles stilled, listening, her words putting him ill at ease for some reason, as if the twist to the story were about to be revealed.

"I would read the reference books my father had on this desk, and eventually I started to see what he saw…only I was better than even he was at detecting it."

"Detecting what, exactly?" Rowles asked carefully.

Joan compressed her lips and glanced to her hands, wringing them once before righting her expression and meeting his gaze unflinchingly. "Forgery."

Rowles frowned. "Forgery?" That answer had taken him by surprise.

"Yes, my father worked for the War Office, assisting with document study for forgery as well as other things that could determine the validity or falsifying of evidence."

"I see." Rowles leaned back in the carriage, studying her, waiting for her to continue and confirm his suspicions. When she said nothing, he prompted, "And now…you work for the War Office?"

"In a fashion," Joan admitted, biting her lip once more. "Not like Morgan does, but…well…he started bringing home missives…things that if they were real…could prove helpful. If they were forgeries, or meant to confuse—for example, sending out two messages, one true and one false—I could tell which was the forgery, at least usually. I've been wrong once or twice. Thankfully, those were not dangerous situations."

"And?" Rowles asked, the initial shock filtering into a cold understanding.

"And I can. So…I've been assisting my brother for a few years."

"Good Lord, you've been at this for years?"

"Er, yes?" Joan answered with an apologetic tone. "It's good work, and I've helped our country quite a bit."

"You're more like Joan of Arc than I originally thought."

"I rather thought the idea was poetic, I confess. But I digress." Her features settled into an expression of seriousness. "Morgan was evaluating three missives. Those were the pages I took from his desk." She withdrew them from under her black cape. "And I noticed something… Come, sit by me so I can lay these on the seat."

Rowles quickly switched seats, the warmth of Joan beside him melting away some of the harsh truth of her words. She laid out the missives and started pointing to a few words.

"The locations are all different, but I noticed they were quite closely clustered together."

"And?"

"And I noted the dates were the same, but something didn't sit right with me. The missives are about securing the 'relic.' But nothing we've done recently has been with this sort of smuggling. And then I started thinking. Why would they give locations all close together? If you were trying to keep someone from showing up at the right location, wouldn't you want them widely scattered so it was more difficult?" she postulated.

"I suppose," Rowles agreed slowly. He was still trying to wrap his mind around the concept that Joan, his Joan, was a spy of sorts. Or at least an aide to the War Office. Good Lord. His chest tightened at the idea, the knowledge of it sitting like a rock in his stomach, weighing him down. She was undertaking dangerous work.

Unaware of his internal struggle, she continued. "They clustered them together because it's a trap. They don't care where the War Office agent arrives. The group of miscreants will all be close enough to do whatever they intend to do. And they used the word 'relic.' Relics are usually holy items from the saints."

"Yes, like the chains from St. Peter in Rome."

"Exactly. Rowles…" She took a slow breath, her body angling to study his face fully. She swallowed, her green eyes troubled. "My name with the War Office is Saint."

Understanding smashed into him like a hammer. "Good God, they're after you?" Rowles's muscles locked down as if preparing for a brawl. So help him, no one would touch her, not as long as he drew breath.

"Which is why Morgan left," Joan continued. "He must have figured it out. I dispatched word to the War Office to send assistance, but I didn't want to linger and wait till they arrived."

"I can't say I agree, but I do understand. I don't like the idea of you being so close to danger."

Joan shrugged. "But this doesn't happen often—the danger part. Morgan will throttle me after I arrive and we take care of the situation. I'm sure I'll endure the lecture of a lifetime."

"He's not the only one who will be lining up to lecture you," Rowles commented softly.

Joan's brow arched, and she met his gaze unflinchingly. "I do not require your approval, Rowles."

The words hit him like a punch to the gut, because at once he knew they were the truth. They were engaged, yes. But not married. And she was her own person, with decisions that were hers alone to make, this being one of them.

And she had trusted him with this secret of hers.

"You're right, but as your impulse is to protect your brother, my impulse is to protect *you*," he answered. "So I will do my best to understand this. I ask you to give me time to adjust as well."

Joan's expression softened. "Forgive me. Yes, of course." She sighed. "It's not an excuse, but aside from my brother, you're the only one who knows, and you're also the only one with an opinion that truly matters to me." Her eyes dropped to her hands as she picked at her gloves. "I know it's strange, and not the usual set of activities for a lady, but I can't imagine doing anything else." She lifted a shoulder.

"And I also know that…my skills…are not conventional. Morgan warned me…so often…about how my involvement with the war office could be taken as less than ladylike, and likely make me the object of scorn. It's not the usual vocation of a gently bred woman. Intrigue is far more dangerous than needlework."

Rowles could easily imagine Morgan's worries; he shared a few as well.

"But I'm not any of those things," she continued. "I'm just…me. And for some reason, God gave me a skill. Not using it to help others seems such a waste. So, here I am."

Rowles nodded once, then reached out, grasped her fidgeting hands within his, and squeezed once, twice, then held her fingers. "One of the very first things that captured my attention about you was your ability to see through me, the world, the injustices that surround us. It makes sense now, that you are able to peel back the lies to see the truth beneath, but I'll never forget how you looked at me, your eyes piercing my very soul while we waltzed that first time and you gave me a lovely gift."

As he spoke, her body relaxed and she leaned against him, her shoulder settling against his arm. She gave a small laugh. "Morgan thought I'd given myself away with that comment. It was too 'telling,' he'd said."

"It was, but not in the way he likely assumed. It gave me hope. It removed the lie that I'd been feeding with my fear. It set me free in so many ways. Because even though I didn't know you well, I believed you."

"I was telling the truth."

"I know." He leaned over and kissed the top of her head, inhaling the sweet scent of lemon. "I know you were. And that's why it was so powerful. There's a verse, one that I use in my lectures quite frequently, especially when we are talking about social issues or current problems—'The truth shall make you free.'"

Joan nodded. "It does."

"Yes, it does. And we don't realize how much of our lives are dictated by the lies we've believed, and we walk around with chains dragging…but truth cuts those away. And you…you did that. And what I'm trying to say is, I'd have to be a truly selfish creature to want to keep that power all to myself and not appreciate how your skill does and will impact the world."

Joan took a slow breath, her body trembling. With an abrupt shift, she lifted her head from his shoulder, tugged her hands free from his grip, then reached up and grasped his chin, pulling it down to meet her lips in a tender and moving kiss.

Her lips captured his, the flavor of salty tears making the kiss even more dear as she cupped his jaw and leaned into him, melting.

Gently, he kissed her back, his hands reaching up to hold her arm and draw her in closer.

He nibbled on her lower lip, savoring its petal-soft texture as his tongue ran along the seam of her lips, only to have the carriage come to a halt.

Stealing one final kiss, he leaned back. "Well, Joan of England...what's the plan?"

Joan's hazel eyes sharpened, and she looked from him to the carriage door and back. "Call me Saint."

And with a determined stiffening of her back, she looked out the window and nodded. "So here's the plan..."

Twenty-six

I do not fear men-at-arms; my way has been made plain before me. If there be men-at-arms, my Lord God will make a way for me to go to my Lord Dauphin. For that am I come.

—*Joan of Arc*

THE PLAN WAS SIMPLE: WAIT TILL SHE WAS CERTAIN Morgan was in that particular location and then intervene. Whomever it was wouldn't be looking for a woman, so she had the element of surprise going for her, as well as the powerful stance of the duke beside her. The goal was to get Morgan out of danger as quickly as possible before anyone was the wiser.

It should be easy.

But Joan's heart was pounding like a drum, and her hands were damp beneath her gloves. She'd never done anything like this before. It was all "what if" whenever Morgan walked her through protecting herself.

Little did he know he was also teaching her to protect him.

"Over there by the inn," Joan whispered as she pointed to three men standing idly next to a hitching post for horses. They had mounts close but seemed restless, as if searching for something. One patted his chest, then rubbed as if ensuring something was secure. She made a mental note.

Rowles nodded. "What if Morgan isn't here, but at one of the nearby places?"

Joan had already considered that. "Give it a few minutes. If I know Morgan, he arrived early and went to the tavern to get a good view of the situation. He's likely inside right now and will come out in a little bit. That way he won't be recognized as just arriving at the determined time, making him appear as the intended target. This location was the most defensible, and he likely guessed it wasn't about picking the correct place, since all would be watched. He'd pick the location that was the easiest to manipulate."

"Never before have I been so grateful for my profession," Rowles replied with a chuckle. "Being a professor may seem boring to some, but it's far less dangerous, with less intrigue."

"Of that we can both agree. And I wouldn't consider it boring. Your job is to teach…what a gift! But I digress. Do you have the time?" Joan asked.

Rowles withdrew his gold pocket watch. "Quarter of five."

"Perfect," Joan responded and nodded to the door of the Hound and Hare. "Look."

Sure enough, Morgan stepped out and glanced at his own pocket watch.

"Follow me." Joan opened the carriage door and allowed Rowles to step out first, then assist her out as well. She'd donned her veil once more, keeping her face hidden from view.

As she took Rowles's arm, she started toward Morgan, who froze as he saw them approach. Swallowing her rising trepidation, she squeezed Rowles's arm as they strolled, and as if reading her mind, he slowed.

"Good sir," he called out. "Thank you for meeting me."

Joan released a sigh of relief. "Yes, thank you," she added. "Will you come with us?"

Morgan's stare hardened, and he looked toward the three men waiting by the hitching post.

"Please, my brother waits to meet you?" Joan implored. The men at the post were nudging one another, as if suspicious, and mounted their horses. With a unified front, they started to approach Morgan. Joan held her breath as the riders came toward them. With a sigh, she shifted to the left slightly as they crossed the muddy street. The riders approached cautiously.

"You, what's the time?" one asked Morgan, the other two riders sidling up beside him. With a loud shriek, Joan slipped in the mud—purposely, of course—and grabbed for the nearest horse's reins, noting the rider was the one who had patted his chest pocket earlier. The horse sidestepped and bucked, dismounting its rider, then bolted down the road. Mud was flung from its hooves as it thundered away, leaving the rider dazed as he sat in the mud.

Joan could see Morgan's approach in her peripheral vision, and with the remaining time till he tried to stop her, she groaned an apology and bent down to dust off the thrown man, as if trying to assist. "Allow me." She offered a hand as Rowles held her elbow. Stepping from him, she wiggled her fingers to the man, praying he'd accept her offering. All he had to do was take her hand; the rest would be simple.

He blinked, as though confused as to why a lady would do such a thing, but he accepted her hand after a moment of debate. With all her strength, Joan hauled him upright, forcing the man forward. With a quick release of his hand, she pressed both of hers on his chest as if to steady him and quickly slipped the missive from his interior jacket pocket, then tucked it up her sleeve before he could notice.

She didn't dare look at her brother, who no doubt had seen everything. She'd have some explaining to do later, but she was convinced once he understood the end, he'd forgive the means.

She hoped.

The man apologized for his loss of balance, and

Joan started to back away, only to bump into a solid chest, yet her body froze and melted all at once, giving her the sweetest sensation of safety.

"I'll assist you, my lady," Rowles stated smoothly, his solid form lending strength to her.

Joan's eyes went to her brother, who was all but curling his lip in frustration as he neared, an icy edge to his scrutiny.

One rider gave chase to the runaway horse, and apparently realizing they no longer had an element of surprise, both the unhorsed man and the final rider backed away slowly and then took off. Perhaps they were convinced they hadn't come upon the proper targets—or so she hoped.

With a defiant glare, she met her brother's hard stare. She looked from the coach to him and raised a brow, hoping he could see it under her veil.

Rowles grasped her elbow and led her toward the hack, his own expression hard and vigilant.

A third set of footsteps had Joan releasing a relieved breath as she turned back to see Morgan following them.

In a moment, they were all seated in the hack.

"Am I to leave my mount here?" Morgan asked in an acid tone.

"For the moment. We can send a footman later," Joan replied softly, keeping her voice low. The hack lurched forward, carrying them back toward Grosvenor Square.

"And while I'm sure I don't want to know, why in the bloody—"

"To save you," Joan cut in, all but tearing off her veil as the tears threatened to spill for the second time that day. Dear Lord, she'd been terrified! Who knew what those men wanted to do to Morgan if they had captured him? What was he thinking, going at it alone like that? She asked him that very question.

"Why? Why would you run headlong into danger like that?"

"I could ask you the very same question!" Morgan all but shouted. "And you, allowing her?" Morgan glared at Rowles.

"He's not my warden," Joan shot back.

Morgan snorted. "Maybe someone needs to be!"

"More like *you* need one! Didn't you read all three letters? They—"

"They were bloody after *you*!" Morgan yelled. "You, Joan! They wanted Saint! What else could I do? I was going to take them all out—"

Joan shook her head. "I know they wanted me, but that doesn't mean you… What do you mean, take them all out? You were going to murder three men? Then what? Wait till more came along after them? Kill them too? No! You leave it and don't make it so easy for them to trap you! Good Lord, Morgan, think with your brain, not your biceps." Joan leaned back and sighed, glancing heavenward, praying for the patience she didn't have.

"I will never, ever allow them to harm you," he vowed.

"They won't. Because I won't do anything as foolish as you—"

"You just did."

"Because I was saving *you* because *you* decided to do something stupid. If *you* don't do something stupid, *I* won't either!" Joan yelled.

Morgan blinked, snorted, and crossed his arms like a petulant child.

"You look like a scolded five-year-old," Joan retorted.

"You sound like an old fishwife."

"You both have no idea how thankful you ought to be," Rowles cut in. Joan turned her attention to him, for the first time noticing the tension in his face, the tight draw of his lips.

Morgan must have sensed it, too, for he fell quiet as well.

"You're so blessed to have each other. Stop your bickering and appreciate the fact you're both alive and well. Good Lord, my heart nearly stopped, watching my betrothed singlehandedly halt horses and pickpocket a thief." He looked heavenward as if also praying for strength.

"You saw that, did you?" Joan asked sheepishly.

"I'd hate to bump into you on Bond Street. You'd rob me blind." He softened the words with a warm tone. "My Joan, a woman of many talents."

Morgan froze, then moved his attention between them. "I gather that he knows?"

"Yes," Joan replied, unable to stop herself from returning Rowles's warm expression.

"I see. I suppose that went better than I expected."

"Although I'd much prefer to be told information before I find myself on the way to perform some rescue in the future."

"Understood." Joan nodded, her smile still firm on her lips.

"Thank you," Morgan added a moment later. "I suppose it's in order to say as much."

"I should think so," Joan replied with a touch of irony. "Please, don't take such action again."

"And have you follow me? I think not," Morgan replied. "How did you discover it, anyway?"

Joan went on to explain how they'd been searching for him, only to remember with sadness the condition of Rowles's mother.

"When we arrived back at home, we should check on your mother," she added, her earlier joy evaporating.

"What happened?" Morgan asked, leaning forward on his seat and resting his elbows on his knees.

"She had an episode. Only this time she confiscated the bottle of laudanum and started to drink…" Rowles's expression closed off, his blue eyes full of walled-off sorrow.

"I'm sorry," Morgan whispered, his brows knitting together as he spoke.

"So far it hasn't been fatal, but that does lead me to the reason we were searching for you." Rowles sighed. "I have an important question for the both of you to consider."

Joan nodded, sharing a look with her brother.

Rowles continued. "Should the laudanum prove fatal for my mother, I'll be in mourning. Which doesn't exactly prevent our wedding, but it might not be looked upon with approval should we wed so quickly after my mother's passing. The question is: In the event that my mother passes, what plan of action do you wish to take?"

Joan released a pent-up breath. She hadn't considered that the duchess's death would inhibit their wedding, yet as Rowles mentioned it, she wondered how she had missed such an obvious problem.

"You could marry by special license tomorrow," Morgan suggested.

"If my mother makes it through the night, yes, but then I would be in mourning for our wedding trip," Rowles added. "I suppose the question truly is, while it matters not for me—my only concern is for Joan's reputation—what do you wish to do? Wait till mourning is over, or marry regardless?" Rowles posed the question to Joan, his blue eyes trying to keep his own feelings on the topic hidden.

Joan reached out and touched his face, cupping his jaw.

Morgan cleared his throat.

"Tomorrow. If your mother makes it through the night, we shall marry tomorrow." Joan stroked his cheek with her thumb, watching as his eyes betrayed his relief at her words. "I don't wish to wait any longer than I need to. You have my heart, might as well give me your name." She bit her lip at her bold words.

He lifted her hand from his face and kissed her fingers. "I'll go to Doctors' Commons in the morning, if possible. If not—"

"We shall cross that bridge when we come to it."

Twenty-seven

THE HACK DELIVERED ROWLES BACK TO WHERE his carriage was waiting. In the interest of propriety, Morgan and Joan took the hack to their home, rather than have Joan accompany him back to his mother's rooms. With a promise to send word, he said goodbye to the two siblings and gave his driver instructions to return to his mother's home. As he sank into the carriage seat, his body slowly relaxed its tension. There was so much information to digest, to process, and he wasn't sure where to begin.

Joan was uncommon, that much he'd known from the start, but her revelation of earlier was far more than an uncommon beauty and spirit. She worked for the bloody War Office as a consultant of sorts because she could differentiate between true missives and forgeries. Of all the astounding things. Had someone told him, he'd never have believed it, yet when it was so apparently true that even the War Office of England trusted her judgment on such matters, how could he do anything but trust her?

He'd be lying to himself if he said there hadn't

been a sharp pain of suspicion trickling into his heart after hearing her confession. His mother's condition had rendered him suspicious and fearful of the unknown. However, he had come to the conclusion that he could trust Joan's confession, because he trusted *her*. And that was enough.

She had told him all her secrets, knowing he could take them poorly or even cast her off. Her bravery humbled him, inspired him, and truly captivated him even more. However, what didn't sit right was the fact that he had a secret he was keeping from her.

Morgan had told him in confidence, giving him the choice to tell or keep silent concerning Joan's parentage. He had decided to tell her, but in light of today's events, it seemed like too much for one day.

Too much truth.

Too much uncovered.

Maybe he would wait till tomorrow.

It had been a taxing afternoon, with the rescue mission for Morgan that was far less eventful than it could have been, but that didn't dismiss the danger Joan had taken on. Rowles shook his head as he considered how she'd taken matters into her own hands.

Which reminded him: what exactly did she retrieve? He forgot to ask, but certainly it was something of note. And how in the world did she know it was there?

Marriage to Joan would certainly not be dull.

No, indeed, marriage would be one big adventure after another. Tomorrow he'd go to Doctor's Commons and procure the license, and likely she and Morgan were already making arrangements for a wedding. It was almost too wonderful to bear—having her choose him, and without delay. Her words had echoed his own sentiments, but he wouldn't pressure her. No, it was on her terms.

A time and season for everything—including weddings—and he wouldn't rush his for selfish reasons.

That wasn't love.

And Joan deserved everything he could offer.

He remembered his words as he had proposed. He wasn't the best man, but his love would be the best love.

And he vowed they would be true.

The carriage halted in front of the town home that housed his mother, and with a deep sigh of concern for what he would find within the doors, he slowly stepped from the carriage and took the steps.

The door opened, and a footman bowed as a relieved expression lit his face. "Your Grace, please come in. The doctor sent word." The footman motioned to the stairs and Rowles nodded, taking the steps two at a time.

As he reached the landing, the older doctor bowed at Rowles's approach. The two nurses from earlier curtsied and stood beside the doctor.

"Doctor."

"Your Grace," the doctor greeted. "I have evaluated your mother's condition and it is in fact deteriorating. I wouldn't expect her to last the night. I wanted you to be aware, should you need to make any arrangements."

Rowles released a silent breath and nodded in understanding. "I see. May I?" He gestured to the closed door.

"Yes, of course." The doctor opened the door and waited as Rowles walked into the room. Candles were lit, giving the room a cheery glow but the air was still, as if death lingered.

The furnishings, all so familiar, gave the room a comforting feel, even with the stillness. The fire burned quietly in the hearth as Rowles stood beside his mother's bed, then kneeled.

Her expression was drawn, her lips tight and unmoving, as if already frozen in that position. He placed a hand on her folded ones, the chill of her skin sending shivers through his body. Her breathing was labored, much more so than earlier; with short pants, she was breathing in and out, quarter breaths rather than full ones, as if her lungs couldn't take in more than a teaspoonful of air at a time.

"Mother?" Rowles asked, whispered, begged.

Her eyelids didn't flicker. The only movement was the short breaths that were both silent and useless.

He squeezed her hands tenderly, his eyes closing against the brimming tears that threatened to fall.

The guilt was as bad as the sorrow because he wouldn't miss who she'd become.

But he'd forever miss who she had once been.

But that...that woman he'd lost a long time ago, long before his brother died. And now all that was left was a shell that wasn't a shadow of who was once the grand Duchess of Westmore.

Saying goodbye was bittersweet. Sweet because she would suffer no longer. Bitter because it meant that he was the last one.

The only surviving member of his family.

He breathed in slowly, the stillness alerting him. He turned to his mother, watching for the panting breaths and finding none.

Stillness.

Frozen.

He held his own breath, waiting to see if she'd take a belated breath, shift, do anything to remind him that she was still present.

A moment later, her body relaxed, releasing its final breath as her chest settled forever, a quiet heart and a mind finally at peace.

Rowles bowed his head, not knowing what to say to the God he'd studied so much.

But study was different than actually knowing someone.

"'He is close to the brokenhearted...'" The

verse floated through his mind on a whisper, and he allowed the tears to far freely, thankful for the privacy of the room as he mourned the loss of his mother. Bittersweet, it was so deeply bittersweet. He kept reminding himself that she wasn't suffering any longer. She was at rest, she was with Robert and their father.

But the hard part about grief was that it was selfish. Because the one hurting wasn't the one who was lost.

It's you.

The one left behind is you.

The one going on with life is you.

The one dealing with the aftermath is you.

The loss is irrevocable.

And there was no way to deal with the pain, but to acknowledge it. So Rowles mourned the fresh loss of his mother, and the earlier loss of his brother, and even the long-ago loss of his father. So much loss.

It weighed on him, like lead weights on his shoulders as he allowed the broken parts of his heart to be heard, as the tears flowed.

Yet the beautiful part of loss is the remembrance.

You lose someone because you once had them in your life, and that was the beauty. You cannot have one without the other, two sides of the same coin. So as the fire burned in the grate, as his mother's body lay at rest, Rowles remembered.

Everything his mother was—good and bad, kind and shrewd, unwell and healthy.

He remembered everything his brother had been, and spent time reminiscing about his father.

The memories breathed, even when the people in them had long ago stopped. As time passed, the fire turned to coals and Rowles stood from his place beside his mother's deathbed and walked toward the door. The doctor had left, probably long ago, and the nurses stood as he exited the room.

"She passed," he stated simply.

"Our condolences, Your Grace," they each said in turn. "We will begin the preparations."

"Thank you. I will be by later. I need to make some further arrangements," Rowles said in a wooden voice, then took his leave. As he descended the stairs, he took a deep, cleansing breath. Soon he was back in his carriage with instructions for the driver to take him home. He needed to inform their solicitor and make arrangements for the burial. But most importantly, he needed to send word to Joan.

There would be no need to take a visit to Doctors' Commons.

As of today, he was in mourning.

Twenty-eight

*It is true I wished to escape; and so
I wish still. Is not this lawful for all
prisoners?*

—Joan of Arc

THE CLOCK HAD STRUCK NINE IN THE MORN-
ing when the butler arrived with a missive. It had
been a difficult night for Joan, and she'd awoken
uncommonly early, only to find her brother in
a similar state. They'd adjourned to the library
after breakfast. Joan took the linen paper from
his silver tray, immediately recognizing Rowles's
seal. She'd been waiting, and she couldn't
open the missive quickly enough to satisfy her
curiosity.

Dearest Joan,

*I regret to inform you that my mother passed last
night. It was a peaceful passing, but I am currently*

*making arrangements for her funeral, which will
take place in two days' time. Hold my heart close;
it's in your hands. I will see you tomorrow.*

*All my affection,
Rowles*

Joan placed her hand over her mouth as she read
the missive again, her heart plummeting as she felt
the sorrow in her beloved's note.

"Is something amiss?" Morgan asked from his
chair near a bookshelf. He set the novel he was
reading aside and stood, his face furrowed in
concern.

"His mother passed," Joan answered, her hand
falling limp at her side.

Morgan paused in his approach and gave a curt
nod. "I see. Well, she's at peace now. Heaven knows
she hasn't been at rest for nearly half a decade. I
suppose it's a blessing."

"It's still a loss, Morgan," Joan chided gently.
"And I'm sure Rowles is hurting."

Morgan shook his head. "Yes, yes, you're correct.
I didn't intend to be hard-hearted, merely logical."

"I understand." Joan quickly forgave him, her
attention straying back to the missive.

"This will mean that he will not procure a special license today," Morgan said softly.

"I know," Joan replied. Her selfish heart had

understood that first off. "I understand and we need to honor his mother."

"The rules of mourning are not hard and fast, Joan. Give it a few weeks for the reading of the banns, and you shouldn't raise too many questions with a wedding. Not to be a cad, but the whole of London knew his mother's condition. They won't expect him to spent the six months in mourning, not fully."

Joan shrugged. "I understand, but I won't let my impatient nature pressure him into anything."

Morgan chuckled. "Ah, dear sister. I don't think you're any more impatient than he is, and that is exactly as it should be."

Joan giggled in spite of herself. "You know, I do believe you've made a correct assessment."

"What was that?" He cupped his ear and grinned. "You said I was correct about something? It is truly a time of miracles. First you come to my rescue, which thankfully was uneventful, and then you give me credit. I can die a happy man."

"You can't die yet, so don't get too comfortable with the concept. Which reminds me…" Joan quit the room and quickly ran up the stairs to her bed-chamber. She had withdrawn the pilfered missive from her widow's cloak and placed it in her desk for safekeeping. She quickly plucked it from her desk drawer and returned to the library where Morgan waited.

"This." She lifted the missive. "I'm not sure what it is, but I noticed the older man, the one I pulled from his horse, patting his chest. He patted his pocket, as if reassuring himself it was still there. I thought it might be important, so I stole it at the first opportunity."

"At one time, I regretted teaching you so much. As it turns out, it was somewhat useful." Morgan stood beside her as she slid open the shallow wax seal. Two letters fell out, and she opened the first. Ink was smeared across the top, as if the letter had been written in haste, closed before the ink fully dried. Joan read the words, her face puckering as she did so.

"Did you ever find out why the false orders sent that prisoner to the London Tower?" Joan asked, rereading the letter.

"I think we may have uncovered it." Morgan's expression lifted as he read over her shoulder.

"Indeed."

"I learned he made a deal with the magistrate to give information, and it seems as if those he named got wind of it."

"So they were going to silence him by making it look like an accident at the London Tower," Joan deduced.

"Exactly, which would likely have worked, had you not discovered the forgery of the sentencing papers."

"I wonder..." Joan opened the second letter. With a gasp, she read through the sentencing paper, so much like the first, but like it a forgery. "They are wanting the prisoner moved."

"From house arrest... Makes sense. It's easy to have an 'accident' when on the move. Any number of things could happen. It could be as simple as sabotaging the wheel of a carriage or spooking the horses."

"Indeed, there are a million ways to do murder. However, this proves their intentions. But these are directions to locate and eliminate this man, Walter Brewer. Is that the name of the prisoner?"

"Indeed," Morgan answered.

"So, those men..."

"Were to intercept you—Saint—to keep you from getting this particular forgery." He shook his head. "Ironic that you stole the very paper they were trying to keep from you." A dark chuckle slipped from his lips.

"But I wonder..." Joan turned the page over, studying it. "Morgan, this paper, the seal...it's forged but done so well... Could someone have infiltrated the magistrate's office?"

Morgan pinched the bridge of his nose. "I would like to say no, but it would most assuredly make sense, especially if this Mr. Brewer could name the traitor."

"That would certainly motivate someone to have him silenced permanently," suggested Joan.

"A traitor in the magistrate's office could easily slip pertinent information to whomever paid highest, or perhaps they were planted in that office to do that very job. Regardless, this needs to be investigated and stopped."

"I suggest you start by talking to Mr. Brewer and finding protection for him. Seems someone wants him dead."

"Indeed," Morgan agreed, then turned to leave the room. "I'm heading to the office. Please, stay here and allow me to do this."

"I always do. I only intervened when you did something half-cocked," Joan replied with derision.

"I will not confirm or deny your allegations, only stay." Morgan pointed, nodded, and then left. "I'll return this evening, and I'll be sure to let you know what we found out."

"Be safe!" Joan called out.

Morgan was already down the hall, calling for his carriage.

Joan sighed. This was the part she hated most, the waiting.

Because between the excitement of it all, there was a great deal of waiting.

Twenty-nine

AFTER DISPATCHING A LETTER TO JOAN FIRST thing in the morning, Rowles sat down with the family solicitor. The arrangements for the funeral were easily delegated to the funeral furnisher, who would see to all the details, giving his mother the remembrance she deserved.

The nurses attending his mother had washed and laid out her body, then proceeded to drape the entire room with black baize cloth. The furnisher would see to the hiring of the mutes, mourners, and jobbers to transport his mother's coffin to the family grave site, where she'd rest forever beside his father.

Rowles leaned back in his chair, closed his eyes, and breathed deeply. The sensation of relief over his mother's death warred against the guilt he suffered for feeling that way, and he was at a loss for how to address either. The funeral would be held the next evening, and he'd say his final goodbyes to the woman who gave him life. He'd choose to remember the good, the times of peace and health—not the slow, methodical destruction the malady had wreaked on her life, and the lives of those around her. It was over, and he'd been fighting for far too long.

He rose from his desk and called for a footman to ready his carriage, then thought better of it. Penderdale House wasn't far, and he needed to move, to walk, to have a moment of fresh air. He would look to the future, and that future held one woman—Joan. He desperately wanted to see her, hear her voice, revel in the intelligent conversation and kind spirit that had utterly taken his soul captive. In a word, he needed her. Collecting his hat, umbrella, and coat, he stepped out the door and started down the elm-lined street toward Grosvenor Square.

As expected, the light English rain was cleansing and refreshing, wiping the air of all the soot and dust and leaving a gentle fragrance in its wake. The leaves of the elms quivered as the small drops landed on them, a soft pattering noise following his progress as the rain touched the sidewalk. In less than fifteen minutes, he paused in front of the Penderdale door, knocking once.

The butler answered quickly, stepping aside to allow him entrance. "Your Grace."

Rowles nodded his appreciation. "Is Lady Joan receiving callers?"

With a nod, the butler led the way to the library. Rowles followed, his heart quickening with anticipation. He stepped into the well-lit room, and his soul immediately found peace as he took in her tender look.

"Your Grace," she said, welcoming him, and approached from her perch on a chair. "I've been concerned. How are you?" She lifted an arm, perhaps to offer comfort, but drew back as if having second thoughts.

Instinctively, he reached out and grasped her withdrawing hand, capturing it and lacing their fingers together as he pulled her a few inches closer. It wasn't exactly proper, but he didn't care. In two weeks, they would be married and he could hold her, kiss her, and love her whenever he chose.

If that wasn't heaven, he wasn't sure what was.

Joan squeezed his hand. "I'll have to adjust to being allowed to touch you, Your Grace."

"Rowles, if you please." He lifted her hand and kissed it softly. "I trust you'll make the transition smoothly. I shall give you abundant practice," he replied with a teasing grin. "It comforts my heart, seeing you."

"I've been worried," Joan confessed. "How are you, truly?"

Rowles shrugged. "As well as can be expected. I'm fighting more against my relief than my sorrow, and my guilt for feeling that way."

Joan's expression grew sympathetic. "You shouldn't bear guilt for such feelings."

"Perhaps, but that doesn't make them less real."

"Indeed. Is there any way I can help?" she asked, gesturing to a sofa and inviting him to sit. "Would you like tea?"

Rowles followed her to the sofa and took a seat beside her, thankful for the allowance of being so near her; betrothal had its benefits. "Yes, tea would be lovely."

Joan rang for tea.

"Now, you were about to tell me how I can help."

"Was I?" Rowles asked, distracted by her perfect lips and the fragrance of lemons that clung to her skin.

"Yes. When is the funeral? You said two days, but I wasn't sure if that changed between now and then."

The subject of the funeral was like icy water poured on his head, instantly cooling his amorous thoughts. "Yes, I've already taken care of all the details and hired those who will address those details."

"So tomorrow night?" Joan asked.

"Yes." Rowles answered.

"I want to go," she stated, her shoulders straightening with resolve.

Rowles paused. "It's…not usually an event women attend." He treaded cautiously, knowing she was certain of her own mind. But the thought of her out at night, with all the potential pickpockets and ruffians who would target such a large group of mourners, set his protective streak on fire.

"I'm more than able to take care of myself, and

I won't leave your side, regardless." She patted his hand, providing immeasurable comfort.

He drew a deep breath. "You might be one of the only women in attendance who is not a hired mourner." He needed to make certain she understood the full scope of her request.

"I'm aware. I attended my brother's and parents' funerals, I'm familiar," she asserted with a firm nod.

In truth, he wanted her to attend as well. To have her bolstering presence beside him as he walked the final steps in saying goodbye to his mother. It was a blessing he hadn't even thought to ask for, yet she gave it. "Very well, thank you. It will be a great comfort to have you there."

Her shoulders relaxed, and she nodded once. "I don't wish for you to walk through it alone. Not if I can help it. Thank you…for hearing me out."

"I will always…at least try," he amended with a lopsided grin, "to hear you out."

"I couldn't ask for more." Joan paused, then lifted his hand to her cheek.

His heart pounded at such a simple gesture that set his body on fire. "Joan." He whispered her name, his attention darting to her lips as he inched forward.

"Ah, Rowles!" Morgan's voice was like the second bucket of cold water tossed on him in the span of ten minutes. Biting back a growl, he gave an apologetic shrug to Joan and turned to his friend, who had a knowing smirk on his smug face. Rowles had never been more tempted to add a black eye to that arrangement.

"Good day to you as well," Rowles answered.

"My deepest condolences." Morgan's countenance sobered as he offered his respects.

"Thank you."

"And the funeral is tomorrow night?" Morgan asked just as his sister had a few moments before.

"Yes, and Joan has asked to attend." Rowles turned back to Joan, whose stare was steady on her brother, as if daring him to challenge it.

"Why am I not surprised," Morgan drawled. "I wouldn't expect anything less from her, I suppose. It's better to take her than to wait for her to sneak out on her own, eh, Joan?"

Rowles turned to Joan, a question on the tip of his tongue before she cut in.

"If my brother had taken me to the funeral he's mentioning, I wouldn't have needed to resort to such measures. Besides, I was perfectly safe. I dressed as a paid mourner, and when I found Morgan, I stuck by his side."

"Ah, that's where you got the widow's garb, and here I thought you kept an arsenal of disguises," Rowles teased.

"A woman never knows when she'll need to blend in," Joan replied with a haughty tone. "Regardless, my brother learned from his mistakes and took me to the next one."

"It's a sorry thing indeed that we've had to attend so many, Joan," Morgan added, his expression sad.

"Indeed, it is," Joan agreed softly. "It is."

"And one more, and let us pray it's the last for quite some time," Rowles finished.

"Will the procession begin at your house or...?" Morgan waited for Rowles to answer.

"Her body is resting at the house I set up for her, so we will travel from there to the grave site," Rowles stated.

"We will meet you at the house an hour before the procession begins." Morgan came to stand beside Rowles and placed a hand on his shoulder. "You'll not walk through this alone."

"Thank you," Rowles said with feeling. A new understanding flowed through him. This...this was his new family. The realization burned bright. They were his family, and he was theirs.

"Well, I need to attend to some paperwork," Morgan stated, as if the emotional atmosphere was too much for to him.

"Thank you for your condolences," Rowles said in parting as Morgan took his leave. With a pause, Morgan turned back and nodded, closing the door partway. Then his face appeared in the opening, and he made a point of narrowing his eyes as if communicating a threat.

Rowles nodded, understanding that the few

minutes of privacy were a gift. But with limits, within which he was fully expected to operate.

"Well, that was surprising." Joan blinked at her brother's disappearing back and turned to Rowles.

"I am forever in his debt," Rowles said as an answer and turned his attention to Joan. "Heaven knows how long I have till the tea arrives." He chuckled. "So, dear Joan, may I kiss you?" he whispered, his countenance softening as he took in the quick parting of her lips, the soft gasp of her breath, and the blush that highlighted her cheeks.

With a small nod, she lowered her gaze shyly.

He placed a finger under her chin, lifting it till her eyes met his. "I see you." He breathed the words, promised them. "I see your strength, your determination, your stubborn nature and fierce devotion. I see your capabilities, your kind heart, and the honesty that flows through your veins. I see the love you have for others, for your family, and beyond all my understanding, the love you have for me, and it touches my soul in ways I never knew existed."

Her green eyes widened, softened, and with the gentlest touch, her lips met his. Her hand cupped his chin, drawing him in as she deepened the kiss.

Rowles was undone.

He made love to her mouth, with every stroke of his tongue and graze of his lips; he worshiped her. His soul fused with hers, his heart matched her cadence as he pulled her in closer, his arms banding around her shoulders as his fingers traced down her arms, only to dance up and down her back, mapping every soft inch he touched.

"I love you," he whispered as he paused between kisses, needing to say the words, hear them in his own voice, speak them over her.

Without breaking contact, Joan said, "I love you."

The clinking of china filtered through Rowles's fevered mind, and after a moment, he kissed her one final time and reluctantly withdrew. He allowed his fingers to trace down her arms, savoring one last touch before he noted with approval her bee-stung lips.

Joan frowned as if confused, but as the maid came in with a tray of tea things, her eyes dawned with understanding as her cheeks bloomed with color anew.

Rowles squeezed her hand and nodded his thanks to the maid, who set the tea service on the small table before them.

Taking up her former place against the wall, awaiting the instructions of her mistress, the maid once again became a silent sentinel keeping watch.

Joan sighed softly; it was a sound of contentment but also wistfulness. "I'll pour. How would you like your tea?"

"Thank you. With cream and sugar, please." And with a grin he whispered, "However, nothing is as sweet as you, so why even bother?"

Her blush gave away her pleasure at the artless compliment.

And as Rowles sipped his tea, he couldn't help but thank the heavens that while he mourned, he was also blessed with the greatest promise of future joy. A life with Joan.

Thirty

JOAN TOOK IN A DEEP, DETERMINED BREATH through her nose as she focused on anything but her reflection.

She would stand by Rowles tonight as he said his final goodbyes to his mother, but in doing so, it would freshen the memories of her own goodbyes.

Her father.

Her mother.

Her brother.

So much loss.

The mourning clothes chafed at her skin, as if reminding her further of the pain of outliving loved ones. But regardless of the pain of her own memories, she wouldn't have Rowles walk the path ahead alone.

Like she hadn't let Morgan walk alone that night they mourned their father.

Or when they'd buried what remained of their brother after the fire that had taken his life.

No. If ever Morgan had needed her, it was when they'd buried his twin. He'd changed that day.

But death coming to an older person didn't make it less powerful in the experience of the loss.

Joan breathed deeply, then looked up. She studied her reflection. The deep-purple hue of the gown made her skin paler, or perhaps it was the effect painful memories have on a person. Her hair was in a simple chignon because tonight was a night when she'd wish to blend in.

With a reluctant sigh, she stood from her place before the mirror and stepped into the comfortable slippers laid out by her maid. The veil she donned next would hide much of her face, but it was still apparent she was a woman, and thus she would stand out since she wasn't going to walk among the hired mourners, who were usually women. No, she'd stay beside Rowles and Morgan.

Exactly where she should be.

It was odd, the fact that women didn't usually attend funerals. It made sense in some distorted aspect, given the low expectation for women's emotional stamina in grievous situations. Was it such a crime to shed a tear, to mourn a loss?

She shook off the indignation at the societal constriction and took her leave. As she took the stairs to the main floor, she noted that Morgan was already waiting. He was dressed in black. As she came to stand by his side, she prayed fervently that this would be the last funeral they would attend for quite some time.

"Are you certain you wish to come?" Morgan asked, even as he led her to the front of the house and their carriage.

"Yes," Joan replied directly.

"Very well, please, stay close—"

"I always have, haven't I?" Joan cut in, meeting his gaze.

Morgan conceded, "Yes, yes, you have. Even when I didn't know you were in attendance. You always stayed close."

Joan took Morgan's offered hand and stepped into the carriage, then took a seat and arranged her skirts. The carriage moved forward, and Joan took another deep breath.

"It's hard, isn't it?" Morgan broke the silence.

"Yes. Yes, it is."

"As much as we've mourned, you'd think we'd be accustomed to it by now."

"I have the distinct feeling that death is the one thing we will never grow familiar with."

Morgan sighed. "And honestly, it would be a detriment to our humanity if we did become so callous."

"Indeed," Joan agreed.

Soon they turned the corner that led them to the square where Rowles's mother's town house was located. Already the mourners were collected outside, lining the street. Black carriages were driven by Friesian horses with the customary black ostrich feather in their headbands. Jobbers stood by the horses, keeping them calm. The mutes waited by the front steps, near the six pages who were all dressed in black from head to toe. It was impressive, the number of people waiting to mourn the duchess. Regardless that most were hired, it was still an impressive number and a glorious tribute that Rowles had created for his mother.

Their carriage paused before the jobbers and rolled to a stop. One of the Westmore footmen stepped from the stairs and helped them from the carriage, then escorted their party to the front door and the awaiting butler. Joan looked around her, noting all the small details that would make the whole day even more memorable.

It would be lovely, if it wasn't a funeral.

Joan followed her brother down the hall and up the stairs. Black baize fabric was draped over every chair and table lining the hall as they approached the late duchess's final rooms. A nurse stood, disappeared into the dark room, then returned. Rowles followed her into the hall.

"Morgan, Lady Joan," Rowles said gently, as if they were the ones in mourning, not him.

Joan wanted to rush forward, place a hand on his shoulder or his cheek, and study his expression. Was he truly as well as he appeared to be? What exactly was going on in that beloved mind of his? Yet decorum reminded her to wait, to observe from a polite distance rather than be invasive.

"Your Grace." She used his formal title, as was necessary for the occasion. Offering a curtsy, she stood and came to stand beside him. "Are you well?" she asked softly.

"I'm better now," he offered, then reached down and grasped her hand. Lifting it, he placed a soft kiss on her gloved fingers. "Your presence is like a balm to my very soul."

Joan put on a brave face, but the concern lingered. A balm she might be, but that didn't eliminate the pain. "We are thankful to be here with you, to share in this with you."

"I'm blessed." Rowles nodded, then turned to Morgan. "Thank you."

"You've stood beside me often enough. I could do no less, my friend."

Rowles nodded and a nurse came from the darkened room. "Your Grace, all is ready."

Rowles turned to her and then to Morgan and motioned for them to step aside. His mother's body rested in her coffin within the sitting room to the left. The coffin was brought out into the hall, carried on the shoulders of the attendants. Rowles followed, and Morgan offered Joan his arm as they moved in behind him, following the procession. As they reached the front of the house, the jobbers assisted the attendants in loading the coffin into the carriage, and the procession began.

The carriage with the coffin started toward the duchess's final resting place as another took its place. Rowles offered his hand to Joan, and she stepped into the darkness of the carriage, followed by her brother and then her betrothed. It was a silent ride to the cemetery within the carriage, but without, the mourners cried, wailed, and called out.

After the carriage halted at the cemetery, Rowles stepped out and assisted her. He offered his arm, and when she grasped it, he drew her in tightly, protectively. It was well known that any sort of funeral processional was a magnet for pickpockets and thieves. All ne'er-do-wells took the opportunity to collect what they could steal in times like these where the crowds were dense and chase was usually not given.

Rowles offered, "Selfish as it is, I'm grateful you're here."

"It's not selfish at all to wish to be with the one you love," Joan replied, squeezing his arm affectionately.

Morgan was behind her. She could hear his footsteps, closer than usual as he took up a protective stance behind them. Joan had a moment of amusement, albeit fleetingly, thinking how it would turn out if some poor thief picked Morgan as a target.

"Something humorous?" Rowles asked as they came to a stop in front of his mother's final resting place.

"I'll tell you later," Joan murmured, realizing it wasn't the time or place to share her amusement, however fleeting.

A curate stood before them, opening his well-worn Book of Common Prayer as he began to read the words of the funeral rite, starting with Psalm 121.

I will lift up mine eyes unto the hills;
from whence cometh my help?
My help cometh even from the LORD,
who hath made heaven and earth.
He will not suffer thy foot to be moved,
and he that keepeth thee will not sleep.
Behold, he that keepeth Israel
shall neither slumber nor sleep.
The LORD himself is thy keeper;
the LORD is thy defense upon thy right hand;
So that the sun shall not burn by day,
neither the moon by night.
The LORD shall preserve thee from all evil;
yea, it is even he that shall keep thy soul.
The LORD shall preserve thy going out, and thy
coming in,
from this time forth for evermore.

The words filtered through the air and landed on Joan's ears with an odd familiarity. While not memorized, they were certainly recognizable. And comforting, reminding the listener that it wasn't the end, but a new beginning.

She liked to think of it that way. Less final, less painful, and full of…hope.

The world could use more hope. The litany continued.

> *O God, whose mercies cannot be numbered: Accept our*
> *prayers on behalf of thy servant the Duchess Westmore,*
> *and grant her an entrance into the land of light and joy,*
> *in the fellowship of thy saints; through Jesus Christ thy Son,*
> *our Lord, who liveth and reigneth with thee and the Holy Spirit,*
> *one God, now and forever. Amen.*

Finally, the coffin containing the duchess's body was lowered into the earth, and with a final word, the curate left his post. Rowles stepped forward, drawing Joan along with him as he approached his mother's final resting place. His shoulders were rigid, and he lowered his head in silent prayer. Joan lowered her eyes, studying the fresh dirt. She offered her own silent words, praying for the troubled woman's soul, hoping it finally found rest. Surely the God of Grace would give her peace. Finally.

As Joan opened her eyes, she studied Rowles, rigid and staunch next to her, a soldier standing guard. She yearned to lay her head on his shoulder, or wrap a comforting arm around his waist, but they had gone against society's customs enough as it was. Rowles led her away, and they watched as torches were lit, and the mourners continued their wailing, but now in more subdued tones. It was finished.

Later, after the mourners had left, they walked back to the carriage that would carry them home. Rowles held himself firm; Joan could feel his bunched muscles in his arm as he escorted her, with Morgan on her other side.

"Thank you for attending." Rowles met Morgan's gaze and turned to meet Joan's. "I know I said it earlier, but it bears repeating."

Morgan gave a curt nod. "It is finished, and I always found that to be a relief."

"Indeed, you are correct," Rowles agreed.

Morgan cleared his throat and shuffled his feet.

"I didn't realize how much so," Rowles began. "But I find I'm…optimistic."

Joan watched him, thankful for his words. "Truly?"

"Yes, it's the final obstacle. Unless you count time," he added.

"Time?" Joan asked.

"Yes, time. Two weeks, to be exact." He tapped her nose with his finger. This time the amusement that lit his features brightened his eyes as well.

"And what exactly happens in two weeks?" Joan played along, lifting a shoulder.

Rowles chuckled. "I'm certain it will be an event that will bear the title of best day of my life."

"That's a heavy expectation."

"And I have no fear of it being fully realized," he said.

"Nor do I," Joan replied, joy from deep within bending her lips in a warm expression. "I'm certain it will be." She tipped her chin. "The hardest days can make the best ones all the sweeter."

Rowles took a deep breath, his brows furrowing in an adorable way that distracted Joan from her earlier thoughts. He squeezed her hand, released it, and cupped her chin tenderly. "That is indeed true. Today was hard, dreadfully so, yet I find that all I want to do is look to the future…because that future holds you."

Thirty-one

ROWLES WOKE THE NEXT DAY WITH A FRESH anticipation that surprised him. Yesterday had been difficult, to say the least, but it was a chapter in the book that was finished and closed. Moving onward, he looked toward a bright future, one that held far more blessings than he ever dared to hope for. With the funeral behind him, he was now able to focus on the wedding, and he couldn't imagine a more worthy endeavor.

After he broke his fast, he sent a missive to Penderdale House. The marriage settlement needed attention, and he wished for Joan to meet with his housekeeper to organize the wedding breakfast.

There was but one damper on his mood, and that was the need to talk with Joan about the secret Morgan was keeping from her. He should tell her today, if she were able to come to him, but the devilish part of him whispered to wait. Didn't he deserve one day without conflict? He'd just buried his mother, for heaven's sake. Couldn't he have one day without some sort of crisis? Yet, did he wish to keep this secret between them, even for a day longer?

The battle warred within him, and when Morgan

replied to his missive that they'd come to visit directly, Rowles's indecision didn't improve.

He was in his study when the butler announced their arrival. Standing, he straightened his coat as Morgan entered, followed by Joan. "Good morning," Rowles said as a greeting, furtively glancing at the clock on the mantel. It was indeed still morning but barely. In a quarter hour it would be noon.

"Good morning, I must say I was surprised you wished to address all this today. I thought you'd want at least a day to recover from yesterday's events." Morgan watched his friend coolly. "Not that I mind."

"I'd much prefer to move forward, rather than dwell in the past," Rowles answered honestly, thinking how such an answer applied to not just his own life at present, but Joan's as well. A hope and a future... Those were the things he would focus on.

"Very well," Morgan replied.

Joan stepped forward. "I, for one, was thankful you didn't wish to tarry. I confess I was hoping you'd welcome us calling upon you," she said shyly as she tugged at her gloves absentmindedly.

"Always," Rowles replied. His restless soul had found peace the moment she stepped into the room.

Her green eyes lifted to meet his, entrancing him. The memory of the flavor of her kiss created a hunger for more, and he gave his head a shake to break the spell she'd woven unknowingly around him.

"How can we be of assistance?" Morgan cut in, rapping his fingers on the desk to defuse the tension in the room.

Rowles shifted his attention to his friend, then sighed. There were indeed tasks that needed attention, and thankfully they all related to Joan, which gave him more ambition in accomplishing them.

"First, I'd like to discuss the marriage settlement. My solicitor drew up the documents and delivered them this morning."

Morgan nodded.

Rowles turned to Joan. "I'd like for you to see them as well."

Joan's eyes widened a moment before a wide, approving expression graced her lips. "Thank you for the consideration."

While it wasn't the norm, he wanted her to know the details of the settlement. After all, it concerned her and their children. Shouldn't she know the particulars? And he knew that Joan would appreciate the gesture. She was far too forward-thinking and self-sufficient to appreciate anything less than full disclosure.

"If you'd take a seat?" Rowles signaled to the chairs in front of his desk and took out the leather-bound folder that held all the particular documents regarding the settlement. Displaying them for the siblings to look over, Rowles returned to his own chair and leaned back, his attention focused on Joan as her eyes darted over the writing.

A delicate furrow pinched her face as she read through the documents, not one of disapproval but of concentration. He loved that he could interpret her facial expressions; it was endearing. Just as he'd taught others, he would become a student of hers. Learning her smiles, unwinding the brilliant way her mind worked, and everything in between. Yes, indeed, he would be a very dedicated student.

"This is…quite generous," Morgan stated as he looked up. "It's more than I had hoped for, for Joan. Thank you. Though I can't say I'm surprised. I have the suspicion that if she asked for a star in the heavens, you'd try to find a way to procure it."

"That might prove difficult, but I'd likely try," Rowles admitted, feeling a bit shy at such a truth being laid bare.

"Thank you," Joan murmured, looking up from the paper and meeting his warm expression. Her green eyes were luminous, captivating him. "Thank you for…everything, but thank you also for including me in the process," she added, her lips dimpling as she turned back to the paper. "I confess I feel as though I don't bring enough into the marriage."

Rowles frowned. He'd never considered she'd look at the settlement with such a perspective. "Joan…"

"I will cut in, only because I have the distinct feeling that I'll feel most uncomfortable with the topic at hand, should it be discussed further. Joan, in return you are giving him *you*...and, dear sister, that is enough. He might not need your dowry, but he does in fact need you." Morgan stood. "Now, I assume this is not the only task that requires our attention?"

Rowles shook his head as he smiled at his friend. "One day you will not be so averse to emotions, Morgan. And I will delight in that day."

"Yes, well, that day is not today so you'll have to wait for such satisfaction."

"Indeed." Rowles smirked.

Joan turned her gaze heavenward as if praying for patience, but she was smiling through her apparent irritation. "Ever the romantic, Morgan. If we're one day to find you a wife—"

"That day is also not today, dear sister," Morgan said with some impatience. "Now, to what shall we set our minds next?"

Rowles stood and arched a brow. "Well, if you must know, I was considering introducing Joan to the staff, especially to my housekeeper so that she can make the needed arrangements for the wedding breakfast."

"An excellent idea," Morgan said with approval.

"It requires no emotion on anyone's part," Joan said with a playful grin.

"Indeed." Rowles sighed. "If you'll follow me, I'll call for Mrs. Adams and she'll meet us in the library."

"Lovely."

Rowles stepped from his study and signaled for a maid to locate the housekeeper and ask her to meet them in the library. The maid quickly left to do his bidding, and Rowles led their party down the hall.

"It occurred to me that you haven't officially had a tour, have you?" he asked as he turned his head to study Joan.

"No, I haven't," she replied, her cheeks flushing slightly. Her eyes trailed along the hall, studying the artwork and decor with interest. "I confess I'd like a tour very much. I'd like some familiarity with the house before it becomes my home." The blush deepened.

Rowles turned his attention forward, needing a moment to let his body cool from the picture she'd painted with her words.

Her home.

Where he'd see her each and every day, and where he'd share her bed every night.

Where he could bask in her glow and the glory of her keen mind, while knowing that the next day held the same delights. Yes, he liked that idea a lot.

"I'd be delighted to show you my home," Rowles answered finally, turning his head to meet her gaze. "I'd enjoy that very much."

"With a chaperone, of course," Morgan added dryly.

"Are you not volunteering for the position?" Joan asked archly.

"I do not feel up to the challenge, nor do I wish to submit myself to such torture," Morgan replied without a hint of humor.

Joan's laughter echoed in the hall, delicate and delicious. "Why am I not surprised?"

"Apparently, I'm averse to emotion, so I suspect you're not surprised, as you say."

"No. I'm not."

"Ah, the library." Morgan walked through the open double doors, giving a warning glare to Rowles as he passed. Something felt off about him, Rowles decided. He was wound tighter than usual. Was he truly struggling with his sister marrying? Or was it that she was marrying *him*? Or perhaps Morgan was tense over wondering if Rowles had told Joan about her parentage.

Of that, they could both be wary.

"Sometimes I think Morgan was born old," Joan said as she passed Rowles in the library.

"I've had the same said about me," Rowles said by way of reply.

"And yet you haven't lost your ability to laugh," she pointed out with a winning smile.

"True," Rowles conceded.

"What is this?" Joan asked, tipping her head slightly as she studied the gold-colored tube resting on a nearby shelf.

Rowles's face stretched into a smile. "That is a kaleidoscope."

"Pardon?" Joan turned to him, her inquisitive eyes dancing.

Rowles lifted the long brass tube from its perch. "Allow me to demonstrate." He first placed the cool metal cylinder to his eye and then turned toward the window, allowing light to filter through the lenses. He twisted to adjust the picture within and lowered it. "Come." He motioned to Joan.

She stood beside him and grasped the brass cylinder as he handed it to her. "Place this end near your eye and look through it while you hold the other end to the light," Rowles whispered, watching with fascination as she followed his instructions. He waited for it, the gasp of wonder that he knew would soon follow.

A moment later, Joan gasped, her lips spreading into a delighted expression of wonder. "Watch this," Rowles whispered, turning the end that moved the colors as they reflected in the interior mirrors, shifting the design into new ones.

"It's magnificent," Joan murmured, distracted by the wonder within.

"It is, isn't it?"

She lowered the glass and turned to him. "Wherever did you find this?"

"This device was invented by David Brewster. I have a colleague in Cambridge who knew him personally, and he gave this to me when I resigned my position at the college," Rowles replied.

"What a lovely gift."

"Indeed. It's unique, but I expect they will be quite commonplace in the future."

Joan lifted the kaleidoscope once more and turned the end as Rowles had, then reacted to the wonder. "It's utterly breathtaking."

"It is," Rowles replied in response to his attention on *her*.

Joan lowered the glass, her cheeks flushing with a rosy hue as she understood his compliment. "Aren't you the charmer today?"

"It's freeing to say what's on my mind rather than try to hide it from prying eyes. I suppose you'll have to grow accustomed to my attentions."

"I think I can manage that," Joan replied shyly. "I think I'll manage that quite well."

Mrs. Adams came into the library and curtsied to the duke. "Your Grace, how may I be of assistance?" she asked. Her dress and pinafore were perfectly ironed and starched, presenting a very capable front. A swell of pride flowed through him. Joan would be aided by a very capable and kind staff, and he was thankful.

"Ah, Mrs. Adams, allow me to introduce you to my betrothed, Lady Joan Morgan." He held a hand toward Joan, who curtsied prettily to the housekeeper.

"A pleasure, Mrs. Adams," Joan said in greeting.

"The pleasure is all mine, Lady Joan. We are

all looking forward to serving you," Mrs. Adams replied.

"Mrs. Adams, would you assist Lady Joan in preparations for the wedding breakfast?" Rowles asked. "And if the rooms are ready, I'd like to give her a full tour as well so she may become familiar with her soon-to-be home."

"Of course, Your Grace. Yes, the staff has been working diligently to prepare the new duchess's rooms, and I hope you'll both find them satisfactory. In the meantime, Lady Joan, I'm sure the staff can attend to every wish you have for your wedding breakfast."

"Thank you," Joan replied, worrying her lip a bit. "I confess I'm not sure where to start."

"If I may, I drew up a possible menu. You may make whatever adjustments you desire and we can start there," Mrs. Adams offered.

Joan's shoulders relaxed slightly as she nodded. "That sounds perfect. Thank you. I can tell already that we are going to get along quite well, Mrs. Adams."

"Of that I'm sure, Lady Joan. If you'll follow me to the kitchens?"

Joan nodded and gave a little wave to Rowles before departing with the housekeeper to attend to whatever details needed her attention.

Rowles savored the sight of it, watching her begin her duties as his wife even before that was official. His mother had delegated most duties to the staff, and they were accustomed to running the estate. This would actually benefit Joan, he considered. Because she wouldn't have to do more than she was ready for, she could gradually assume those duties she wished to do and delegate the rest to a very competent staff.

"She left five minutes ago, and you're still staring at the door," Morgan stated as he poked Rowles in the shoulder. "Should I be concerned? Or simply thrilled you love her that much."

"The latter." Rowles blinked, then met his friend's expression.

Morgan lowered his voice as he spoke. "Have you told her?"

Rowles knew to what he was referring. He gave his head a slight shake.

"I thought not. She'd have laid into me had she known, but I wanted to ask. Tell me." He paused and met Rowles's eyes with a forthright stare. "Are you going to tell her? Have you decided on a course of action?"

Rowles took a deep breath. "I'll tell her. I don't wish for there to be secrets between us, and should she find out one day and discover I *knew*, that will not go well."

Morgan sighed and nodded once. "I understand. I suppose it's for the best. I…"

"Yes?" Rowles encouraged him when Morgan didn't continue.

"I looked for any documentation, in case she had questions, should you tell her."

Rowles eyes widened slightly before he asked. "And? What did you find?"

"Very little, but there was a small blanket with a lamb embroidered on it. It was hers, but all other documents were destroyed, I'm assuming."

"That would make sense, since your parents didn't want her to know. Why is that, I wonder?"

Morgan shrugged. "I think it's because they didn't want her to feel like she was any less a Morgan because she didn't share the same bloodlines as the rest of us. You know how the members of the *ton* are…and it could easily be an issue if a suitor"— Morgan speared a look at Rowles—"decided that a person's pedigree was more important than the person herself. I think perhaps they wished to spare her that as well."

"They obviously put a lot of thought into it."

"Yes, my parents weren't ones to take matters like this lightly."

"Nor will I. I will take the utmost care when I talk to Joan."

"Talk to me about what?" Joan asked, her brows furrowed as she searched a bookshelf near the door. "Mrs. Adams said there was a fantastic book that had different menus and recipes. Do you know which one she's referring to?" Joan asked. "Found it!" She withdrew the book and glanced to Rowles, then her brother. "Wait…" she said, her head tipping like a sparrow.

Rowles could see it then, the way she read his look and shifted her eyes to her brother, who immediately looked away. *Guilty*, he thought as his friend avoided his sister's scrutiny.

There was nothing for it. He wouldn't lie to her or pretend they were talking about something else.

So much for waiting a day and having some peace.

No. Today he'd dive in and pray this revelation wasn't as damning as it could potentially be.

"Joan, when you're finished with Mrs. Adams, I'd like to take you on a tour and then...we can talk."

Her sharp stare settled on him. "Why does that sound ominous?"

"It isn't," Rowles was quick to answer, and honestly, it wasn't ominous, it wasn't bad, it was knowledge. In truth, it changed nothing.

Joan nodded and took her leave, the wary expression never leaving her eyes.

Rowles watched her depart, his mind affirming that it changed nothing, her parentage changed nothing at all.

But while he was convinced he was making the right decision in telling her, just because it was right didn't mean it was easy. Not at all.

Thirty-two

IT WAS A LESSON IN SELF-CONTROL FOR JOAN AS she patiently worked with Mrs. Adams to organize the wedding breakfast, rather than rush through the planning to get to the bottom of whatever was being discussed in the library in her absence. Whatever it was, it truly didn't change anything… for Rowles. But that made her still wonder if perhaps it changed something for her.

"And we will, of course, serve champagne," Mrs. Adams added.

"Yes, thank you," Joan replied with a determined tone. "I think this is going to be perfect. Thank you for all your assistance."

"It's my pleasure. The late duchess, God rest her soul, didn't involve herself with many matters in the house. It's a delight to have company and set our minds to tasks we haven't had the pleasure to tend to for years." Mrs. Adams clapped her hands once. "We will truly make every effort to assist you, my lady."

"I believe it, and you, Mrs. Adams. Thank you." Joan gave her a warm, heartfelt smile. How difficult it must have been to attend to a bachelor house with a duchess who needed constant care and watching.

Joan rose and quit the small sitting area beside the kitchens, then took the stairs to the main floor. She approached the library quietly, hoping to eavesdrop on any current conversation. Perhaps she might pick up a clue as to their earlier discussion. But the library was silent, and with a frown, she surveyed the room.

"My lady, the duke is in his study," a footman explained as he bowed upon entering the library.

"Thank you," Joan answered, following the footman's lead down the hall and taking the opportunity to study her environs. The home was lovely, furnished sumptuously but also tastefully, grand yet not so grand it was cold. She approved of all she saw. She tried to imagine herself as the duchess, her heart bursting at the thought. As beautiful as the house was, she truly found the most joy in knowing with whom she would share the home.

Rowles.

As if thinking his name had also voiced it, he looked up the moment she stepped into his study. "Ah, Joan. Thank you." He nodded to the footman, dismissing him. "Morgan and I are finishing up the signatures needed for the marriage settlement."

"The wedding breakfast is all planned as well," she said in a cheerful tone. "I must say, we are accomplishing much today."

"Indeed we are!" Rowles agreed. "And with your brother's permission, I'll take you on that promised tour. Mrs. Adams will act as a chaperone, if that's satisfactory?"

"It is indeed," Morgan replied. "I'll see you tonight, Sister." He gave Joan a quick wave and took his leave.

Rowles sent for the housekeeper, giving Joan a precious few moments in privacy with him. Her body was at war with her mind over what to spend those precious moments doing. She wanted to kiss him, feel his arms around her, banded and strong, while her mind whispered that now was a good time to ferret out any secrets he wished to share. Torn, she took a step toward him, but didn't know how to begin.

"First, I think it would be wise to show you to your rooms," Rowles cut in before she could make up her mind. "And then I'd love to show you every inch of my home, hoping you'll love it as much as I do." Rising from his place behind his desk, he came to stand beside her. Wrapping his warm hand around hers, he pulled her in tightly and held her. With his chin resting upon her head, she could hear and feel his heart beating, and that soothed her soul.

"I love you," he whispered softly into her hair, then kissed the top of her head. "More than anything."

Joan melted at the sound of his voice. "I love you too," she whispered into his chest, speaking the words directly to his heart. "But I confess, I'm a little afraid."

He pulled back slightly, enough to read her expression. "Of?"

Joan glanced down, studying a button on his chest. "Of whatever had Morgan refusing to look at me."

"Did you ever consider that it has more to do with his fear than yours?" Rowles asked, using a finger to lift her chin up so her eyes met his.

She blinked. "No."

"Sometimes we react more to our own fears more than to anything else," Rowles answered. "And all in good time. We will talk, but not now when I have limited time before my housekeeper walks through the door." He softened his tone.

"I suppose that's wise," Joan conceded.

"I have my moments," Rowles added sagely.

Joan swatted him playfully and took a step back as the housekeeper came into the study. "A tour?" she asked.

"Indeed." Rowles shared a smile with Joan, one

that calmed her fears a little. If he was at peace with whatever it was, shouldn't she be as well?

He offered her his arm, and she placed her hand on his jacket as he led them from the study into the hall. The housekeeper tagged along behind.

"Westmore House has been in my family for five generations," Rowles began. "The first Duke of Westmore was given his title by Queen Elizabeth. In return, when the house needed renovations, the duke made plans to commemorate the queen's generosity by designing the modifications in the shape of an E, in her honor. So you'll find that there are three wings that meet along a long single one, making the shape," he explained.

"I'm sure the queen took notice," Joan replied, taking on a new curiosity. Could she decipher the shape from this hall? she wondered.

"The queen and several others. It became a more common modification in houses for a while." Rowles chuckled.

"I would imagine."

Rowles paused along the hall. "Here is one of the wings. This is the middle of the E, which is the two-story library. The first arm of the E is the vaulted ballroom, which was put in the front of the house so that it made entertaining guests more efficient. It's close to the door, you see."

"Ah, brilliant really."

"When one entertains, at least. The last wing of

the E has the family apartments. It's quite a long trek from there to the other wings." He lifted a shoulder and let it drop. "If we had entertained more, I suppose I would better appreciate the layout of the house, but as it is, it keeps me quite active moving about from library to apartments and back and forth." He shrugged once more.

"Our home is much smaller, so I didn't think of the amount of space that needed to be traversed from one place to the next. Ours is all quite close together."

"Yes, and offers a warm and welcoming atmosphere. I'm afraid Westmore House can be chilly in that aspect."

"Then I shall try to find ways to warm it up," Joan announced, squeezing her fingers along his arm.

"Your presence alone does that very thing, Joan." Rowles lifted her hand and kissed it, then placed it back on his arm. "Let's take the stairs, and I'll show you to the rooms that will be yours."

The housekeeper followed them up the grand staircase, and as Rowles came to an ornate wooden door, he paused. The housekeeper gave him a nod, as if assuring him that all was right within, and on silent hinges, the door swung open to reveal a room filled with sunlight.

Joan wasn't sure what she was expecting, but it wasn't all the light that spilled into the room, making it feel as if it were a courtyard rather than a bedroom. The farthest wall had four windows, all identical and close together, the source of the bright light that cast the rest of the room in a cheery glow. Roses lined the vanity in crystal vases, and the hearth boasted a glowing fire. Joan covered her mouth as she smiled far too widely for polite company and gave her head a slight shake. "It's… perfect," she murmured.

"I thought you'd like it. In a way, it reminds me of you," Rowles said softly.

She turned. "How so?"

"It's warm, cheery, and sheds light on everything it can."

"You are in fine form today… Such a pretty compliment. Should I expect a sonnet later?" she teased, then turned her attention back to the room. There was a delicate writing desk in the corner and a large vanity with an oval mirror. On the opposite wall was the bed, a four-poster and canopied confection in pink roses that looked as soft and inviting as a bowl of whipped cream. "I can't imagine one thing I'd change." She turned to Rowles and then the housekeeper. "Thank you. I can see there was much thought and care put into its preparation."

Mrs. Adams stood up a little straighter with the praise. "Thank you, my lady."

Joan turned to Rowles, one question filtering through her mind. "Was this your mother's room?" She kept her tone light, but she was curious.

Rowles shook his head. "A long time ago, yes. But she moved to a separate room when my brother took over the title." Rowles looked down at the mention of his late brother.

Joan bit her lip, her heart hurting for his loss.

For her losses as well.

Death had a way of becoming a bold reminder of the preciousness of life.

"Thank you for showing me. I truly adore it," she added, changing the subject back to a cheerier topic. "What else would you wish to show me?"

Rowles beamed at her. "I don't believe you've seen the ballroom, and I have a lovely hall that is lined with art, but first, tea. Don't you agree?"

At the mention of tea, her stomach gave a silent churn of hunger. "Tea is an even better idea."

"Mrs. Adams?" Rowles asked. "Please have tea sent to the blue parlor."

"Of course, Your Grace." She left to do his bidding, casting a backwards look as if worried about leaving them unchaperoned. Then, as if deciding that she trusted her master, she disappeared down the hall.

"I think Mrs. Adams is concerned about my reputation since we're alone," Joan whispered teasingly.

"You've found a champion in her, that's for certain." Rowles gave his head a shake. "I can see who will be the favorite, and it won't be me."

"I'll put in a good word for you," Joan flirted

back as he led them out of the room and down the hall back to the stairs.

"It pleases me that you like it here," he confided.

"It pleases me that you want me to love my new home," Joan replied.

Rowles put on a brave face, but the light didn't quite reach his eyes. It was a silent few moments as he led them to the parlor, then closed the door all but a few inches. "Joan, sit with me?" He signaled to a sofa near a table ready for tea.

"Of course," Joan replied, swallowing her tension.

Rowles took her hands in his, his thumbs smoothing over her wrist, then her palm, as if soothing her before he even spoke.

"Hurry up, it's making me more nervous by the minute," Joan said, her chest tight.

Rowles gave a wry grin. "My apologies. I'm only trying to do this well and…I'm not sure I will."

"I appreciate a frank word as much as kind one," she offered.

Rowles sighed. "Morgan told me something that I feel is important for you to know about, since it pertains to you, dear Joan. And I have vacillated between telling you and not telling you because it doesn't change anything concerning your future with me, my love for you, or anything of the sort. But…I think it's wise that we have this conversation so that if it ever did come to light later in life, it wouldn't be something I was intentionally keeping from you. I want no secrets between us, Joan."

Joan nodded, her throat dry. "Go on… I trust you, Rowles."

"I have but one question. Do you wish to know? After hearing that it won't change anything, do you still wish to know?" He took a breath. "You trust me, but I also trust you, Joan, and I will abide by your choice in this matter."

Joan frowned. She hadn't truly considered that she didn't *need* to know. Curiosity burned through her, but…in the end, did it need to be satisfied? "Morgan told you, but hasn't ever told me?" she asked, piecing together some of his earlier words.

"Yes."

"And my parents knew, I assume?" she questioned further, a twinge of understanding pulsing through her chest.

"Yes." Rowles gave a single nod.

As with a puzzle missing the most crucial piece that gave the design clarity, understanding snapped into place.

She breathed deeply, letting her heart and mind adjust to the concept, to the idea that had never once entered her mind till that moment. But so much of it, so many different details made sense.

She'd always felt sorry for her mother. She'd been the last child they had been able to conceive, left feeling like it was her fault, that she'd harmed her mother in some way.

Except…she wasn't.

Because she wasn't a Morgan by blood.

No.

She'd been adopted.

Thirty-three

ROWLES'S CHEST BURNED AS HE REALIZED HE'D been holding his breath. He released the pent-up air and intentionally breathed in, and out, all the while keeping his complete focus on Joan.

Watching as she gained comprehension without him even telling her. Yes, he'd been right in saying something. She was far too keen of understanding and aware of others to have this secret remain buried. It was a miracle that she'd not discovered it earlier. Morgan was stealthier than Rowles had given him credit for.

"Who knows?" she asked, turning eyes full of warring emotions upon him.

"Morgan and myself," Rowles answered gently. "Your parents didn't wish for you to know, and as Morgan explained it to me, I can in some part understand why."

"Why, then?" Joan asked, but without the harsh tone that could have accompanied such a question.

"Because pedigree can be prized, and they didn't want you to feel that pressure or have to succumb to society's cruel gossip in such matters should the truth come to light," he answered. "It was all in effort to protect you. It changed nothing concerning their love or devotion to you, or yours for them, so I think they felt that there was no true benefit in you knowing."

"Except that it was withholding the truth," Joan answered, but without heat or a bitter edge. "I understand why, but that doesn't mean I can agree with it." She released a silent sigh, her shoulders caving slightly as if the knowledge was a real weight upon her shoulders.

Rowles's mind grasped for something comforting to say but came up empty. So instead he squeezed her hand within his, continuing to rub her palm with his thumb. Sometimes actions spoke louder than words.

"Is there any information about my birth?" she asked after a moment, her attention lingering on their intertwined hands.

Rowles shrugged. "Not much. Your parents had most of it destroyed, from what Morgan has told me. They didn't want any of it traced back to you."

"I suppose that makes sense."

"Morgan went searching for information back at your home. That's what we were discussing earlier in the library."

Joan's eyes flashed up to him. "Did he find anything?"

Rowles shook his head. "No, not much at least. He wondered, first of all, if I was indeed going to tell you about it. I told him my instinct was to tell you, and from there he said he'd found a blanket. It had been left with you at the church. There's a lamb embroidered on the corner."

Joan sighed. "I'd like to see it."

"I'm sure Morgan will show you. And I'm also sure you will have questions for him. I'm sorry he won't have many answers for you."

Joan bit her lip. "Odd how questions seem to multiply. I have about a million." She hitched a shoulder and took a deep breath. "I suppose it will take time for me to fully grasp this."

"That's understandable. But, Joan…" Rowles lifted a hand and tipped her chin so that they were eye to eye. "I meant what I said earlier. While your parentage is most certainly a part of you, it matters not to me that you're not a Morgan by blood, or that your parentage is somewhat unknown. You…*you* are who I love. Not your bloodlines." He spoke the words like a vow, praying she understood the truth in them.

Her eyes held his for a moment. Then she smiled, softly and gently, warming his soul with her acceptance of his words. "Yet another reason I love you."

The housekeeper bustled into the room, the sound of lightly clanking china punctuating her steps as she set the tea tray on the nearby circular table. "Ah, here we go. I waited an extra few minutes so that you'd have the warm biscuits directly from the oven." She arranged a plate and saucer.

"Thank you, they smell divine," Joan replied. "How would you like your tea... Wait. I remember." She turned to the tea service.

"Cream and sugar, and at least three biscuits," Rowles answered anyway and thought about how they would often sit and take tea with each other, the simple domestic bliss of it all seeming underrated.

Joan served him and then herself. When she bit into one of Cook's biscuits, Rowles watched her surreptitiously, waiting for her reaction. She didn't disappoint. Her eyes closed and her lips tipped upward as her other hand reached up to catch a crumb from the delightfully crisp confection.

"Oh my, I may marry you for the biscuits," she teased.

Rowles chuckled. "By whatever means necessary. I'm certainly not above bribing you with biscuits."

"I shouldn't be so easily bought, but biscuits are indeed a weakness." She sipped her tea.

His heart swelled with pride and love for her. She'd been given a startling truth, and yet her perspective was still joyful. She'd have questions, and likely as soon as tea was finished, she'd want to return home to talk to her brother. He'd offer to go with her, but she'd want to do it on her own.

She was quite independent, his Joan.

And he loved her for it.

Like her namesake, she was a warrior at heart.

Thirty-four

JOAN WAS TORN BETWEEN WANTING TO SEE THE rest of Westmore House and spend time with Rowles, and going home and pelting her brother with questions. In the end, she chose the latter, and Rowles offered to take her in his curricle, with the promise to return later that afternoon, should she feel up to a stroll in the park.

She was quite certain she would delight in a stroll; however, she had been quite certain of a lot of things that morning and those had changed dramatically.

"I understand," Rowles said as she conveyed her tumultuous thoughts. "I'm here whenever you need me. Just send word." He helped her from the curricle and kissed her hand.

She could feel his stare on her back as she took the stairs to her home. Turning to give one final wave, she wondered how any other man would have reacted, had they found out about her questionable parentage. Would they have still loved her? Wanted her? Or would they have cried off?

Rowles returned her wave, a solid pillar of honesty. She gave him a brave nod and turned back to the door. Straightening her shoulders, she walked into the house.

"Where is Lord Penderdale?" she asked a footman as he took her pelisse.

"His study, my lady," the footman answered.

Joan nodded and headed in the direction of Morgan's study, her boots making determined little clicks on the wooden floor as she closed the distance.

As she walked into the room, she paused, at odds about where to even begin.

"He told you," Morgan said by way of greeting as he finished signing a document. Blowing across the ink, he waited a moment for it to dry and then set it aside. "Your stride gave you away. Quite a determined sound, I must say."

Joan narrowed her eyes at her brother.

"My question is..." He rose and stepped from behind his desk and started toward her. "Am I going to answer questions or get attacked by them?" he asked playfully, then paused, holding up a hand as if to stop her from answering. "I'm sorry. For all of it. I should have told you, but I did not. I'm not sure how Rowles addressed it, but for what it's worth, it truly changes nothing. You're my sister. Simple as that. I couldn't love you any more or less. I love you like I loved Percy, and that hasn't ever changed nor will it. Mother and Father loved you as much as they loved Percy and me as well. There was never any discrimination between the three of us. You were equal in every way." He glanced down, all earlier humor and teasing gone. "And for fear that you'd question that truth, we decided to keep it from you."

Joan nodded, her eyes stinging with tears as she listened to her brother's words. "Rowles said as much," she admitted finally.

"He was always quite good with words and difficult situations. He'd talk himself out a fight—"

"And you'd knock out the aggressor." Joan smirked even through her tears. Yes. What Morgan said was true. There was no change in their relationship. Morgan was her brother in every way that mattered. "I still wish you had told me sooner," she confided, still irked because they hadn't.

"I'm sure you do, and for that I apologize. Mother and Father wished to keep it secret."

"Just as you want me to trust your love for me, I wish you had trusted my love for all of you," Joan said, her brows pinching. "You're still my brother, and our parents were still my parents. The truth might have raised questions, but it never changed the most important thing—my love for you."

"I realize that now." Morgan nodded, his brown eyes meeting hers. "Forgive me, Joan."

"Forgiven," she replied quickly. "Rowles said you looked for information and other things. He mentioned a blanket?" she asked, her curiosity burning.

Morgan quickly swiped his hand across his eyes as if removing tears and nodded. "Indeed, follow me." He led the way from the study to the stairs. "It's in the old nursery."

Joan followed him down the hall to the room they hadn't used for years, not since she'd been out of leading strings. As Morgan opened the door, memories of her childhood flooded her mind. It had been a good one, filled with pestering her older brothers and adoring her parents. In adopting her, they'd given her a gift she didn't even understand.

And even more, she owed the mother of her birth. Whomever she was, she had given her daughter the best life possible, without even knowing. She'd been selfless, surrendering her child—if it was anything like with most foundlings at the hospital. Joan knew what drove women to make those difficult choices. And it was hope.

Hope that their child would live.

Hope that their child would thrive.

Hope that they were giving their child a future they couldn't give themselves.

"Here." Morgan had opened the wardrobe and withdrawn several boxes, one wooden with a lock. "The key was lost years ago, or so Mother had said. I broke into it a few days ago, when I was certain that Rowles would tell you."

Joan nodded, then had a question pop into her mind. "Why Rowles? Why did you ask him to tell me, instead of telling me yourself?"

Morgan took the wooden box to a nearby table and

considered her with a weary expression. "I didn't know how, or where to begin, and in truth, I was afraid." The honesty of his answer rang through his words. "But it was a matter of honor to tell Rowles. I know him well enough that he wouldn't cast you aside because of your adoption. Heaven knows he'd marry you if you were a scullery maid, and damn the consequences."

"He's romantic like that."

"Call it what you will, but notwithstanding, I knew I could trust him, and he needed to know since he was to be your husband."

Joan's irritation simmered. "I find it difficult to understand how my future husband needed to know something I did not."

Morgan paused. "When you put it that way, I have no good answer. It seemed logical at the time, but that won't suffice now, I understand."

"At least you admit it," Joan said with less fire.

"My humility knows no bounds," Morgan said with a little sarcasm, enough to be teasing.

"For that, I have no response." Joan gave a soft chuckle. "What's in the box?" she asked, her irritation soothed slightly.

Morgan lifted the lid and set it aside. Within was a dirty white blanket, knit in a tight weave with an embroidered lamb in the corner. "You were wrapped in this. And there was a letter, but we don't have it any longer."

"Do you know what it said?" Joan asked, lifting

the blanket from the box and holding it. The fabric was a thick wool, slightly stretchy against her skin as she rubbed her fingers over it.

"All I know is that the letter was in French, which was distinctive since we'd been at war with Napoleon. Maybe your mother was escaping the war, only to be caught up in it here as well? Maybe she was a British sympathizer. I suppose we will never know. The letter was short, simply a plea to have you cared for."

"At least she wanted me cared for." Joan sighed. "I suppose that's more than some ever have."

"It is indeed, and from that we can deduce that she loved you and wanted something better for you than she could give."

"All good qualities to have in a mother, even one I never knew."

"And all good qualities she likely passed on to you," Morgan added, and in a rare show of affection, gave her an awkward side hug.

Joan leaned her head on his shoulder for a moment. "Thank you, I know this isn't easy for you either."

"No, it's not. But there's one more thing." He sighed and stepped back. "At dinner the other night with Rowles, you mentioned a name you were searching for at the Foundling Hospital."

"Yes." Joan nodded. "Agneau."

"Lamb," he translated. "The name Agneau, or something quite similar was pinned to your blanket when they found you on the church steps."

"So that might be *my* family name?" Joan asked, shocked.

"It's possible, but it could also be a decoy since it's a common surname. I'm not sure, but I thought you should know," Morgan added.

Joan nodded. "Thank you." She sucked on the corner of her lip as she absentmindedly clutched the blanket to her chest. "Morgan, you said I was found at a church, and I realize I haven't asked how Mother and Father even found out about me."

Morgan's shoulders relaxed. "Ah, that is a story I do know." He had a relieved expression. "Come, sit down with me." He pointed to a pair of rocking chairs in the corner by a bookshelf.

"Mother couldn't have any more children, not after Percy and I were born. The doctors said it was a miracle she survived our birthing at all." Morgan frowned as he stared at his folded hands. "I'll admit I've carried years of guilt over that, but at the same time, it was that very reason that Mother and Father adopted you, so I couldn't feel too guilty. I was far too happy to have you…most times." He winked.

"I did enjoy pestering you."

"Did? As in past tense? You still enjoy it, and far too much so."

"This is true and not going to change. I'm utterly unapologetic about it." She cast him a saucy grin.

"Nonetheless, they never gave up wanting more children, and one spring, Father decided to skip the season. There wasn't much need for him in London, so we stayed in our estate in West Sussex, near Chichester."

"Oh! I love that place. Wait, is that why we didn't go there often? Were Mother and Father concerned that the vicar would somehow let the secret out?"

Morgan nodded. "They were quite certain it wouldn't be divulged, but rather than test that theory, they decided that if you were out of sight, you were equally out of mind."

"I see. Continue, please?"

"Well." He leaned back in the chair and rocked a few times. "The Church of the Holy Trinity had finished their evening service, and as the vicar was about to close the doors, he heard a cry. In the bustle of people leaving the service, no one had noticed someone leave a baby in a basket to the side of the front entrance. The vicar took you in and read the note attached to your blanket."

"How old was I?" Joan asked.

"I'm no expert, and I was young myself, but I think quite new. A week, maybe?"

"I was so small," Joan added, unable to imagine being all along and so young.

Morgan continued, "The note requested you be brought to Thomas Coram's Foundling Hospital, but it so happened that the vicar had met with Mother a week earlier. She'd asked for him to pray for her to have more children. It was a brave step for her, but that tells you her desperation. Father didn't even know she'd made such a request."

"So the vicar contacted Mother?"

"Yes, and it didn't take more than moment for Father to be completely in agreement. They picked you up that night when it was dark, in a hired hack so no one would suspect. The vicar took care of the paperwork, and it was done."

"That's quite the story."

Morgan nodded. "And because we'd skipped spring season, when we returned with an almost one-year-old girl in tow, people simply assumed that Mother had been in confinement and that was why they'd skipped the season. Mother and Father never corrected people's assumptions."

"That worked out quite tidily," Joan remarked.

"Indeed, as if God planned it so."

Joan nodded, her mind whirling with all the implications and details. All the things that could have gone wrong but went so very right instead. "It's incredible, really."

"I thought so. And Percy and I were so young that we didn't really know what was going on. For all we knew, that's how babies were made and how we came to be in the family as well." He snickered. "It wasn't till later we found out, which led to other questions, and I can still remember Mother scolding us for asking how babies were made, since they weren't only picked up at a church."

Joan burst into a laugh. "Oh my, I can't imagine Mother doing anything but blushing a crimson red."

"She did that, and then sent us off to our father. Who explained some, but not much."

"Speaking of which…"

"No. That is a conversation you will have with your husband when the time is right. I am not up to that challenge."

"You delegate quite a few things to my future husband for being so dead set against my interest in him to begin with." Joan placed a hand on her hip.

"I had my reasons, and all of them are no longer necessary. I stand by my decision."

"You would." She held the blanket to her chest, then gently placed it back into the box. "Well, I suppose I'll never truly know. But…I wonder." She tipped her chin and looked at him. "I wonder if I would have been handed over to the Foundling Hospital. Maybe there was some deep part of me that knew, and that's why I was drawn to help there."

"Perhaps. It's impossible to say, but you have a tie to those children, and that is a lovely thing, Joan. I'm sorry that this has all presented you with more questions than it has answered." He sighed.

"Yes, but it also gave me answers I didn't know had questions," she replied.

"Yes, well, I'm sure Rowles is curious how all this went. Would you like to invite him for dinner?"

Joan nodded. "Yes, I think that's an excellent

idea." She closed the box and wiped a gentle and loving caress over the top before turning to her brother. "I'm not sure how I feel about it all."

"It's a lot to consider, that is to be certain."

"I–I think I'm glad…that I didn't know sooner. I think I would have questioned much and now, looking back, I didn't have the burn of that truth when I was too young to grasp it."

"I'm glad you feel that way. For better or worse, we thought we were doing the right thing." Morgan took the box and put it back in the wardrobe.

"I know. Which makes it easier for me to accept." Joan studied her brother. "Though I must say, it is impressive you kept this a secret from me." She frowned.

"Indeed, it was a challenge to say the least. I had to be very careful not to look at you, to avoid any conversation about your birth, but generally that was pretty easy." Morgan hitched a shoulder. "Now, if you're ready, I'm sure your betrothed is impatiently waiting to hear from you. I must say, it's a wonder he's waiting to have the banns read."

"His patience is far more impressive than my own. But it's two weeks. I think we can survive that," Joan answered bravely.

Two weeks… It wasn't *that* long.

Except, in her heart, it felt like an eternity.

Thirty-five

FOR ROWLES, THE NEXT WEEK PASSED WITH EACH day a test in fortitude and patience as one day bled into the next with exasperating slowness. Each day, he'd break his fast and then go over to Penderdale House, or Joan and Morgan would come to Westmore. Mrs. Adams and Joan had made considerable progress on arrangements for the wedding breakfast, and the final fitting for Joan's wedding dress was tomorrow afternoon. She'd said as much yesterday, with a great amount of enthusiasm. It was going to be a day above all others. Today, Rowles had one important task to accomplish: arranging the wedding trip.

Deliberately, he'd waited till it was only a week away, lest his impatient nature overtake his good sense. It was a time of celebration, one where he and Joan would celebrate their marriage and enjoy every ounce of intimacy it offered. His heart pounded as his blood raced through his veins at the thought. He'd never wanted a woman so much in his life, never experienced the overwhelming need and ache for anything like he wanted Joan. For those reasons, he'd waited to plan the time he'd fully explore those delightful pleasures. But he'd put that off long enough, and it was time. Steeling himself against the onslaught of tempting thoughts, he forced himself to think clearly.

At first, he'd considered his estate in Bath. She'd mentioned wanting to visit the Roman ruins, but upon further consideration, he decided that precious little sightseeing would happen on the wedding trip. It would be better to visit a place where they could be comfortable and not feel the pressures of exploring anything but each other. So, for that reason, he penned a letter to his butler in Cambridge. The house wasn't grand, but it was homey and comfortable. It was cozy, intimate, and everything he'd loved about his past combined with everything he loved about his future.

If they wished to get a bit of fresh air, he could take her to the college, show her where he'd worked and studied, and share that side of his life with her. It was perfect. So with a few strokes of his pen, he let the housekeeper know to prepare the home for his arrival with his new bride, with a few particulars for Cook to procure—champagne and a plethora of biscuits. He'd remembered how much Joan loved them at Westmore House, and the same recipe was used at his Cambridge house.

Content with his choice, Rowles thought about Joan in his Cambridge home. It was a perfect picture in his mind, one that brought a swell of peace and love to his spirit. Cambridge was where he'd truly felt at home, and Lord willing, one day he'd be able to return and do more than visit.

"Your Grace." The butler came in with his silver tray, a missive with the Penderdale seal resting in the middle. "There's a messenger awaiting a reply."

"Thank you." Rowles lifted the missive and set it on his desk. With a brass letter opener, he peeled the wax and unfolded the letter.

Rowles,

There's been a development, and I require Joan's assistance. However, since you are aware of her involvement with my line of work, I thought it the right thing to let you know and seek your permission, of sorts. Likely Joan would have my head should she know I was asking you. However, I know that if the tables were turned, I'd wish to know as well. Please reply with your sentiments concerning the situation.

Regards,
Morgan

Rowles frowned as he reread the letter. He understood what Morgan was asking and was unsure how he felt about it. It was one thing to be there on a mission, another to trust her without his presence, without seeing to her safety with his own eyes. She'd not needed him before, and he was certain she'd like to continue assisting the War Office even when they were married, but that didn't mean he didn't feel concern.

He scribbled a reply and sent it off, praying he'd made the right choice. It had been a simple reply, only four words: *Do what you must.*

But they conveyed a thousand meanings.

He refused to be the domineering husband who controlled his wife's every move, and Joan wouldn't have loved him had he been that sort of man. But it was at great cost to his mind and heart that he sent those words.

Yet he also knew Morgan. He'd not put his sister in danger and would forfeit his own life, should it come to that, to keep her safe. That assurance gave Rowles the power to let her go.

He grinned to himself even as he thought the words.

As if he could stop her in the first place.

It was for that reason, and many more, that she'd captured his heart.

Thirty-six

If I am not in the state of grace, may God place me there; and if I am, may God so keep me.

—*Joan of Arc*

JOAN STUDIED THE MAN BEFORE THEM. WITH hands bound and resting on the well-worn table, his mannerisms were easy to interpret, at least so far. Morgan's foul mood radiated within the room like a blazing fire as he pelted the man with questions. There had been another attempt, another forgery sent to try to move the prisoner from house arrest to another prison. Morgan had intercepted it, and Joan had confirmed their suspicions. There was nothing left to do but interrogate the criminal that others wanted silenced forever.

"Who?" Morgan asked, leaning forward on the table separating them from Walter Brewer. "Who were you in contact with before your arrest?"

The man appeared different from what Joan had expected. A man with a gentleman-like manner and cool blue eyes that studied them both with extreme mistrust.

Then again, if she'd been nearly sent to the London Tower after having only a sentence of house arrest, she'd be suspicious as well. Little did he know that the reason he *wasn't* sent to London Tower was because *she* had found the forgery. Irony never ceased to amaze her.

"I was locking up the magistrate's building, maybe seven months ago. I was about to leave when a figure in a dark cloak stopped me and demanded I reopen the doors." He lifted his hands.

Joan listened with fierce intensity. "And? What did you do?" she asked, forgetting that she was usually a silent member of the interrogation.

"Well, I didn't wish to lose my life that night, and he carried a wicked-looking knife. It probably would have been better though. Quite a bit of trouble my cooperation has led me to. I let him in, and he took a few documents, then said if I cooperated, I'd be rewarded." He shrugged. "I'm not above a little reward, you see."

"I can imagine. Go on," Morgan intoned. "Was there a name? Can you remember anything distinctive? Perhaps draw his face."

"I can give you the name. It's Penderdale."

Morgan froze.

Joan sucked in breath, then calmed her reaction so as not to give anymore away.

"Penderdale?" Morgan repeated, the word sounding foreign, even though it was so familiar.

Was someone pretending to be him? Framing him? Or was it simply a very unlucky coincidence?

"Aye. That's what I said." The man leaned back in his chair, watching them with a speculative glare. "Bloke said he worked for an investigator, so I didn't think I was doing anything that would be wrong."

Joan had to remind herself to breathe.

Morgan tapped the table. Joan watched as his body radiated tension. "Then why were you convicted, if you were assisting one of us?"

"I'm not sure. And you can imagine my panic when they sent me to the bloody tower..."

"Yes, well, turns out someone determined you had betrayed them and tried to do away with you before you could tell your tales."

"I figured. That's why I told you just now." He shrugged. "Sorry for scaring you, miss." He turned to Joan.

"We will see that no harm comes to you, Mr. Brewer." Morgan stood and nodded. "The officer will see you back to your house, and we will confirm your story."

"Will I go free when it checks out?" Mr. Brewer asked, lifting his shackled hands.

"We shall see," Morgan answered, then gestured for Joan to leave the room ahead of him.

It wasn't till they were in the carriage that

Morgan spoke again. "Well, this has been an inter-esting afternoon." He released a long sigh. "What I thought would be a confirmation of the story we'd heard from our informant turned into a twisted story of someone using my name."

"There's...there's no one else with that title, is there?" Joan asked, curious and concerned at the same time. If someone was masquerading as her brother, heaven only knew what else they would do, and how it could affect Morgan.

"The title is my own, but it could be someone's surname. It's possible—not likely, but possible. I need to inform the War Office and see if they have any information that could add clarity. For all we know, there could be another Penderdale who works for king and country."

"I hope it's the latter, rather than someone using your name. Heaven only knows how that could end up badly."

"It's my title, not name, so I'd worry less." He reached over and patted Joan's hand. "Thank you for your assistance."

Joan sighed. "I don't feel like I was much assis-tance. He was a pretty simple person to read. You could have probably figured out what his body lan-guage meant without my help."

"It's always good to have two perspectives."

"True."

Morgan paused, his fingers fiddling with his hat

as he sighed. "I want you to know I sent a missive to Rowles this morning regarding this meeting."

Joan tipped her head, waiting for him to continue. That he told Rowles wasn't all that surprising. "And?"

"And I thought you'd like to know how your betrothed replied." He lifted his attention from his hat to her face. "It was four words, and I thought they carried a bit of weight. He said, 'Do what you must.'"

Joan's lips spread into a grateful smile, and she gave her head a slight shake. How blessed was she? Not only to find a worthy husband who loved her, but to find one that understood her need to contribute. Four words, but they spoke volumes. They spoke of his trust in her, his respect for her work, and his faith in letting her be herself.

"That is utterly romantic." Joan sighed delightedly.

Morgan frowned. "Well, I suppose it can be thought of that way. I was only thankful he isn't a closet tyrant. I didn't expect him to be, but it pleases me that he values your experience and skill."

"Like I said, romantic."

Morgan huffed a laugh. "I do not think I'll ever understand women."

"That is a very likely truth." Joan chuckled.

"If I haven't said it yet, I'm happy for you, Joan. You and Rowles. I couldn't part with you for anyone less." He reached across the carriage and patted her hand.

"I love you too," Joan replied as she squeezed his hand.

Thirty-seven

ROWLES WAS WAITING IN THE BLUE SALON, READ-
ing a book but seeing nothing of the words, listening for the return of Morgan and Joan. He'd arrived
a quarter hour ago, based on the information that
Morgan had sent concerning the time, but upon his
arrival, the siblings still hadn't come home.

So he waited.

And each moment stretched on to the next, tor-
turing him. Was Joan safe? Did they need help?
And good Lord, he should have asked where they
would be in case he did need to assist.

"And that, dear sister, is a very relaxed gentleman," Morgan said as he entered the room, his
voice dripping with sarcasm. "Could you be wound
any tighter, Rowles?"

Rowles narrowed his eyes at his friend, but the
relief was too overwhelming for him to muster any
other sort of reaction to Morgan's teasing words.
He looked for Joan, and the moment he saw her, his
heart skipped and then resumed its regular cadence.

She was well.

"I think I may have worried a few years of my life
away," Rowles said as he stood to greet her.

"My brother should have given you more information. Then you wouldn't have worried so." She glared at her brother, but there was something comforting about her tone and her look.

"Am I allowed to ask how things went? Or am I not privy to such information?" Rowles asked, his body slowly unwinding from the earlier tension.

Joan turned to her brother, allowing him to answer the query.

"It was an interrogation of sorts, but the arrested man wasn't a threat. I suspect he was arrested for protection."

"I hadn't thought of that." Joan gasped. "It makes so much more sense, if—" She paused and closed her mouth as if preventing herself from saying too much.

Rowles sighed, reminding himself that this would likely be the first of many more such conversations they'd have.

Morgan nodded. "Exactly. I'll explore the concept more tomorrow."

Rowles looked back and forth between the two siblings, then reached out a hand toward Joan. Immediately, she relaxed her rigid posture and moved forward to hold on to him. He pulled her in for a hug, earning a disapproving glare from her brother, but nothing more.

His body relaxed at touching her, finding home and heaven at the same time. "I'm much better now, and I will try not to be as tense in the future," he told her.

"Truly, I don't do this sort of thing often. So there will not be much need for you to be concerned," Joan said against his chest, holding him tightly as if she needed his touch as much as he needed hers.

Rowles kissed her head and slowly released her. "Now, tell me what I can know."

Joan and Morgan dove into the conversation, and before they had finished, dinner was announced. Rowles listened, amazed with all the information they had gleaned and its possible meanings.

Once again, he was thankful for his chosen profession. Books and students were far more appealing than criminals and espionage, in his humble opinion. But he couldn't deny the delight and fascination he found in watching Joan's animated conversation with her brother on those subjects. She thrived, her captivating mind doing acrobatics around ideas and scenarios and possible motives in ways that had him nearly dizzy, yet harboring deep respect for how her mind worked. It truly was a gift, one she used to bless others, to bring justice to their country, and did so without any recognition or accolade.

"We're utterly monopolizing the conversation. My apologies," Morgan stated after a moment, directing his words to Rowles.

"I'm entertained, listening to the two of you. It

makes me content with my profession, I must say," Rowles replied, giving voice to the thoughts he'd had only moments before.

"Speaking of which, are you thinking of going back to Cambridge anytime soon?"

Rowles looked to Joan. "Actually, quite soon. I've decided that it will be a delightful place to visit."

Morgan choked on the sip of wine he'd taken.

Joan shot him a glare and then turned a gloriously happy expression to Rowles. "Truly? I... Yes, I've never been to Cambridge. I had to think about it for a moment. Will you show me the college? I've heard so much about it, especially when Morgan was attending with you and the Duke of Wesley," she said excitedly.

"That is one of the main reasons I thought it would be a good place to spend some time." Rowles didn't disclose the other aspects, that it would be an easy place to stay sequestered in one room or another, enjoying the newfound pleasures of marriage. But judging by the quick arch of a brow from Morgan, he had deduced those aspects as clearly as if they had been spoken.

"Lovely, I can't wait."

"Me either," Rowles answered honestly, earning a quick flaming blush from Joan and an eye roll from Morgan.

"And on that note, I think we'll adjourn to the parlor. Whist, anyone?"

Rowles nodded, earning no little satisfaction from Morgan's reaction. He only delighted in the hope that one day the tables would be turned and Morgan would find someone who made him throw caution to the wind.

Love had a way of making even the most stoic-hearted soft. And Morgan might be love's greatest challenge yet.

But as Rowles assisted Joan from her chair and escorted her to the parlor, drinking in the sight of her smile, the beloved weight of her hand on his arm, he knew that what the Apostle Paul had written was utter truth: *Love is patient, love is kind. It does not envy, it does not boast, it is not proud. It does not dishonor others, it is not self-seeking, it is not easily angered, it keeps no record of wrongs. Love does not delight in evil but rejoices with the truth. It always protects, always trusts, always hopes, always perseveres. Love never fails.*

Thirty-eight

About Jesus Christ and the Church, I
simply know they're just one thing, and
we shouldn't complicate the matter.

—Joan of Arc

THE DAY OF THE WEDDING DAWNED BRIGHT AND sunny, with a few scattered puffy clouds that promised to disappear before noon. Joan was vibrating with anticipation and excitement. After waiting what seemed like forever—though it had only been a few weeks—finally the day had come.

What had started with giving her heart would now be finalized as she took his name. She'd awoken early to prepare for the ten o'clock wedding and was struggling to remain still while Mary weaved seed pearls into her hair in a lovely design that would perfectly complement her dress.

And oh, her dress.

It was a lovely confection of pale-blue silk with an empire waist and puffy cap sleeves that set off her shoulders. Long, lacy gloves matched the gown, along with blue slippers the exact color of the silk.

The modiste had sewed in seed pearls along the hem of the gown and added a satin sash that tied at the back below the row of pearl buttons.

When Mary finished with her hair, another maid was brought in to help her dress for the occasion. After donning her soft new underthings, all lacy and delicate in a way she'd never worn before, she leaned over the chair to allow the maid to tie the corset. Then it was time for the dress. When they helped her step into it, the fabric made the softest whisper as it trailed up her body and sat along her shoulders.

"Oh, my lady, it's lovely," Mary whispered.

"Simply lovely," the second maid echoed.

They helped her step into her shoes and, with a final assessment, declared her ready.

A knock on the door sounded. "May I come in?" Morgan asked.

"Yes," Joan answered, lifting her dress ever so slightly so as not to rumple it, but so she could turn to face her brother, giving him the full effect of the dress.

Morgan stepped into the room and paused, his hand coming to his heart. "You're a vision, dear sister."

"Thank you," Joan said, then grinned. "I know."

"And humble," he teased as he approached her. "I have a gift for you. Well, it's already yours but Mother wished me to save it for this special day." He held out a hand and released a few fingers, and a pearl necklace dangled from his grasp. "And I have the earbobs as well." He held out his other hand, which held a small wooden box.

Joan's eyes filled with tears as she fanned her face to keep them from spilling. "Oh, Morgan. I remember these."

"Yes, I thought you might. May I?" he asked, and when she turned, he latched the pearl necklace on her neck. "Perfect."

Joan considered herself in the mirror. The necklace was the perfect complement to her gown and hair. "Thank you."

"I'll let you put these on." He handed her the box with the earrings.

Joan nodded wordlessly, not trusting her voice as she carefully put in the precious earrings.

"I...couldn't let you go to a man less worthy," Morgan said after a moment of silence. "And I'm thankful that if you're marrying someone, it's my best friend."

Joan turned to regard him. "He's a good man. I couldn't imagine loving anyone else."

Morgan nodded, then rocked on his heels. "Are you ready?"

"Indeed." Joan stood up straight and nodded her assent. "Lead the way."

Morgan offered her his arm and led her from her rooms. Already the maids were packing her belongings.

Morgan helped her into the carriage and instructed the driver to head to St. George's.

They had debated on sending out invitations and, in the end, decided to keep it a quiet affair. A few friends would be in attendance, Miss Bronson and her family, for example. The carriage paused before the church at five till ten, and the guests were already within the church and waiting.

Morgan helped Joan alight from the carriage and led her up the stone steps to the church. After they passed through the foyer, the sanctuary came into view.

Joan's heart pounded feverishly, and it only slowed its cadence when she caught sight of Rowles.

"Are you ready?" Morgan asked for the second time that day.

Joan nodded, her eyes captivated by the man at the end of the aisle who was gazing at her with a depth of love she'd never hoped to experience.

He cut a handsome figure in his white linen shirt, dark-blue breeches, and black pump shoes. His jacket was dark blue with a swallowtail cut, and his white silk cravat was complemented perfectly by his top hat, but even with all the masculine glory, Joan couldn't get over his gaze.

And the love that shined through it.

Morgan led her down the aisle, step by step, and finally he was offering her hand to Rowles. Her beloved grasped her hand in a gentle yet firm grip that said *I shall never let go*.

And she believed him.

The bishop started with a prayer, but Joan heard none of the words, only whispered a prayer of thanks herself for the man holding her hand and promising to hold her for his entire life.

The bishop recited their vows, and as Joan repeated hers, the power of her vows hit her anew: *In sickness and in health, to love, cherish, and obey till death us do part.*

In a word, forever. Her whole life, she'd offer everything for the man before her.

And by some miracle, he swore to her the very same.

"With this ring I thee wed, with my body I thee worship, and with all my worldly goods I thee endow. In the Name of the Father, and of the Son, and of the Holy Ghost. Amen."

His life, his breath, his love, forsaking all others.

For the reading of Psalm 128, she focused on Rowles, whispering the vows of her heart into the sanctuary of her mind as she met his expression, praying he could read her heart with her gaze.

Then came the announcement.

"May I present the Duke and Duchess of Westmore," the bishop said, and with the gentle applause of the few in attendance, Joan went with her new husband from the sanctuary into the ante-chamber of the clerk, where she'd register her new name into the annals of the church.

After it was made official, Rowles squeezed her hand and led her to their carriage.

After so much loss.

So much heartbreak.

So much mourning.

It was time to celebrate.

Finally.

Epilogue

Cambridge, England

WOULD THERE EVER COME A TIME WHEN THE touch of her lips wouldn't set him on fire? He doubted it, and as he leaned into his wife's kiss, he had a rather deep regret.

Regret they'd dared to leave home, even for a few hours.

At the time, it had been a lovely idea, to get out and show her the beloved Christ's College where he'd taught for several years, but as Joan's hand pressed against his chest, her fingers wrapping around his jacket and pulling him in tighter, he decided it was a foolish idea to be anywhere but his bedroom.

Her velvet tongue danced along his lower lip, and he all but shuddered with the need for more. Yet as the carriage hit a rut in the road, he was reminded that all those needs would have to wait.

"You'll be the death of me," he murmured against her lips a moment before he recaptured them in a searing kiss, branding her once against as his and his alone. Good Lord, she was so sweet; he'd never recover from loving her.

"And you're the only one burning, are you?" she asked, withdrawing slightly, enough to tease him into leaning forward, searching for her lips. "It was *your* idea to get some fresh air. I was perfectly content at home."

Rowles opened his eyes and was greeted with a teasing grin from his far-too-tempting wife. He glared at her, even though her words painted such an erotic picture he had difficulty keeping the playful scowl in place. "You'll pay for that later," he vowed, then captured her lips once more, devouring her answering smile.

"I'm sure I will. I hope so," she mumbled against his tormenting kiss.

The carriage slowed and rolled to a stop. Rowles swore softly at being interrupted in kissing his delightful wife, but upon realizing the sooner they finished their outing, the sooner they could return home, he reluctantly released her lips and sighed. "I suppose we've arrived."

"That's generally what the halt of a carriage means, Your Grace," she teased, then gave him one final quick kiss.

"Is that so? I hadn't noticed." He injected his words with a hint of joking sarcasm. Then he took a moment to straighten his rumpled coat, and as his eyes lifted to Joan, a deep swell of satisfaction filled him. Her bee-stung lips were evidently well-loved and her dress was only slightly mussed, but enough that he felt pride in knowing it was all his doing.

And it would be his undoing later.

"Am I presentable?" Joan asked tucking a stray hair behind her ear. "Or is it that obvious you assaulted me on the carriage ride over?"

Rowles frowned playfully. "If I remember correctly, *you* assaulted *me*."

"Details." She waved a hand dismissively.

"Yes, details," he replied with a flick of her fingers. "If you're not presentable, it's entirely your fault."

"How so?" she asked, but her tone was light and playful.

"Because you're entirely too tempting, and I cannot be expected to resist any of your charms, ever. So let that be a warning not to tempt me in a way I cannot refuse."

Joan's scrutiny lowered to her lap as a blush tinted her cheeks a fetching pink. "I'll take that as a compliment."

"It's a compliment that's the raw truth, my love." He lifted her hand and kissed it. "And another truth, I hate gloves. I much prefer your skin," he murmured against her wrist.

"Well, I must say I prefer your skin as well, but in public, social constraints require them."

"Unfortunate, that."

Joan shook her head. "Are we ever going to leave the carriage or should we turn back? Wait. No, I didn't say such a thing." She laughed.

"Well…"

"No, we must go and see your beloved college, or I fear I'll never get the official tour you've promised. I wish to see the places you love so well." She shook her head amusedly.

"My wife, a wise woman." He gave a curt nod of approval. "Shall we?" He stepped from the carriage onto the cobbled stone of St. Andrew's Street. The white stone buildings lined the walk where people bustled by, likely on the way to a lecture or the library.

Rowles offered his hand to Joan; she took it and stepped down. Her hat was askew, so he tipped it slightly for her, gently so as not to tug too much on the pins holding it in place.

"Thank you," Joan offered, her skin highlighted by the pale green of her day dress that made her green eyes seem more emerald than usual.

"You're beautiful." Rowles kissed her hand before placing it on his arm.

"You're quite handsome yourself," she replied.

Rowles laughed. "This will be the quickest tour in the history of all of Cambridge." He led them down the street. "To distract myself from you, I'm going to explain a little history about Christ's College."

"I do love learning from you."

Rowles turned to her. "I suggest you pay attention since this will be the only time I'm letting you out of our bedroom for the rest of the trip."

Joan made a show of closing her lips and nodding.

"Very well." Rowles sighed, trying to collect his wayward thoughts. "So, Christ's College is one of the many constituent colleges of Cambridge University. It was established as 'God's House' by William Byngham in 1437. Later, its name was changed to Christ's College. It houses several different buildings, all with different specialties, and has its own choir, like many other of Cambridge's colleges."

"Fascinating. I've heard much about it," Joan noted, looking over the buildings and the lawn between them.

"Here's the Great Gate." Rowles gestured to the wide break in the white stone buildings lining St. Andrew's Street. "Inside is First Court, a well-known garden area." He paused before the gate and watched Joan's reaction.

Wonder and excitement filtered through her expression. "Is this where you taught?"

"Yes, would you like to see the room? I can take you through the old chapel as well."

Joan watched him with her wide green eyes. "I'd love to see it."

Rowles led her through First Court, along the gravel path so as not to disturb the grass. They took the northwest entrance to the chapel. "And to the right is the Master's Lodge, and directly behind us is the Mountbatten Room where smaller conferences and the like are held." He gestured to the side and behind him, then stepped aside for a few people to pass before opening the door to the chapel for Joan.

The white and black tiles along the floor were a stark contrast of light and dark. The old pews that lined the narrow aisle were well worn with hundreds of years of use, the halls of the chapel ghosting a century of music below the hallowed arched ceilings.

"I can feel it." Joan closed her eyes as she stepped inside a pew and sat. "I can feel the peace here, the echoing of years of worship."

"It was one of my favorite places. So much of what I taught was based on the Bible, but here... here it all came to life."

Joan nodded, having no words for what they both felt so deeply.

With a slow breath, she stood and turned to him. "And where did you teach?"

Rowles gestured to the hall that led from the chapel. "This way. I doubt we will be able to go inside—a lecture may be taking place—but I can at least give you a closer look."

"Wouldn't they welcome you touring the college? You taught here not too long ago, and..."

"As a former Fellow and a duke, they would likely

have the choir sing in response to my presence, should I let them know I was here, but I didn't." He shrugged. "I wanted to blend in and focus on my time with you. I wanted you to see the place that is so close to my heart, but I didn't want any fanfare. Just...you." Rowles paused before a wide wooden door. "It's empty. We can go in, if you'd like."

Joan nodded. Heavy wooden desks lined the creaking floor as they walked into the vacant room. Wide chalkboards lined the farthest wall, and Rowles inhaled deeply of the scent of erased chalk and the knowledge it represented.

How he missed teaching!

He led Joan to the front and pulled out a chair for her behind a student desk. Then he went to the front and looked over the lecture hall. Closing his eyes for a moment, he could picture it filled with students, all hungry for information and eager to understand.

"You miss this," Joan stated, breaking the silence.

"Yes, but it's not my season." Rowles opened his eyes and studied his wife. Yes, he missed teaching, but if he hadn't resigned, he'd likely not have met her.

Joan's very presence warmed him. "You know..." She stood and walked toward him, her hand reaching out to grasp his. "When we were becoming friends, I had that same thought. There truly is a season for everything."

"Ecclesiastes."

"Yes, and maybe this isn't your season for teaching, but that doesn't mean that someday the season won't make a full circle back. And should that time come, I want you to take that opportunity, Rowles." Joan cupped his face gently.

"Thank you," he whispered. "Seasons do tend to shift, don't they? And I must say, this past season had more than its share of difficulties, but it also had its greatest blessing."

"Oh? And what is that?" Joan asked, tugging his hand toward the door.

"I'm talking about you," Rowles answered, chuckling as he caught up with her and opened the door leading to the hall.

"Yes, but I delight in hearing you say it over and over," she whispered as they walked back through the chapel doors, into the courtyard, and to the Great Gate leading to St. Andrew's Street.

"And where are you taking me now?" he asked, fully knowing the answer.

"You know very well where I'm taking you," she teased, biting her lip in the way that he loved.

"I do know, but I love hearing you say it over and over again," he said, casting her earlier words back to her.

"You have some promises to keep, Your Grace. I'm only making sure you honor them."

Rowles helped her into the carriage, deciding that the ride back home was far too long to wait, but also enjoying the heady anticipation. "Is that so? Are you afraid I'll go back on my word?" he asked, nibbling at her lip as the carriage moved forward toward home.

"No, simply impatient for you to begin," Joan mumbled against his hungry lips. "I love you."

"I love you," he said, then leaned back. "I started loving you the moment you told me I wasn't like my mother. And I loved you more when you captivated my mind with your sparkling debate." He paused and shook his head. "Joan of Arc saved a nation. Joan Morgan, you've saved me," he whispered.

Joan regarded him tenderly and pulled him into a kiss that said far more than words ever could.

In the end, three things remain.

Faith, hope, and love.

But the greatest of these, by far, is love.

Author's Note

The Regency era was a time of sparkling social events and glamour, but there was also a darker side. In this story, I address the societal norms that are challenged by a noblewoman with dementia. Unfortunately, the care for someone in that era with that illness was entirely dependent on the fortune and family of the one affected. In this case, the duke's mother was the one with the malady, and with care and great historical research, I navigated the path of what this sort of illness could look like in this time. I also wished to portray what love for a family member suffering with dementia can look and feel like.

Unfortunately, mental health in the Regency era wasn't viewed with the understanding we have today. In a time where suicide by laudanum overdose was a dark problem, and Bedlam was filled with ill people on parade (I won't go into detail; it's been an emotionally difficult aspect to research), we can all shudder at the lack of available care that many people needed. Mental health was just beginning to be recognized during this time, but for many, care for mental illness was too little and too late. No matter when people lived, it was always important that those affected by mental illness have support and the understanding that they were not alone. That is especially important today. There are resources available, and heaven only knows how many of us need to use those resources to manage the shifts in our world. There's no shame in that, only a road to healing and recovery.

Here are some resources available, should you or a loved one ever need them:

- National Suicide Prevention Lifeline: 1-800-273-TALK (8255)

- SAMHSA Treatment Referral Helpline: 1–877-SAMHSA7 (1-877-726-4727)

- National Veterans Hotline: 1-800-273-8255

- National Alliance on Mental Illness (NAMI) HelpLine: 1-800-950-6264, info@nami.org

- National Institute of Mental Health (NIMH): 1-866-615-6464

- Crisis Text Line: Text CONNECT to 741741

Acknowledgments

There are so many people who help cultivate, create, refine, and then repeat the process in bringing a book to life. I'm so thankful to each editor, proofreader, cover artist, publisher, and all the parts in between that make books like this possible. THANK you, Sourcebooks, for making the process a dream. Thank you to my family, who patiently works together to give me time to pursue this dream and write, and thank you to every reader!

FORTUNE FAVORS
THE DUKE

First in the sparkling new Cambridge Brotherhood series
of Regency romance from author Kristin Vayden

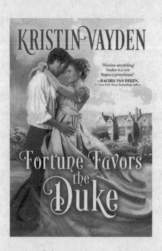

Quinton Errington is happy teaching economics at Cambridge.
But when his eldest brother dies in a tragic accident, Quinton
becomes Duke. Between being head of his family, mourning his
brother, and trying not to fall in love with his late brother's fiancée,
Quinton will need some help...

**"Flawless storytelling! Vayden is a
new Regency powerhouse."**
—Rachel Van Dyken, #1 *New York Times* bestselling author

For more info about Sourcebooks's books and authors, visit:
sourcebooks.com